Bloom Duel

Jenna King

Published by Jenna King, 2024.

BLOOM DUEL

First edition. November 15, 2024.

ISBN: 979-8230074236

Written by Jenna King.

Chapter 1: Petals of Rivalry

The morning sun spilled golden light over Riverview, casting a warm glow on the cobblestone streets that danced with the laughter of children and the chatter of neighbors. As I arranged the flowers in my shop, Bloom & Co., the world outside felt alive, pulsing with the rhythm of spring. The vibrant hues of my blooms—iridescent tulips, delicate daisies, and velvety roses—created a symphony of colors that drew in passersby like moths to a flame. I could almost hear the whispers of admiration as they admired the floral arrangements displayed in my window.

But the thrill of anticipation was dulled by the bitter tang of rivalry. Across the street, Jude Hale was erecting his booth, a striking display of emerald foliage and fiery orange marigolds. I could feel his presence even before I saw him; it was as if he had a magnetic pull, drawing the attention of the crowd. The way he moved—confident, almost arrogantly—sent a prickle of annoyance along my spine. Jude, with his devil-may-care attitude and a smile that could melt the stoniest heart, was everything I loathed in a competitor. Yet, there was a twisted sense of thrill in the way he challenged me, igniting a fire in my belly that I couldn't ignore.

"Nice booth you've got there," I called out, my voice laced with feigned sweetness as I straightened the petals on my best-selling bouquet. He turned, a smirk playing at the corners of his lips.

"Thanks, but I doubt it'll hold a candle to mine," he shot back, his voice smooth and rich, like dark chocolate melting on the tongue.

His eyes sparkled with mischief, and I hated how the flutter in my chest betrayed me. This was not the time for a heart-thumping attraction; I had a business to protect and a title to claim. The reigning champion of the Floral Festival was a title I intended to wear with pride, and I wasn't about to let Jude snatch it away from me.

With a final huff, I tossed my hair over my shoulder, forcing a smile that was all business. "Well, we'll see who walks away with the trophy this year."

The annual Floral Festival had become an unspoken contest between us, a battlefield of blooms and creativity. Last year, Jude had narrowly defeated me with his stunning floral installation—a tower of blossoms that resembled a whimsical waterfall. This year, however, I had an arsenal of ideas that would make my display unforgettable.

As the sun rose higher in the sky, casting a warm glow over the bustling festival, the atmosphere grew electric with excitement. Vendors set up stalls, children darted between booths, and the tantalizing aroma of fresh-baked goods wafted through the air. I immersed myself in arranging the flowers, my fingers dancing over the soft petals as I created a masterpiece that would leave a lasting impression.

But the moment I glanced up, I found Jude watching me, leaning casually against his booth, arms crossed, a playful smirk on his lips. "Nice technique, but I'd recommend a little less chaos in your arrangement. Too many colors can be a bit... overwhelming."

I narrowed my eyes at him. "And I'd recommend you focus on your own work instead of critiquing mine. Maybe then you wouldn't have to rely on a gimmick to attract customers."

The words slipped out sharper than intended, and the air between us crackled with tension. There was a moment, brief yet potent, where our eyes locked, and I could see the challenge reflected in his gaze. It was maddening how a simple exchange could turn my heart to mush and make me second-guess every competitive instinct I had.

The festival began in earnest, and as the sun climbed higher, a throng of visitors descended upon our booths. I fought to maintain my focus, attending to the customers who marveled at my creations, their faces lighting up with delight. Every compliment fueled my determination to outshine Jude. Each time I glanced over at him, I noticed the way he engaged effortlessly with his customers, flashing that disarming grin that could sell ice to an Eskimo.

I tried to ignore the nagging thought that flickered through my mind: was there something more to Jude than just the rivalry? Beneath the competitive facade, I sensed a depth in him, a layer of complexity that was both fascinating and infuriating. It was an unsettling feeling, and I quickly pushed it away, reminding myself of my goal.

As the afternoon wore on, I overheard snippets of conversation from festival-goers, their laughter mingling with the scent of flowers. "Did you see Jude's display? It's incredible!" "I love Bloom & Co., but there's something magical about Jude's arrangements." Each compliment felt like a dagger to my pride, fueling my competitive fire.

With determination surging through my veins, I grabbed a bundle of iridescent peonies, determined to craft a centerpiece that would draw the crowd's eye. As I worked, I became lost in the rhythm of arranging flowers, my thoughts swirling around my strategy for the competition. Suddenly, a playful voice broke through my concentration.

"Need a hand, or are you planning to single-handedly win this thing?" Jude leaned closer, his breath warm against my ear.

"Just making sure my arrangements don't look like a toddler's art project," I shot back, trying to mask the thrill his proximity ignited.

He chuckled, the sound rich and genuine. "Well, if you ever want to learn how to create something truly breathtaking, I'm just a few feet away."

I met his gaze, and for a heartbeat, the rivalry faded, replaced by a flicker of connection that left me momentarily disarmed. "Thanks, but I prefer to figure it out myself. I wouldn't want you to steal all the glory."

With that, I turned back to my flowers, trying to suppress the warmth creeping into my cheeks. It was ludicrous how one little conversation could turn my world upside down. As the competition unfolded, I knew I was in for a battle—not just against him, but against the stirrings of unexpected feelings that threatened to disrupt my carefully curated plans.

As the festival progressed, the air thickened with the scent of earth and blooms, a sensory overload that should have been invigorating. Instead, it felt like a tightrope walk between elation and anxiety. I twisted the strands of my hair around my fingers, stealing glances at Jude's booth, which somehow seemed to draw an endless parade of admirers. It was infuriating—like watching a rival athlete steal the spotlight at a championship game.

"Gorgeous day for a floral battle, isn't it?" came a voice, breaking through my swirling thoughts. It was Claire, my best friend and the unofficial cheerleader of Bloom & Co. She appeared like a breath of fresh air, her colorful sundress swirling around her like a field of wildflowers. "You're not going to let Jude's antics get to you, are you?"

"Antics? It's like he's got a spell over them," I replied, nodding toward the small crowd of festival-goers who were cooing over his marigold-laden creations. "I swear he's got some kind of pheromone thing going on. Either that or he's secretly a magician."

"More like a smooth-talking charmer. But you know, you have something he doesn't."

"What's that? An aversion to flashy showmanship?" I shot back, my tone sharper than intended. "Because if that's what it takes to win, I'm out."

She rolled her eyes, nudging me with her shoulder. "No, silly. You have heart. Your arrangements tell a story. Look around—you've got real artistry here, not just a pretty face with some flowers."

The sincerity in Claire's voice warmed my heart, but the flutter of doubt still buzzed in my mind. I surveyed my display, a carefully curated selection of blooms that embodied the essence of spring. Each bouquet felt like an extension of my soul, crafted with care and love. Yet, here I was, up against a showstopper.

With a sigh, I turned my focus back to my booth. I needed to channel my energy into something productive, something that would show the world what Bloom & Co. was truly about. I began rearranging my peonies, adjusting their placement to create a more inviting tableau.

"Don't forget the secret ingredient," Claire teased, stealing a small sprig of lavender from my table and tucking it behind my ear. "Confidence. You've got this."

"Confidence, right. And maybe a dash of luck," I replied, catching a glimpse of Jude laughing with a group of customers. It was like watching a scene from a rom-com where the charming lead was winning over hearts left and right.

"Speaking of luck, I heard he has a special arrangement he's revealing later. Something spectacular." Claire leaned closer, her voice dropping to a conspiratorial whisper. "I think he's trying to pull out all the stops this year. You know how he loves to be the center of attention."

"Great. Just what I needed. A dramatic reveal from Mr. Perfect." I tried to mask my irritation, but the words slipped through clenched teeth. "What am I supposed to do? Start juggling flowers?"

"Maybe a little flourish wouldn't hurt." Claire's eyes sparkled with mischief. "Or you could simply remind everyone why you're the best. Your blooms are heartfelt, and that's something no gimmick can replicate."

"Heartfelt? I'll take it." I straightened up, mentally shaking off the heaviness that had settled on my shoulders. "I just need to focus on what I do best."

With renewed determination, I threw myself back into my work, weaving together a new bouquet of wildflowers, the colors bursting forth like the very essence of spring itself. Time slipped away as I lost myself in the rhythm of my creativity, the clinking of glass vases and the soft rustle of petals providing a soothing backdrop.

But the moment of tranquility shattered when I heard a loud gasp from the crowd, followed by an enthusiastic cheer. I glanced up, my heart racing. Jude was unveiling his centerpiece—a massive floral structure that twisted and spiraled like a fantastical vine, adorned with exotic blooms I couldn't even name. It was breathtaking, a riot of colors and shapes that seemed to defy gravity. I felt the air leave my lungs as the crowd erupted in applause.

I swallowed hard, trying to keep my composure. "Great, just great," I muttered, forcing a smile even as envy clawed at my insides. "Is that even legal? How can one person have so much talent?"

"Talent? Or a knack for showmanship?" Claire whispered back, crossing her arms. "You can't let him get to you. Remember, you're in it for the artistry, not the theatrics."

Just as I was about to respond, a woman approached my booth, her expression curious yet friendly. "These are beautiful! You must be the artist behind these arrangements," she said, gesturing toward my display.

"Thank you!" My heart soared at her praise. "I put a lot of love into them. Each arrangement tells a story, a little piece of who I am."

"That's lovely. I'm actually looking for something special for my daughter's wedding next month. I've seen some of Jude's work, but I'm drawn to yours." She glanced over at Jude's booth, a hint of uncertainty flickering in her eyes.

"Yes! A wedding! Let me show you some options," I said, excitement bubbling within me as I dove into my sales pitch, showcasing the delicate beauty of my creations. This was what I thrived on—connecting with customers, sharing in their joy.

But as the conversation flowed, I couldn't shake the feeling that Jude's presence loomed over me like a shadow, an ever-present reminder of the rivalry that stirred the pot of my competitive spirit. Just then, I caught him out of the corner of my eye, leaning against his booth with that infuriatingly charming smile, casually chatting with another group.

A wave of defiance washed over me, igniting my determination. If I was going to rise above this rivalry, I needed to create something that was not just beautiful but meaningful, something that would resonate with people long after the festival ended.

"Let me show you a special arrangement that could be perfect for your daughter," I suggested, my voice firm yet inviting. As I turned to gather the flowers, I felt a surge of purpose flood my veins. I was ready to reclaim my ground, and for the first time, the competition felt less like an obstacle and more like a catalyst for my creativity.

With renewed vigor, I began to create a breathtaking centerpiece that would encapsulate the spirit of love and beauty, hoping it would not only impress the festival-goers but also leave a lasting impression in the heart of one special customer. The festival was far from over, and I was just getting started.

With each passing moment, the buzz of the festival intensified, the atmosphere crackling with excitement and the sweet sound of laughter echoing through the streets. I poured my energy into the centerpiece, combining delicate white roses with vibrant lilacs and cheerful sunflowers. The soft rustle of petals and the earthy scent of fresh blooms calmed my racing heart, reminding me of why I loved this craft so much.

"Wow, that's stunning!" Claire exclaimed, her eyes wide as she took in the arrangement. "You really have a knack for this."

"Thanks!" I beamed, my spirits lifted. "This is going to be special for someone. I can feel it."

Just then, a familiar voice cut through the chatter, low and teasing. "What do you think you're doing? Trying to steal my thunder with that little concoction?"

I turned, my heart sinking as I faced Jude, his presence as magnetic as ever. He leaned casually against his booth, a teasing grin plastered on his face, the kind that could charm a snake off a tree. "I didn't realize you were attempting to create something worth stealing."

"Oh, I assure you, my creations are worth more than your flashy display," I shot back, my voice laced with playful defiance. "At least mine have substance."

His laugh was like music, a wicked melody that twisted my stomach in knots. "Substance is nice, but don't forget that sometimes, all it takes is a little sparkle to grab attention."

"Sparkle is just glitter's desperate cry for help," I quipped, waving my hands dramatically. "And everyone knows I'm not about that life."

He stepped closer, the playful banter charged with an energy I couldn't quite place. "You know, beneath that tough exterior, I think you're just scared of being overshadowed."

"Scared? Hardly. More like motivated." I crossed my arms, refusing to let him see the way his words rattled me. "Besides, you've got nothing to worry about. Your ego is already so inflated it could float away."

With a chuckle, Jude raised an eyebrow, unfazed. "A little fire in you today, huh? I like it. Just don't burn yourself out before the judging."

As he walked away, the spark of our exchange lingered in the air, mingling with the sweet scent of the flowers. My heart thudded in my chest, a chaotic mix of annoyance and exhilaration. Did I really just flirt with my rival? I shook my head, forcing myself to refocus on the arrangement in front of me.

Hours passed, and the festival buzzed with life. I watched customers weave through the booths, their laughter ringing out like chimes in the breeze. With each compliment on my arrangements, I felt my confidence swell, inching closer to the sense of accomplishment I craved.

Just as I was about to catch my breath, a commotion erupted from Jude's side of the street. Curious, I glanced over to see a group of festival-goers gathered around his booth, their faces alight with excitement. Jude stood in the center, his expression one of triumphant satisfaction as he unveiled a grand floral creation that eclipsed everything else.

It was a breathtaking archway of blossoms, a vibrant cascade of color that flowed like a waterfall, each petal meticulously arranged to create an enchanting spectacle. Gasps of awe rippled through the crowd, and for a brief moment, I felt my heart sink, envy twisting in my gut.

"Isn't it magnificent?" a woman exclaimed, her voice laced with wonder.

"Yes! Absolutely stunning!" another chimed in, eyes gleaming.

I clenched my fists, fighting against the wave of frustration crashing over me. How could I compete with that? As I struggled to rein in my thoughts, Claire stepped up beside me, sensing my turmoil.

"Don't let it get to you," she urged, placing a reassuring hand on my shoulder. "You have your own style, your own story. People appreciate authenticity."

"Authenticity won't win me the trophy," I murmured, my gaze still fixed on Jude's blooming spectacle, the crowd completely captivated.

"Look, just focus on what you can control. Create something that speaks to you, not what you think people want," Claire said. "You have the talent; just let it shine."

With a deep breath, I nodded, trying to absorb her words. As the festival continued, I refocused my energy, adding the final touches to my centerpiece. The sun hung low in the sky, casting a warm glow that bathed everything in a golden light, and for the first time, I felt a flicker of excitement stirring within me.

I decided to incorporate some unique elements—dried flowers and herbs that told a story of resilience, a tribute to the seasons that had shaped my journey as a florist. It was a personal touch, one that represented not just blooms but the struggles I had overcome. I arranged them meticulously, letting my heart guide each movement.

As I stepped back to admire my work, I felt a sense of pride swell in my chest. This was my piece, my identity. In that moment, I resolved that it didn't matter how grand Jude's display was; what mattered was that my creation resonated with authenticity.

Just as I was reveling in my newfound confidence, the announcer's voice boomed through the festival grounds, interrupting my thoughts. "Ladies and gentlemen, it's time for the annual Floral Festival judging! Please gather around the main stage!"

A mix of anticipation and dread bubbled up inside me. I hurriedly finished my last few details, heart racing as I made my way to the stage, the crowd thickening around me like a tide rising with the moon. My pulse quickened as I stood among the other contestants, Jude's competitive gaze locked on me from across the stage.

"May the best florist win," he called out, a hint of mischief in his voice.

"Don't worry; I plan to," I replied, matching his playful tone, but my heart thundered in my chest.

As the judges began to walk around, inspecting each arrangement, I forced myself to breathe. I couldn't let my nerves overtake me. The moment the judges approached my display, I straightened my spine, ready to share the story behind my creation.

But just as I opened my mouth, a loud crash echoed through the crowd, and the earth beneath us seemed to tremble. Gasps erupted, followed by chaos as people began to scatter. I turned to see Jude's magnificent archway tilting dangerously, a cascade of flowers falling in a colorful avalanche toward the ground.

"Watch out!" someone yelled.

In that split second, time slowed. Jude dove forward, instinctively reaching to save his creation, and I felt an unexpected pang of concern for him. But then, amidst the chaos, something else caught my eye.

A small figure darted through the crowd, slipping past festival-goers with an urgency that sent a shiver down my spine. Who was that? Why were they here?

The atmosphere thickened with tension as I realized that this wasn't just a mishap; it felt like a harbinger of something deeper, a storm gathering on the horizon. As the judges looked on, bewildered by the unfolding spectacle, I knew that today was far from over. The real competition wasn't just about flowers anymore; it was about to reveal secrets that lay hidden beneath the petals, and I was ready to uncover them.

Chapter 2: The Garden of Secrets

The festival sparkled like a thousand fireflies, an elaborate tapestry of laughter, vibrant colors, and the tantalizing scent of roasted chestnuts wafting through the air. Each stall overflowed with treasures, but I was entirely consumed by my own floral creations. Each bouquet was a labor of love, an extension of my very being—sunflowers, daisies, and delicate lilies woven together in a way that whispered of summer's eternal charm. My fingers, sticky with sap and dusted with pollen, moved deftly as I crafted, each arrangement a little piece of my soul offered to the world.

Yet, despite the intoxicating atmosphere, there was an unsettling awareness prickling at the nape of my neck. Jude. He was there, his presence a constant shadow, sharp and unyielding. I could almost feel his eyes tracing the curves of my designs, examining not just the flowers but the heart that beat behind them. I'd seen him from a distance, his handsome features framed by the dim glow of lantern light, laughter playing around him like a soft caress. But there was something more—an intensity, a depth in those stormy eyes that seemed to hold secrets.

"Is there something on your mind, Elara?" Jess, my best friend, asked, snapping me from my reverie. She leaned against the wooden table, her arms crossed, a knowing smirk on her lips.

"Just trying to figure out the mystery of the universe," I replied with a light laugh, but my gaze strayed back to Jude. He was in the middle of a conversation, the playful banter disguising something deeper.

Jess followed my line of sight. "You know, you could ask him to help you with those arrangements. A little collaboration could go a long way."

"Collaborate? With Jude? You must be joking," I scoffed, though a flicker of intrigue danced in my mind. The very idea of working with him made my stomach flutter, and not entirely in a bad way. The way he spoke, confident and assured, had a magnetism that drew people in. "He's a competitor, Jess. He'd just as soon run me off the road as help me sell a bouquet."

"Or he could help elevate your work," she pointed out, raising an eyebrow. "You can't tell me you're not the slightest bit curious about what he's up to. You're practically vibrating with tension."

Tension, indeed. I felt it coiling around me like a vine, squeezing tighter with each passing minute. As I arranged the last of my blooms, I couldn't ignore the whispers of uncertainty that danced through my thoughts. My instinct had always been to protect my heart, to shield myself from distractions, especially when they came in the shape of a man like Jude. He was too charming, too enigmatic. And there was something else—something lurking beneath the surface that made me hesitate.

Later, as the sun dipped below the horizon, surrendering the sky to a cascade of stars, I found myself wandering toward Jude's booth. The festival's sounds faded into a gentle hum, and curiosity—insatiable and fierce—drove me closer. The twinkling lights illuminated his booth, casting a soft glow on the various arrangements he had crafted.

"Beautiful, aren't they?" Jude's voice cut through the stillness, a rich baritone that sent shivers down my spine.

I blinked, surprised to find him leaning against the table, arms crossed, watching me with that intense gaze. "You know, for a competitor, you have a remarkable way with flowers." I tried to sound nonchalant, but the words felt heavy in the air, charged with an electricity that made my skin prickle.

"Flattery will get you everywhere," he replied, a playful grin tugging at the corners of his lips. "What brings you to my side of the festival? Is it my stunning arrangements or my undeniable charm?"

"Maybe a little of both," I countered, forcing a lightness into my tone, though my heart raced. "I was just curious. What are you really doing here?"

His laughter was warm, but it didn't reach his eyes. "You think there's a conspiracy afoot, don't you? That I'm plotting to take over the flower kingdom?" He stepped closer, the scent of cedar and citrus enveloping me like a warm blanket. "I assure you, my only plan is to survive this festival without being trampled by the competition."

"Survival, huh?" I raised an eyebrow, skepticism dripping from my words. "You don't strike me as someone who plays by the rules. I overheard a couple of folks saying there's more to you than meets the eye."

"Ah, the rumor mill," he mused, rubbing his chin thoughtfully. "You know how it goes. People love a good story. Makes them feel important."

A knot tightened in my stomach. What if the rumors were true? What if beneath that charming exterior lay something dark? But before I could ponder further, he leaned in, lowering his voice conspiratorially. "You're right to be curious, Elara. There's a garden of secrets buried beneath this festival, and I have a feeling you're only scratching the surface."

I felt a shiver of excitement mixed with apprehension race through me. Secrets? What kind of secrets? I found myself caught in his magnetic pull, unwilling to back away despite the warnings screaming in the back of my mind. What if I uncovered something that changed everything? What if I ventured too close and got burned?

"Are you inviting me to dig?" I asked, my voice softer now, intrigued against my better judgment.

"Maybe," he replied, his eyes gleaming with mischief. "But only if you promise to be careful. Some things are best left buried."

His words hung in the air like a challenge, and I couldn't help but wonder what lay beneath the surface of our tangled lives. I stepped back, the weight of his gaze making my head spin, unsure whether I was on the verge of discovery or disaster.

The stars glimmered like scattered diamonds against the deep velvet sky as I stepped closer to Jude's booth. The festival, now winding down, exuded a palpable magic, the lingering scents of flowers and roasted nuts intertwining in the air. Jude stood at the edge of his display, a casual grace evident in his posture, as if he belonged there, a prince among peasants, commanding both attention and intrigue.

"Careful now, Elara," he teased, tilting his head slightly as I approached. "I might think you've come to steal my secrets. Or worse, my flowers."

"Steal your flowers?" I laughed, unable to resist the playful banter that sparked between us. "You'd have to catch me first, and I'm fairly quick on my feet. Besides, I prefer my blooms untainted by whatever shadows cling to your business dealings."

"Touché," he replied, the laughter in his voice warm but his expression suddenly serious. "But shadows can be deceiving. Sometimes they hide the most beautiful things." He gestured toward a cluster of midnight-blue hydrangeas, their color almost ethereal under the twinkling lights. "Wouldn't you agree?"

I shifted on my feet, feeling the weight of his gaze as he studied me, something simmering just below the surface of his charming facade. "Perhaps," I responded cautiously, "but the beauty of a flower doesn't change the fact that it grows in soil rich with secrets."

"Ah, the soil," he mused, a smile playing on his lips. "A necessary evil, I suppose. But if we're going to dig deeper, I'd prefer we do it together. You can help me cultivate my blooms, and I'll help you uncover whatever mysteries you're chasing."

"Is that your way of inviting me into your garden?" I shot back, unable to keep the teasing tone from my voice, though part of me was undeniably intrigued by the proposition. The other part, the one that had built walls higher than any castle, recoiled at the thought.

"Only if you promise not to run away when it gets messy." His eyes gleamed with mischief, and I could feel the air crackle between us, a current pulling me closer despite my reservations.

"Messy is an understatement when it comes to dealing with secrets," I replied, suddenly more aware of the night air that seemed to hum with possibilities. "And besides, I'm a florist, not a gardener. I prefer my hands dirty only in soil and water."

"Yet you're here, risking your well-earned reputation for a glimpse into my world. That sounds like the spirit of a gardener to me," he said, his voice smooth as silk. The way he spoke made my heart race; it was like he could see right through me.

"I'm here for the flowers, Jude. Nothing more." I tried to sound resolute, but the teasing glint in his eyes made my heart flutter in a way I'd never experienced before.

"Is that so?" he murmured, stepping slightly closer, the space between us shrinking. "Then perhaps you should see what lies beyond the blooms."

The challenge in his tone ignited something within me, a curious flame that flickered with both fear and excitement. "What are you suggesting?" I asked, playing coy even as my pulse quickened.

He reached down, plucking a delicate white orchid from one of his arrangements, its petals glistening under the lantern light. "Come with me. I promise it'll be worth your while."

I hesitated, the sensible part of my brain warning me to retreat, to keep my distance from the man wrapped in layers of charm and mystery. But the curiosity that bubbled beneath the surface was impossible to quell. I felt as if I were being pulled into a story I didn't quite understand, yet I yearned to discover every hidden twist.

"Fine," I said, summoning what little courage I had left. "But only for a moment. I don't have the time or the energy to get tangled up in your web of secrets."

He smirked, the corner of his mouth quirking up, and my heart raced at the sight. "You might find the web rather comfortable, Elara."

Before I could voice my concerns, he turned and led me deeper into the festival grounds, past the flickering lights and the distant laughter of revelers. The world around us began to fade as we stepped into a quieter area, the sounds muffled by the lush greenery that encircled us.

"There's something you should see," he said, glancing back over his shoulder, eyes sparkling with mischief. We entered a small garden hidden away from the festival's hustle, a secret enclave filled with wildflowers that danced in the cool evening breeze. The air was heavy with the heady scent of jasmine, intoxicating and serene.

"This is your secret garden?" I asked, impressed despite myself. The flowers were free and vibrant, untouched by the confines of formal arrangements.

"More like a refuge," he replied, kneeling down to pluck a small flower, its petals a brilliant shade of violet. "A place where I can escape the expectations and judgments of the world."

"Seems lonely," I remarked, a tinge of sympathy slipping into my voice.

"Perhaps," he said, looking up at me, his expression shifting. "But it's my choice, and choices are often made for good reason." There was a weight behind his words, a hint of sorrow that lingered just beneath the surface.

"Your choices can't all be for the best," I challenged gently, curious about the man behind the flowers. "You're drawing yourself away from everyone."

His gaze held mine, intense and unyielding. "Maybe I'm protecting myself. Or maybe I'm just tired of the games."

"Games?" I echoed, taken aback. "Is this a game to you? To pull me into your world, to dangle secrets like bait?"

He sighed, pushing a hand through his tousled hair. "Not a game, Elara, but a gamble. I'm not sure what I stand to lose or gain, but I've been watching you. You have a fire, a passion that I admire. I thought perhaps... perhaps we could help each other."

"Help each other?" I repeated, incredulous. "You mean me helping you cover up whatever it is you're hiding?"

"Or you discovering that the shadows you fear might not be as dark as you imagine," he countered, stepping closer again. "What if I told you that I'm not the villain you think I am?"

"Prove it," I said, my heart racing at the challenge.

His lips curled into a smile, a genuine warmth spreading across his face. "Then let's start with trust. You'll see the truth, but only if you're willing to step beyond your own garden of secrets."

The night felt electric, charged with the possibility of unraveling something profound. I could almost taste the intrigue in the air as Jude extended a hand, inviting me to step into a world where every bloom could whisper a secret, and every glance could spark a revolution. My heart raced at the thought of what lay ahead, the thrill of the unknown lacing every moment with tension and promise.

The moon hung low, casting a silvery glow over the hidden garden, where wildflowers swayed like whispers in the gentle breeze. I stood at the threshold, a world of blooms unfurling before me, vibrant and alive. Jude's invitation hung in the air like a promise, and as he extended his hand, I felt a mixture of trepidation and excitement surge within me. What lay beyond this moment? What secrets were hidden among the petals?

With a hesitant breath, I took his hand, my pulse quickening as his fingers closed around mine. The warmth of his touch sent ripples of electricity up my arm, and I caught the flicker of amusement in his eyes as he led me deeper into the garden. "Welcome to my sanctuary," he said, his voice low and inviting. "Here, the only rules are the ones we make."

"Are there rules?" I challenged, a playful spark igniting within me. "Or is this a free-for-all?"

"Depends on what you want to discover." He paused, regarding me with an intensity that made the air shimmer. "I can show you beauty or chaos; the choice is yours."

"And you think I'm equipped to handle either?" I shot back, trying to mask my intrigue with bravado.

"From what I've seen, you can handle much more than you let on," he replied, a teasing lilt in his voice. "You have an adventurous spirit beneath all those flowers."

A soft chuckle escaped my lips, disarmed by his words. "Adventurous? I prefer to think of myself as practical. I craft floral arrangements, not chaos."

"Yet here you are, in the depths of my secret garden. Doesn't that scream adventure?" He plucked a small blossom from a nearby bush and held it out to me. "This is a moonflower. It blooms only at night, revealing its beauty when the world is asleep. Much like us, don't you think?"

"Are you comparing me to a flower that blooms at night? That's a bold compliment," I replied, accepting the delicate flower and twirling it between my fingers.

"Only if you're willing to embrace the darkness, Elara." There was something in his tone that hinted at layers I hadn't yet uncovered, a depth that drew me closer to the edge of my curiosity. "But beware; not all secrets are meant to be unveiled."

"I'll take my chances," I said, my voice steadier than I felt. The thrill of the unknown surged through me like a tempest. "What's the worst that could happen?"

He smirked, leaning in as if to share a conspiratorial secret. "You might find yourself entangled in more than just petals and vines. There are shadows lurking here, and sometimes those shadows hold the most dangerous truths."

As the words hung in the air, a rustling sound pierced the stillness, shattering the intimate bubble we'd created. I turned, heart racing, scanning the garden for the source. "What was that?"

"Just the night," Jude replied, but his expression shifted slightly, a shadow flickering in his eyes. "Sometimes, the night holds its own surprises."

I felt a knot of tension form in my stomach, the thrill of adventure rapidly overshadowed by an encroaching sense of unease. "You said this was your sanctuary. Shouldn't it feel safe?"

He hesitated, the weight of something unspoken lingering between us. "Even sanctuaries can be vulnerable."

Before I could respond, a figure emerged from the trees at the edge of the garden, silhouetted against the moonlight. My heart leaped into my throat, instinct screaming at me to flee. Jude's grip on my hand tightened, grounding me in place.

"Stay close," he murmured, his voice low and steady, though I could feel the tension radiating from him.

The figure stepped forward, revealing a tall woman with dark hair cascading over her shoulders like a waterfall of night. She wore a long, flowing gown that seemed to shimmer in the moonlight, and her eyes sparkled with a predatory glint. "Jude," she said, her voice smooth and honeyed, yet edged with something sharp, "I thought I might find you here."

"Valentina," Jude replied, his tone clipped. "What are you doing here?"

"I was looking for you, darling," she purred, taking a step closer, the air thickening with unspoken tension. "The festival is a terrible place for secrets, don't you think? You shouldn't hide away in a garden when there's so much more to explore."

"Maybe I like it here," he countered, his voice firm. "And maybe I'm not in the mood for your games tonight."

Her laugh was melodic, yet there was an undercurrent of menace. "Oh, sweet Jude, you know I don't play games. I just collect what's mine." She turned her gaze toward me, eyes narrowing slightly, assessing. "And who might this be? Another flower in your garden?"

"I'm Elara," I introduced myself, forcing a confident smile despite the unease curling in my gut. "Just admiring the blooms."

"Admirers can be so easily distracted, can't they?" Valentina replied, her smile sharp, almost predatory. "Careful, Jude. You wouldn't want your little flower to get lost among the thorns."

"Stop it," Jude snapped, his demeanor shifting to something more protective. "You don't need to threaten her."

"Threaten? I'm simply stating a fact," she retorted, her tone turning icy. "These gardens are not as safe as you think. Secrets have a way of blooming into something far more dangerous."

A chill swept through me, the air growing heavy with unspoken implications. My heart raced as I felt the weight of her gaze, a blend of curiosity and malice that made my skin crawl. "I think it's time for you to leave, Valentina," Jude said, his voice low and firm.

"Why? So you can play house with your little florist? That's rich, Jude," she scoffed, her gaze flicking dismissively between us. "But remember, some secrets can't stay buried forever."

With that, she turned, gliding away into the darkness like a specter, leaving behind a suffocating silence that hung heavy in the air. I glanced at Jude, whose expression was a mixture of frustration and concern.

“What was that about?” I demanded, my voice barely above a whisper, the unease growing like a thorn in my chest.

“Just a warning,” he replied, his eyes scanning the shadows. “Valentina has a knack for digging up trouble. We need to be careful.”

“Careful?” I echoed, my heart racing. “You brought me here, Jude! I didn’t sign up for this kind of chaos!”

“It’s not just chaos, Elara. It’s something much bigger,” he admitted, his voice barely concealing the tension beneath the surface. “And I’m afraid you might already be in deeper than you realize.”

Before I could respond, a rustling came from the opposite side of the garden, more urgent and erratic than before. My breath caught in my throat as I turned, fear clawing at the edges of my composure. Something was lurking just beyond the shadows, and my heart thundered in my chest, pounding with the realization that the night held more than just secrets—it held dangers waiting to be uncovered.

“Jude—” I began, but before I could finish, a figure lunged from the darkness, and the world around us erupted into chaos.

Chapter 3: Thorns and Blossoms

The scent of caramel corn wafted through the air, mingling with the crisp autumn breeze, infusing the festival with a sense of warmth that belied the chill of the season. Twinkling fairy lights danced above the bustling crowd, casting a gentle glow that made everything seem magical, yet somehow distant. I maneuvered through the throng of festival-goers, my heart pounding with each step, every laughter and cheer intensifying the thrill that coursed through me. It wasn't just the festival that set my pulse racing; it was the thought of Jude, his sharp wit and disarming smile lingering in my mind like an intoxicating melody I couldn't quite place.

As I passed by a booth filled with handmade jewelry, my fingers brushed against the cool metal of a ring. It sparkled like stars trapped in silver, and I had to resist the urge to buy it—not because I couldn't afford it, but because I was momentarily lost in thoughts of Jude, a boy who seemed to have made it his mission to disrupt my carefully constructed world. I could still hear his laughter ringing in my ears, a sound that both delighted and infuriated me.

Our earlier encounter had been charged, a battle of wits where every playful jab felt like a step closer to something profound and unsettling. I had expected Jude to be a mere nuisance, another face in the crowd. Instead, he had unraveled some of my defenses with a single, devil-may-care grin. His confidence was a force of nature, sweeping away my initial irritation and planting a seed of curiosity where there had been none before. I found myself wondering if perhaps I had misjudged him, if there was more to the boy whose very presence ignited a flurry of conflicting emotions within me.

"Are you going to stand there all day, or are you going to try that pumpkin spice latte I've heard so much about?" A voice cut through my reverie, pulling me back to reality with the precision of a well-aimed dart.

It was Max, my friend since forever, with his tousled hair and perpetually mischievous grin. He always seemed to appear just when I needed a distraction, and today was no exception.

"Are you kidding? It's like drinking syrup!" I shot back, folding my arms defiantly as I tried to suppress a smile.

"Only if you're too afraid to embrace the seasonal bliss," he retorted, wiggling his eyebrows dramatically. "Besides, it's practically a rite of passage at this festival. You can't tell me you're above such things."

Max had a knack for pushing my buttons, and while I feigned annoyance, I couldn't help but admire his infectious enthusiasm. With a resigned sigh, I rolled my eyes and let him pull me toward the coffee stand, trying to shake off thoughts of Jude as we joined the line.

The barista, a young woman with bright pink hair, greeted us with a beaming smile. "What can I get you guys?"

"Pumpkin spice latte, please," Max replied, as if he'd just ordered a rare delicacy.

"Make it two!" I added, half-heartedly conceding to his persuasion. As the rich scent of spices wafted toward me, I wondered why I let Max lead me into these sugary traps. Yet, when the first warm sip met my lips, I couldn't help but moan in delight. "Okay, fine. This is amazing!"

"Told you so!" Max beamed, enjoying his small victory.

Just as I began to relax into the sweetness of the moment, a familiar figure emerged from the crowd, his presence electrifying the air around us. Jude was leaning against a nearby stall, arms crossed and a smirk plastered across his face, the epitome of casual confidence.

"Ah, if it isn't the latte lovers," he called out, his voice teasing yet melodic, like music played just a touch too loud.

Max glanced at me, his eyes dancing with mischief, as if he were waiting for the inevitable explosion. "Looks like we've been caught, huh?"

"Not surprised you'd choose something so basic," Jude continued, eyes glinting with mischief as he stepped closer, his gaze landing on me like a warm caress. "Didn't take you for someone who followed trends."

"Maybe I just enjoy delicious things, unlike you," I shot back, my heart racing despite myself. "But it's hard to see anything delicious when you look like you just rolled out of bed."

Jude's laughter was genuine, a sound that sent a flutter through my chest. "At least I'm not afraid to show my true self," he replied, leaning in as if sharing a secret. "Not everyone can pull off that overly polished look you rock, you know."

It was an unexpected compliment wrapped in a challenge, and it made me feel oddly seen in a way that both thrilled and unnerved me. "Oh please, don't flatter yourself. I'd rather be polished than a rough draft," I countered, my voice steady even as a blush crept up my cheeks.

The air thickened with tension, a blend of rivalry and undeniable chemistry. I couldn't pinpoint the exact moment when our jabs morphed into something deeper, something that flickered beneath the surface like fireflies just out of reach. A flicker of vulnerability shone in his eyes, and for a moment, the playful banter transformed into an intimate exchange. It was as if we were speaking in a language all our own, one filled with layers of meaning that eluded the others around us.

As I turned away, my heart raced, not from anger but from the heady realization that what had begun as rivalry was shifting. The festival, with its vibrant colors and joyful chaos, mirrored the tangled web of emotions we were weaving. Somewhere amidst the laughter and celebrations, our paths had crossed in unexpected ways, forging an uncharted connection that left me breathless and wanting more.

Max and I navigated through the festival grounds, our pumpkin spice lattes in hand, weaving past booths showcasing artisanal crafts and local treats. The kaleidoscope of colors—from the deep oranges of pumpkin decorations to the vibrant reds and golds of fallen leaves—painted a picture of autumn's embrace. Laughter rang out from a nearby hayride, where kids scrambled to find their seats, their parents capturing the moment on smartphones. I caught a glimpse of a little girl with pigtails, her infectious giggles making me smile.

"Okay, spill," Max said, his voice a conspiratorial whisper as we stopped beside a stall selling caramel apples. "What was that back there with Jude? You two were practically sparring."

I shrugged, feigning nonchalance, but inside, my thoughts were a tangled mess. "It was just... banter," I replied, but my heart didn't quite agree. "He knows how to push my buttons, that's all."

"Sure," Max chuckled, eyeing me knowingly. "But the way you were looking at each other? You could practically see the sparks fly. You're telling me you didn't feel that?"

My cheeks warmed as I remembered the way Jude's gaze had lingered on mine, the way he made me feel alive and infuriated all at once. "Fine, there might have been some chemistry. But that doesn't mean I want to go on a picnic with him."

"Who said anything about a picnic? It sounds like you're on the verge of a very intense game of verbal tennis. I could even place bets on who serves up the best insults." Max grinned, his eyes sparkling with mischief.

"Let's just focus on the festival, okay?" I shot back, but a smile tugged at my lips. The truth was, every time I crossed paths with Jude, my defenses crumbled a little more. He was maddening, yes, but there was something magnetic about his presence.

We stopped at a booth adorned with delicate glass ornaments, shimmering in the golden light like captured raindrops. I absentmindedly reached out to touch a dainty glass owl, its eyes twinkling back at me. "You know, this would make a great gift for my mom," I mused, imagining her delight.

"Or you could keep it for yourself," Max suggested, leaning closer to examine it. "That way, you could admire it every day while secretly plotting your revenge against Jude. It's the perfect battle trophy."

I laughed, the sound bubbling up from deep inside. The playful banter between us was familiar, a comfort in the whirlwind of the festival. But as I marveled at the beauty of the ornaments, I couldn't shake the feeling that I was caught in a much larger game, one that involved not just Jude and me, but layers of complexity that I hadn't yet begun to unravel.

Our laughter drew the attention of a nearby couple, who were busy trying to win a giant stuffed bear from a ring toss game. Their enthusiasm was contagious, and before I knew it, I found myself cheering them on, completely swept away by the moment. When they finally won, the squeals of delight were infectious, and I couldn't help but feel a flutter of happiness for them.

As I clapped and joined in their celebration, I felt a tap on my shoulder. I turned to see Jude standing there, an amused grin plastered across his face. "Looks like you've found your true calling—cheering for random strangers," he quipped, hands stuffed casually into his pockets.

"Better than being a sarcastic commentary on everything," I shot back, but my tone was light, almost teasing.

"Oh, but I do that so well." His laughter mingled with mine, and for a moment, the competition between us faded into something softer, more genuine.

"Are you just going to hover, or do you want to join the festivities?" I challenged, my bravado masking the fluttering nerves in my stomach.

"I was about to ask you the same thing," he replied, stepping closer. The space between us charged with unspoken words. "What do you say we try that haunted house over there? I promise to keep you safe."

I raised an eyebrow, fighting a grin. "Safe? From what? Your terrible jokes or the actual ghosts?"

"Both," he retorted, a mock-serious expression settling on his face. "But mostly, the ghosts. I've heard they prefer girls who scream at every little thing. Should be a good time for both of us."

"Fine," I agreed, curiosity piqued despite myself. "But if I scream, it's only because you're lurking behind me like a shadow."

He feigned offense, placing a hand over his heart. "I'm wounded. But I'll allow it for the sake of adventure."

As we approached the haunted house, a rickety structure cloaked in cobwebs and adorned with flickering lights, I felt a thrill race through me. The line was long, but it only gave us more time to exchange jabs and banter. Each quip seemed to pull us closer, and the tension between us was palpable, like a coiled spring ready to snap.

When we finally stepped inside, the dim light illuminated a hallway lined with ominous paintings that seemed to watch us as we walked past. I could feel Jude's presence beside me, warm and inviting, yet laced with mischief.

"Promise me you won't grab my arm too hard," he murmured, his voice low enough that only I could hear.

"Only if you promise not to yell like a little girl," I shot back, half-teasing, half-challenging.

He laughed, the sound echoing in the eerie silence of the haunted house. "Deal."

As we ventured deeper into the maze of scares, shadows danced along the walls, and the air turned thick with suspense. Each corner we turned brought fresh surprises—a ghostly figure jumping out from the darkness, a chilling laugh echoing through the halls. My heart raced, not just from the fright, but from the exhilaration of being so close to Jude.

"Didn't think you'd actually come in here with me," he said, stealing a glance at me as we turned a corner.

"Didn't think you had the guts to ask," I replied, a smirk playing on my lips.

"Touché."

But as the next scare hit us, I instinctively grabbed his arm, the contact sending a jolt of electricity through me. The moment hung between us, charged and heavy, as I pulled away, breathless. For a heartbeat, the playful rivalry morphed into something deeper, an awareness that crackled in the space between us.

Suddenly, the world outside the haunted house faded into the background, and it was just the two of us, teetering on the brink of something we couldn't quite name.

We stumbled into the next room, where darkness enveloped us, and for a moment, I couldn't tell where the boundaries of reality ended and the haunted house began. A sudden gust of wind rushed past, followed by a ghostly wail that sent shivers down my spine. I barely had time to brace myself before an apparition appeared from the shadows, its chains clinking ominously. I jumped, reflexively grabbing Jude's arm again, my heart hammering like a wild drum.

"Relax," he whispered, half-laughing, half-sarcastic. "It's just a guy in a sheet trying to get paid."

"Easy for you to say," I retorted, my pulse racing not just from fear but the warmth of his skin beneath my fingers. "You're not the one getting haunted."

The ghostly figure lunged forward, and I let out a yelp, burying my face in Jude's shoulder, entirely ignoring the twinge of embarrassment that shot through me. He chuckled softly, his laughter vibrating against me, a soothing balm amidst the chaos. I could feel his breath hitch slightly as he struggled to maintain composure, and I had to bite back a smile, feeling oddly comforted by the ridiculousness of the situation.

"You really scream like a banshee, don't you?" he teased as we navigated through more unsettling twists and turns.

"Only when I'm being attacked by invisible chains," I shot back, trying to muster all the bravado I could. "What kind of person thinks a haunted house is a great idea anyway? This is just a trap for us to scream and get embarrassed."

"Oh, come on. Embrarrassment is half the fun!" he replied, his eyes sparkling with mischief. "Besides, we'll have a great story to tell when we survive this."

"Survive?" I echoed, suddenly aware of the shadows creeping closer, lurking just out of sight. "Is that supposed to make me feel better?"

"Hey, we're in this together. Just keep holding on to me like that, and I'm sure we'll make it out alive."

As we ventured deeper, we encountered a series of jump scares and eerie sound effects, each more ridiculous than the last. At one point, a mechanical spider dropped from the ceiling, and I let out a squeal, twisting away from Jude and clutching his shirt in a panic.

"Are you trying to strangle me or just get closer?" he teased, amusement dancing in his eyes.

I couldn't help but laugh, my nerves slowly settling into a giddy exhilaration. "Maybe both. Just shut up and let me cling to you for dear life!"

"Your wish is my command," he said, his tone mockingly dramatic as he stepped forward into the next room, a grand hall adorned with cobwebs and flickering candles. It was unexpectedly beautiful, an artist's rendition of terror, complete with a chandelier that swayed eerily overhead.

"This place is so cheesy," I whispered, my voice reverberating slightly against the walls. "I almost feel bad for the people who worked on it."

Jude nodded, a playful smirk on his lips. "Well, at least they're committed. And you know what they say: fake it till you make it."

"Yeah, but what if it fakes us out first?" I shot back, feeling a thrill ripple through me.

Suddenly, the lights flickered, plunging us into near-complete darkness. The soft murmur of the crowd faded away, replaced by an unsettling silence. My breath caught in my throat, the atmosphere shifting from playful to something far more intense.

"Jude?" I said, my voice barely above a whisper.

"Right here," he reassured me, his hand finding mine, warm and steady.

Just then, an eerie howl echoed through the hall, sending chills racing down my spine. A shiver of genuine fear coursed through me, and I tightened my grip on Jude's hand, my pulse quickening.

"What was that?" I asked, my heart pounding as panic crept into my voice.

"No idea," he replied, his voice tinged with uncertainty. "But I'm sure it's just part of the act."

As if in response, the floor beneath us shook slightly, and I felt a jolt of electricity in the air. I glanced at Jude, and his expression shifted, the teasing glint in his eyes replaced by something far more serious. "Maybe we should get out of here," he suggested, the gravity of his tone pulling me back to reality.

We turned to leave, but the way we came in was suddenly blocked by a thick, heavy curtain that had not been there moments before. I frowned, my mind racing. "Jude, that wasn't there before. Are we trapped?"

He glanced at the curtain, then at me, his eyes wide. "Okay, that's not good."

The air felt heavy with tension, and the realization that we might be in real trouble settled in like a cold weight. The haunted house had transformed from a lighthearted adventure into a claustrophobic maze with no clear escape.

"Let's go back the way we came," I suggested, heart racing as I tugged him back toward the hallway, but we were met with another wall of black.

"Seriously?" Jude exclaimed, his voice rising in pitch. "What kind of haunted house does this?"

One moment, we were mere participants in an autumn festival, and the next, we were part of a sinister game that felt all too real. Panic threatened to bubble over as the howling noise grew louder, echoing through the corridor, vibrating in my chest.

"Jude!" I exclaimed, adrenaline surging through me. "What if we really can't get out?"

"Don't freak out," he said, voice steady despite the chaos. "We just need to think. There's always a way out."

I could feel his resolve, his determination to protect me, and yet my heart raced with fear. The shadows closed in, each flicker of light casting sinister shapes against the walls. "But what if this is part of it?"

Before he could answer, the lights flickered back on, revealing an exit sign glowing ominously in the distance. But just as quickly as it appeared, it began to dim.

"Let's go!" Jude shouted, his grip on my hand tightening as we sprinted toward the sign.

But as we dashed forward, a wall of mist enveloped us, swirling and thick, and I felt an unyielding force pulling us apart. "Jude!"

I screamed, reaching out, panic slicing through me as the world around us faded into darkness.

His voice cut through the haze, laced with urgency. “Don’t let go! I’m right here!”

The mist thickened, wrapping around me like a shroud, swallowing the light until I could barely see. Just as I stumbled, my heart racing, I felt a sudden pull—a sharp tug of resistance as I struggled to break free. And in that moment, everything changed.

As the world slipped away, a piercing scream echoed through the darkness, merging with the howl from before, and I was left with only the sensation of falling into the unknown, the weight of uncertainty pressing down on me like a heavy fog.

Chapter 4: Dark Petals

The aroma of freshly brewed coffee enveloped me as I stepped into the cozy little café, its familiar warmth a welcome distraction from the chaos that had consumed my floral shop. The air was thick with the scent of roasted beans and sweet pastries, but all I could focus on was the knot in my stomach. It was a gathering storm, one I knew I had to face head-on. I spotted Jude in the corner, his tall frame slouched against the wall, an espresso cup cradled in his hands like a shield. The sunlight streaming through the window highlighted the sharp angles of his jaw, casting shadows that seemed to mirror the tension brewing between us.

"Jude," I greeted him, my voice a mixture of resolve and hesitation. He looked up, his expression shifting from surprise to a guarded semblance of irritation. The café buzzed with life around us, yet our corner felt like an isolated island, the weight of our unresolved issues pressing down like an anvil.

"Did you come to accuse me again?" His tone was laced with sarcasm, a clear defense mechanism.

"Accuse you? I'm simply seeking answers," I replied, crossing my arms as I leaned against the table, feeling the rough wood beneath my palms—a tangible reminder of the grounding reality I was desperate to cling to. "Why have your arrangements been sabotaged? I know you've been behind this."

"Really? You think I'm some petty criminal, sneaking into your shop to ruin your flowers? That's rich." He leaned back, his blue eyes narrowing, a spark of challenge igniting in their depths.

"You have a motive, don't you?" I pressed, my frustration bubbling to the surface. "You're trying to take my clients. Riverview is a small town; people talk. It's not just the flowers going missing; it's the way you've been acting."

"You mean the way I'm trying to run a business?" he shot back, the tension crackling in the air like static electricity. "Maybe I'm simply better at it than you."

"You think that's what this is about? A competition?" My voice rose slightly, drawing the attention of a few nearby patrons who paused mid-conversation to listen. I took a deep breath, willing myself to calm down. "This isn't just business, Jude. It's my livelihood."

He leaned forward, the intensity in his gaze unyielding. "And what makes you think it's not mine?"

The world around us faded, and for a moment, I could only hear the rhythmic thud of my heart against my chest. Beneath the simmering anger lay an undeniable tension that I could no longer ignore. Part of me wanted to dismiss him entirely, to throw myself back into the safe embrace of my flower arrangements, where emotions could be translated into vibrant colors and fragrant blooms. But the other part— the part that had grown curious about the man across from me—pulled me deeper into the complexity of our rivalry.

"Do you even care?" I blurted out, the words escaping before I could rein them in. "Or is it just about the competition for you?"

His eyes flashed with surprise, and I sensed a shift, a crack in the facade he'd carefully constructed. "Of course I care. This town...this industry—it's not just a game for me. I'm here to make something of myself, just like you."

"Then why the sabotage?" I challenged, my voice softer now, almost pleading for clarity.

"It's not me," he insisted, the sharpness in his voice giving way to something more vulnerable. "I wouldn't do that. But it seems like you want to think the worst of me. Why? Because I'm your rival? Because I'm a man trying to make my way in this world?"

A flush crept into my cheeks, caught between my desire to defend myself and the dawning realization that I might have misjudged him. "It's not that simple. You come off like you're...invincible. Like nothing matters to you but winning."

Jude's expression softened slightly, a hint of amusement flickering in his eyes. "And you come off like a princess guarding her castle. Maybe there's more to both of us than meets the eye."

The unexpected intimacy of his words sent a jolt through me, awakening a strange mix of frustration and intrigue. Did I truly see him as a villain? Or was there a flicker of something else—a deeper connection that we were both too stubborn to acknowledge?

Before I could respond, a commotion at the café entrance drew our attention. A group of women burst in, laughing and chattering, their arms laden with shopping bags, oblivious to the tension radiating from our corner. One of them, a regular customer of mine, spotted us and approached with a bright smile.

"Hey! Are you two finally working things out? I thought this rivalry was going to ruin Riverview's flower scene!" She laughed, oblivious to the undercurrents swirling between us.

Jude and I exchanged a look, a silent understanding passing between us—a shared realization that we had become more than just competitors. The façade of rivalry had begun to fracture, revealing layers of complexity neither of us had anticipated.

As the conversation turned toward trivial matters, I found myself glancing at Jude out of the corner of my eye, noticing the way his lips curled into a wry smile as he responded to the women. The lightness of the moment was a welcome distraction from the weight of our earlier confrontation. Yet, beneath the banter, the unresolved tension lingered like the scent of coffee and pastries in the air.

When the group finally moved on, leaving us in our bubble of uncertainty, I felt the pull between us strengthen—a strange gravitational force that defied all logic. Could it be possible that beneath our rivalry lay the seeds of something more profound? The notion fluttered in my mind like a butterfly caught in a gust of wind, beautiful yet elusive.

"Let's call a truce," Jude suggested suddenly, his tone unexpectedly earnest. "We both have shops to run. I don't want to sabotage you, and you don't want to sabotage me. Maybe we can figure this out without all the drama?"

I stared at him, weighing his words carefully. "And how do you propose we do that?"

"Team up. At least for the upcoming spring festival," he said, a glimmer of hope lighting up his features. "We can showcase our flowers together, create something extraordinary instead of tearing each other down. Who knows? It might even boost our sales."

The idea hung in the air, fraught with possibilities, and as I considered it, my heart raced. Could it be that in the heart of Riverview's competitive spirit lay the potential for collaboration? The thought felt both exhilarating and terrifying, a dance of light and shadow. But what if working together could lead us to a place where our rivalry transformed into something far more complicated?

"Let me think about it," I finally replied, the weight of my decision heavy on my shoulders. As I turned to leave, a strange mix of anticipation and uncertainty settled within me. The fight wasn't over; it was merely shifting. I could almost sense the dark petals of our connection unfurling, revealing secrets yet to be discovered.

The following days blurred together like watercolors bleeding into each other. Each morning I would unlock the door to my flower shop, stepping into the fragrant embrace of roses and lilies, but my heart felt heavy with uncertainty. The blooms were a vivid contrast to the shadow looming over my business. Missing petals and sabotaged arrangements were not mere inconveniences; they were direct assaults on my passion, and the whispers among the townsfolk grew louder with each incident. I could practically hear them behind my back, speculating, judging, and wondering if the Riverview Flower Studio was on the brink of collapse.

In the midst of this turmoil, I couldn't shake the notion that Jude was somehow orchestrating this chaos, though I had no proof beyond my gut instinct. Every stolen flower and ruined bouquet seemed to point back to him like an arrow seeking its target. It was absurd, I knew that, yet here I was, entangled in this web of rivalry and confusion.

As I arranged a fresh batch of daisies, their cheerful yellow heads nodding in the sunlight, my thoughts drifted back to our heated conversation. Jude had suggested teaming up for the upcoming spring festival—a prospect that sounded both promising and utterly terrifying. Could I really work alongside my rival, the man who had made my life as vibrant as the blooms I cherished and as thorny as their stems? It was a tantalizing idea, but one that felt drenched in complexities and unspoken truths.

That afternoon, while I was fussing over the display in the shop window, the bell above the door chimed, and in walked Clara, my best friend since childhood. Her dark curls bounced as she rushed over, a storm of energy wrapped in a vintage floral dress that seemed to mirror the very essence of spring.

"Okay, spill! What's the drama?" she demanded, her hands on her hips, her eyes glinting with mischief. "I heard there's been some sabotage at the flower shop. What kind of villainy are we dealing with?"

I couldn't help but chuckle at her dramatic flair, even as my heart twisted. "I think I might be embroiled in a very personal war with Jude. He's been sabotaging my work, or at least, I think he is."

"Ah, the handsome rival trope," she teased, rolling her eyes playfully. "What is it with you and your penchant for brooding, handsome men? Do you need a dramatic tension meter to help you choose between love and rivalry?"

"I don't need a meter; I need a detective. This isn't some romantic comedy, Clara. My business is at stake!" My voice rose slightly, the frustration spilling over. "And every time I think about teaming up, I can't shake the feeling that he's got something up his sleeve."

Clara leaned in closer, her voice dropping to a conspiratorial whisper. "Have you considered that maybe this rivalry is just a cover? Perhaps you two are like those classic foes in literature who secretly harbor a fiery passion beneath all that animosity."

"Oh please," I scoffed, though a part of me tingled at the thought. "I can barely stand him half the time."

"Exactly," she replied, her tone smug. "That just means there's some unresolved chemistry bubbling under the surface. Have you tried flirting back? A little tension can be good for business."

"Flirting? With Jude?" I shook my head, but a smile crept onto my face. "He'd probably throw a pot of daisies at me and call it a flower fight."

"Sounds like an entertaining scene to me! You know, your life could use a little more spontaneity. Why not shake things up?"

"Right, because that's exactly what I need—a flower fight to make my shop the talk of the town." My sarcasm hung in the air, but beneath it was a flicker of intrigue. What would happen if I threw caution to the wind? If I leaned into this absurd rivalry and let it take me where it would?

As we chatted, the bell jingled again, and I glanced up to see Jude stepping through the door, his expression a blend of determination and something else I couldn't quite place. He scanned the shop, his gaze landing on me, and I felt the air thicken with unspoken words.

"Am I interrupting something?" he asked, his voice smooth like honey but laced with an edge of challenge.

"Not at all. Clara was just giving me some...interesting advice," I replied, a playful smile on my lips as I shot Clara a glance.

"Interesting, huh?" Jude arched an eyebrow, stepping further into the shop. "Care to share?"

"Not a chance," Clara interjected, a grin spreading across her face. "But I'd love to hear your side of the story. How's the competition treating you, Jude?"

He chuckled, a sound that resonated deep in my chest. "The usual. Trying to win over the hearts—and wallets—of Riverview. But I might need a little help," he said, his gaze lingering on me. "Which is why I came here. I wanted to talk about the festival."

I felt Clara's eyes dart between us, a mixture of excitement and mischief dancing in her gaze. "Oh, you mean the joint venture?"

"Yes, the joint venture," Jude said, his tone suddenly serious. "I think it would be beneficial for both of us. It's the biggest event of the season, and we can showcase our work together instead of tearing each other down."

The suggestion hung in the air, potent with possibility. I could see the sincerity in his eyes, yet my instinct screamed caution. "And what makes you think I wouldn't be setting myself up for failure?"

"Because we both have something to gain," he countered, a hint of a smile playing at the corners of his mouth. "Imagine the impact we could make, two rival florists uniting for a common goal. We could create something beautiful."

"Or a disaster," I shot back, half-amused and half-serious. "What if it flops and the whole town laughs at us?"

"Then we'll drown our sorrows in cake at the bakery across the street," he replied with a casual shrug. "I'm not afraid of a little risk if it means achieving something great."

His confidence was infectious, and I could feel the tension shift in the room, almost like the calm before a storm. Clara clapped her hands together, grinning widely. "Well, I for one am in favor of this partnership. I say you both give it a shot! What's the worst that could happen? You become Riverview's dynamic floral duo?"

"Or become infamous for the greatest flower fiasco in history," I muttered, the corners of my mouth twitching with a reluctant smile.

Jude stepped closer, his voice dropping to a softer tone. "Trust me. We can make it work. It's time to stop playing this game of rivals and start being allies."

The weight of his words settled over me, mingling with the intoxicating aroma of flowers and coffee. What if this was the chance I had been waiting for—a way to not only save my business but perhaps also uncover the truth of my feelings for Jude? The very thought made my heart race, both from fear and excitement.

"Okay," I finally said, my voice steady, yet my heart thundered in my chest. "Let's do it. But if this goes south, I'm holding you responsible for the outcome."

"Deal." His eyes sparkled with mischief, a challenge lacing his words.

As we exchanged glances, I couldn't help but think that perhaps, just perhaps, this was the beginning of something entirely new—not just for our businesses but for us. And as Clara winked and slipped out of the shop, I felt the air shift, charged with a spark that promised adventure, chaos, and a connection I was only beginning to understand.

The sun dipped low in the sky as Jude and I began to sketch out our plans for the spring festival, the café around us bustling with life and chatter. Despite the tension that had hung between us just days before, the atmosphere now crackled with an electric sort of energy. We sat at a small table, our ideas colliding like the vibrant colors of the blooms we both cherished.

"I'm thinking we could create a joint display that highlights both our styles," Jude suggested, his brow furrowed in concentration. "Something that represents the essence of Riverview—like a local flower garden, but on a larger scale."

"Like a competition of sorts, but a friendly one," I replied, feeling the flicker of enthusiasm spread through me. "We could use sunflowers, daisies, and maybe some wildflowers to keep it rustic. It's what people expect at the festival."

"Great idea! We can set up a photo booth area too," he added, his eyes gleaming with inspiration. "A backdrop of flowers where families can take pictures. It'll make our stall the centerpiece of the event."

As we brainstormed, laughter spilled from the nearby tables, and the aroma of cinnamon pastries wafted through the air. Each passing moment eased the weight of our earlier confrontation, replaced instead by a budding collaboration that felt surprisingly comfortable. Yet, beneath that comfort, a lingering apprehension gnawed at me. Could I truly trust him after everything that had happened?

Just as we were sketching our ideas, a commotion erupted from the door. A small group of women, some regulars at my shop, burst in, their faces flushed with excitement. One of them, Maggie, a spirited florist from a neighboring town, rushed toward us, her eyes wide.

"You won't believe what just happened!" she exclaimed, barely able to catch her breath. "I heard from Alice that flowers are going missing all over Riverview, not just at your shop. It's chaos out there!"

I felt a chill run down my spine, the nagging suspicion I'd harbored about Jude flaring up again. "What do you mean, going missing?" I asked, my heart racing.

"It's like someone is intentionally stealing them. Alice said she found her whole shipment of peonies gone! They were supposed to be for her arrangements at the festival."

Jude's expression shifted to one of concern, a flicker of empathy crossing his features. "How many other shops have been affected?" he asked, his tone more serious now.

"Five so far, and rumors say there might be more. People are starting to panic. If it keeps up, the festival will be a disaster!" Maggie's voice was a mixture of excitement and alarm, and I could see the gears turning in her mind as she tried to gauge the implications.

As the realization sank in, I exchanged a glance with Jude, a silent understanding passing between us. This was bigger than just our rivalry now; the very foundation of our businesses was at stake.

"We need to investigate," I said, determination edging into my voice. "If someone is stealing flowers, we have to figure out who it is and why."

Jude nodded, his expression resolute. "Together then?"

"Together," I affirmed, though the word tasted bittersweet on my tongue. The irony of our situation wasn't lost on me; here we were, rivals forced into an alliance by circumstances beyond our control.

As we stepped out of the café, the fading sunlight cast long shadows on the cobblestone streets. The air was thick with anticipation, and I could feel a rush of adrenaline as we walked side by side, heading toward the heart of Riverview. Our destination was the community center, a hub for the festival planning, where I hoped to find more information on the flower thefts.

"Do you think it could be anyone we know?" Jude asked, his voice low, almost conspiratorial.

"Honestly, I wouldn't put it past anyone in this town," I replied. "Competitiveness has a way of bringing out the worst in people, especially when money is involved."

Just then, I spotted Clara leaning against the community center's doorframe, her eyes scanning the crowd. She waved us over, her expression a mix of concern and curiosity. "There you are! I've been looking for you two. The rumor mill is in overdrive, and people are saying the thefts are connected to the festival somehow."

"Connected how?" I pressed, my heart racing at the thought of a deeper conspiracy at play.

"Some believe it's a rival florist trying to sabotage everyone to claim the spotlight for themselves. There's talk that someone is even planning to expose all the shops that fail to provide a stunning display," she explained, her voice lowering as if sharing a secret.

"Great, just what we need—a floral villain lurking in the shadows," Jude muttered, his hands clenching into fists.

"What do we do now?" Clara asked, her eyes wide with intrigue.

"First, we need to gather more information. Talk to the other florists affected. See if we can find a pattern or any common threads," I suggested, the plan taking shape in my mind.

As we delved deeper into the heart of the community center, I could feel the pulse of anxiety in the air. We split up to cover more ground, Jude heading toward the main hall, while Clara and I checked the smaller rooms where vendors were setting up.

In one of the side rooms, I found Alice, her face pale as she recounted her own experience. "I've never seen anything like it. I had an entire shipment ready for the festival, and by the time I went to check on them, they were just...gone. No sign of a break-in or anything."

My instincts kicked in. "Were there any strange people hanging around before it happened? Any odd deliveries or visitors?"

She shook her head, frustration evident in her expression. "Not that I noticed. It was just a regular day until everything went wrong. I thought I had everything under control."

As we continued to gather information, I felt a sense of urgency building. This wasn't just about the flowers; it was about our livelihoods and the very spirit of Riverview. If we couldn't stop whoever was behind this, the festival would be a disaster, and our reputations would be at stake.

Finally, I regrouped with Jude and Clara, their expressions mirroring my concern. "What's the plan?" Clara asked, her brow furrowed.

"We need to keep a close eye on our shops and set up a stakeout," Jude suggested, a spark of determination in his eyes. "If we can catch whoever is behind this in the act, we might be able to stop them."

"Or we might end up as their next victims," I warned, the weight of my words hanging heavy in the air.

"Better to risk it than to let them win," Jude replied, his voice steady.

As we began discussing our strategy, a sudden commotion erupted outside the community center. Shouts rang out, and the sound of breaking glass shattered the night.

"Stay here!" I ordered, my heart racing as I rushed toward the door. My instincts screamed that whatever was happening outside was connected to the thefts.

I burst into the cool evening air, my eyes widening at the scene before me. A crowd had gathered, murmurs of shock rippling through them. In the center of it all, a figure darted away, their silhouette illuminated by the streetlights. Clutching something in their arms—was it flowers?

"Hey! Stop!" I shouted, adrenaline pumping through my veins as I took off after them, the world narrowing to the rhythm of my pounding heart.

Just as I was about to close the distance, the figure turned a corner, vanishing into the shadows. I skidded to a halt, panting, frustration mixing with the thrill of the chase.

Jude caught up with me, breathless. "Did you see who it was?"

"No! They got away too quickly!" I replied, scanning the area for any sign of them.

Clara rushed to join us, her expression a mix of fear and excitement. "What was that all about?"

"Someone just ran off with a load of flowers," I said, my heart still racing.

As we surveyed the crowd, I spotted a familiar face in the throng—a face that sent a chill racing down my spine. It was the last person I expected to see here, someone I thought had nothing to do with the festival at all.

My heart sank. It was a face I knew well, a face that could change everything. The very presence of that person threatened to unravel all the threads we'd been trying to weave together, igniting a new layer of chaos that none of us had seen coming.

"Jude," I whispered, my voice barely audible. "I think we might have a bigger problem on our hands than we realized."

Chapter 5: Tangles and Twists

The vibrant streets of Riverview came alive under the golden glow of the late afternoon sun, casting playful shadows that danced along the cobblestone pathways. The scent of blooming jasmine mingled with the crisp autumn air, wrapping around me like a warm embrace. Yet, beneath this picturesque facade lay a tangled web of intrigue that I couldn't quite untangle on my own. As I navigated through the market square, the vibrant stalls filled with the season's finest flowers—deep crimson dahlias, golden chrysanthemums, and lush green ferns—I felt the weight of the mystery pressing down on me like a thick fog.

Jude had become an unexpected ally in this chaotic quest. Just days ago, he had been my rival, a thorn in my side with his obnoxious smirk and clever retorts. Now, with sabotage wreaking havoc on my shop and his, we were thrust into a reluctant partnership. Our banter felt like a dance; a combination of playful jabs and sharp comebacks, it was somehow exhilarating. Jude had a knack for getting under my skin, yet I found myself intrigued by the depths of his character that I'd never noticed before.

"Why don't you just admit it?" Jude said one afternoon, his eyes glinting with mischief as we stood in front of my shop, surrounded by the aftermath of yet another unfortunate incident—another delivery of wilted flowers. "You need my help because you can't do this alone."

"Excuse me?" I shot back, my voice sharp enough to cut through the air. "I had everything under control until your petulant little tantrum sent everything into a tailspin."

He leaned against my flower cart, arms crossed, a lopsided grin tugging at the corners of his mouth. "My tantrum? Please, you're the one who nearly knocked over a shelf of irises when I pointed out that your last arrangement looked like a flower explosion."

"Maybe I'd have arranged them better if you'd kept your comments to yourself," I retorted, although a smile threatened to break through my defensive facade.

Every time I opened my mouth to retaliate, there was a flicker of something more, something unexpected, hidden beneath our constant sparring. As the days passed, the underlying tension shifted from pure irritation to a palpable attraction that both exhilarated and terrified me. It was confusing—Jude was infuriating, but his charm was disarming, wrapping around my senses like a vine. With every shared moment, I could see glimpses of his kindness and protectiveness, revealing layers to his persona that I hadn't anticipated.

The golden leaves crunched underfoot as we strolled through the park, investigating potential leads on who might be responsible for the sabotages. I clutched a notepad, scribbling down the names of potential suspects, our discussions punctuated by bursts of laughter and heated arguments. Each interaction felt charged, electric, as if the very air around us was thick with unspoken words. I caught myself sneaking glances at Jude—how his hair tousled in the breeze, how the sunlight caught the edges of his jaw, sharp and defined.

"Do you ever stop to think that maybe, just maybe, you're a little too obsessed with flowers?" he teased, leaning closer as we examined a suspicious vendor's stall filled with wilted plants and fading petals.

"Excuse you," I shot back, feigning shock, though a laugh bubbled up. "You're the one who's spending his time trailing behind me like a lost puppy."

"Maybe I like trailing behind you," he said, his voice dropping an octave, making my stomach flutter. "You know, to protect you from the shady characters lurking around."

I rolled my eyes but felt the heat rise in my cheeks. "Right, because you're so noble," I retorted, but my heart raced at the thought. It was absurd how his presence made me feel safe, despite our endless bickering.

Our search led us to the old town library, a creaky, charming building filled with the scent of aged paper and secrets long hidden between the pages. Together, we sifted through old town records, maps, and newspaper clippings, our fingers brushing against one another occasionally, sending jolts of awareness through me each time. I could feel my heart hammering against my ribcage as we delved deeper into Riverview's past, uncovering stories of rivalry between florists, hidden romances, and whispered tales of jealousy that might explain our current predicament.

"What's the worst that could happen if we found out who's behind this?" Jude mused, leaning back in his chair, eyes sparkling with mischief. "Maybe we'd finally get a moment to ourselves without the chaos."

I raised an eyebrow, curiosity piquing within me. "You mean to plot your revenge on your enemies? I thought you were more about charm and wit."

He chuckled, the sound rich and infectious. "Oh, I can be charming and witty. But sometimes, a little chaos is needed to shake things up."

"Is that your excuse for messing with my arrangements?" I shot back, leaning closer, my heart racing.

"Consider it a warm-up for what's to come." His expression turned serious, a flicker of something deeper passing between us. "But I'd like to think we're a team now. A team that's meant to go down swinging."

I blinked, startled by the intensity of his gaze. It was a moment where the air thickened, the background noise fading away, leaving only the two of us—two unlikely allies entwined in a quest that had become more personal than I ever anticipated.

As our investigation continued, I couldn't shake the feeling that beneath the layers of rivalry and sarcasm lay something deeper—a connection that had begun to grow in the chaos of our situation. With each stolen glance, each accidental brush of hands, the fabric of my emotions unraveled further, leading me down a path I never expected to tread. I found myself drawn to Jude in ways I couldn't comprehend, and with each step deeper into Riverview's tangled underbelly, I feared what might happen if I fully surrendered to the pull of my heart.

The following days blurred into a whirl of frenetic energy and half-finished thoughts, each moment slipping through my fingers like the petals of the flowers I cherished so dearly. Each morning brought a renewed determination as Jude and I convened at my shop, the scent of fresh blooms mingling with the faint aroma of the strong coffee I relied on to fuel our investigations. The mornings were our sacred time, a stolen moment amidst the chaos of sabotage that had threatened our livelihoods. Yet, I couldn't ignore how our partnership was morphing into something richer—something that sent thrilling shivers down my spine with each shared glance and playful jab.

One particular morning, the sun streamed through the large windows, illuminating the flower arrangements I had carefully crafted. Jude stood at the door, his usual swagger softened by a hint of vulnerability. "You know," he began, pushing his hands into the pockets of his worn jeans, "this place could really use a splash of—"

"Stop right there," I interrupted, hands on my hips, a mock scowl on my face. "If you say something ridiculous like 'sunflowers,' I might have to reconsider our partnership."

He laughed, the sound warm and inviting, melting away my defenses. "Okay, okay, no sunflowers. But maybe some of those fiery red zinnias?"

I pretended to consider his suggestion seriously, tapping my chin thoughtfully. "Zinnias? Bold choice. I didn't know you had an eye for such things."

"It's all about the flair," he quipped, raising an eyebrow. "And I know how much you love a good arrangement."

"Flair, huh? Is that what you call it?" I shot back, a smile creeping onto my face despite myself.

As we began to piece together our investigation, the playful banter felt like a shield against the underlying tension that continued to build between us. We scoured every nook and cranny of Riverview, visiting other florists, combing through suppliers, and even interviewing eccentric townsfolk with their outlandish theories about who might wish us harm. Each conversation revealed a new layer of the community, a tapestry woven with secrets, rivalries, and the occasional unexpected ally.

It was during one of these excursions—a visit to a small, dusty flower shop on the outskirts of town—that our partnership reached a tipping point. The shop, nestled between a quirky antique store and a bakery that wafted tantalizing smells into the air, seemed to hold its breath as we entered. The owner, an elderly woman named Mrs. Petunia, regarded us with her sharp, discerning gaze, as if she could see straight through our motives.

"What brings two rival florists into my humble abode?" she asked, folding her arms, a knowing smile dancing on her lips.

Jude stepped forward, an earnest expression washing over his features. "We're investigating some issues with our shops, Mrs. Petunia. We believe someone's trying to sabotage our businesses."

"Ah, the age-old rivalry," she mused, tapping her chin. "Tell me, do you really think it's competition that drives people to such extremes?"

I exchanged a glance with Jude, the weight of her question lingering in the air. "We just want to get to the bottom of this," I said, my voice firm.

Mrs. Petunia's eyes sparkled with mischief. "Sometimes, you find that the fiercest rivalries hide the deepest connections."

Before I could respond, Jude chimed in, "You sound like a fortune teller. What's next? A crystal ball?"

The old woman chuckled, clearly unfazed by Jude's bravado. "Just consider this a friendly warning, dear boy. Sometimes the enemies we create are just reflections of our own insecurities."

As we left the shop, the weight of her words hung heavily between us. Jude's easy confidence faltered for a moment as he turned to me, a furrow in his brow. "What do you think she meant by that?"

"Honestly? I think she has a point," I replied, a tinge of vulnerability creeping into my voice. "There's more to our rivalry than just flowers. It's personal."

He nodded, his expression serious. "Maybe it's time we confront what's really driving us."

In that moment, I felt an urge to bridge the gap between our hearts, to peel back the layers of animosity that had built up over time. "And what if we find out it's not just competition, but something more?"

Jude stepped closer, his breath warm against my skin. "Then maybe we'll need to reevaluate everything we thought we knew about each other."

Before I could respond, a commotion erupted nearby, pulling us back to the present. A crowd had gathered, their murmurs rising into a crescendo of excitement and concern. As we rushed to investigate, we discovered a local celebrity, a renowned chef who had come to Riverview for a pop-up restaurant. He was surrounded by reporters, and the camera flashes illuminated the street like starlight.

"Look at this," Jude murmured, eyes sparkling with intrigue. "Maybe he can help us get the word out about the sabotage."

"Or maybe he's just here for the attention," I replied, rolling my eyes but unable to suppress a grin.

"Let's see if we can get his attention," Jude suggested, his charm flipping back on like a light switch.

We pushed our way through the crowd, exchanging knowing glances and whispers as we approached the chef. As Jude initiated a conversation, I felt a surge of adrenaline course through me. Here we were, two rival florists, standing shoulder to shoulder in front of the very man who could help us expose the threats to our livelihoods.

But as Jude spoke to the chef, I noticed something shift in the crowd. A figure emerged from the throng, and I felt my heart drop. It was Lily, my former best friend turned formidable rival.

"Fancy meeting you here," she said, a smirk playing on her lips as she stepped forward. "What are you two up to? Plotting more mischief in your little flower kingdom?"

Jude glanced at me, concern flashing in his eyes, and I could feel my blood boil. Lily had always had a knack for getting under my skin, her condescending tone stoking the fires of our rivalry.

"We're just gathering intel, Lily," I replied, my voice steady despite the anger bubbling beneath the surface. "What brings you here? Looking for a chance to gloat?"

She feigned innocence, tilting her head. "Oh, I'm just here for the food. But it's interesting to see you both so... cozy."

The tension in the air was thick, palpable, as we exchanged glances. This wasn't just a confrontation; it was a reckoning. I had spent so long locked in a cycle of competition with Lily, and now, with Jude by my side, everything felt different.

"Maybe it's time you realized that Riverview is big enough for all of us," Jude said, his voice firm, stepping slightly in front of me as if to shield me from her barbs.

Lily's eyes narrowed, but I sensed the shift—this time, we wouldn't be cowed by her words. This was no longer just about flowers; it was about standing together against the shadows threatening to envelop us. As I squared my shoulders, I felt a rush of determination. It was time to unravel the threads of rivalry and deception that had tied us all together, and with Jude by my side, I knew we could face whatever came next.

The tension hung in the air like the scent of jasmine on a warm evening, thick and intoxicating. Jude and I stood toe-to-toe with Lily, the spark of confrontation crackling between us. I could see the wheels turning in her mind, her eyes darting between Jude and me as if she were calculating her next move, plotting the best way to assert her dominance in this social chess game.

"Cozy? Is that what you call it?" I shot back, my voice steady, but my heart raced beneath the surface. "Maybe it's time you got used to the idea that we're working together now."

Jude's arm casually brushed against mine, a gesture that sent an electric jolt through me, grounding me in the moment. "Yeah, Lily," he added, a teasing lilt in his voice. "Just because you can't keep a partner doesn't mean others can't find their way."

Lily's expression soured, but her smirk never faltered. "How adorable. You two think you're going to solve this little mess? You have no idea what you're up against." Her words dripped with a mix of disdain and amusement, and I could sense her delight in our predicament.

"Maybe you can enlighten us," Jude challenged, stepping forward slightly, the playful glint in his eyes sharpening into something more serious.

"Ah, but then I'd lose all my fun," she replied, flipping her hair back over her shoulder with a practiced elegance. "Let's just say, Riverview has its share of secrets, and not all of them are flowers and sunshine."

I clenched my jaw, fighting the urge to retort with something cutting, yet knowing that engaging with her would only draw me deeper into the petty rivalry. Instead, I glanced at Jude, who seemed unfazed by Lily's taunts. "We're going to find out who's behind the sabotage," I asserted, my voice firm. "And when we do, we'll be ready."

"Good luck with that," Lily said, her laughter ringing out like the chime of a distant bell. "I wouldn't want to be you when the truth comes to light. Some things are better left buried, you know."

With a flick of her wrist, she turned and sauntered away, her confidence palpable, as if she thrived on the chaos she left in her wake. I watched her go, a knot of uncertainty twisting in my stomach. Jude's presence beside me was a comfort, but as we turned back to our mission, I couldn't shake the feeling that we were swimming in dangerous waters.

"Are you alright?" Jude asked, his voice low and gentle, pulling me from my thoughts.

"Yeah, just peachy," I replied, but the sarcasm didn't mask the tremor in my voice. "Lily's always been good at rattling my cage."

"She's good at rattling a lot of cages," he countered, a light smirk playing on his lips. "But you held your own. I like that about you."

"Flattery will get you everywhere," I said, the corners of my mouth lifting despite the lingering tension. "Now, back to business. We need to focus."

We retreated to my shop, where the atmosphere was vibrant with the colors of my creations, but the joy was muted by our shared uncertainty. As we rifled through notes and ideas, I felt an urge to delve deeper, to peel back the layers of the mystery that had entangled us both.

"Do you think it's someone from within the community?" I asked, glancing up at Jude, who had settled into a chair, his brows furrowed in thought.

"Could be," he replied, fingers tapping rhythmically on the table. "But there's also the possibility it's someone outside, someone trying to provoke us into a fight. You know, create chaos."

"Wonderful," I murmured, running a hand through my hair in frustration. "Just what we need—a puppet master pulling our strings."

"I've faced worse," Jude said, and there was an unexpected sincerity in his tone. "But I think we can outsmart them. Together."

A warmth unfurled in my chest at his words, a swell of something more profound than friendship. "Right, together," I echoed, allowing the sentiment to linger. But as the moment stretched, the gravity of our situation pressed down on me once again.

As we returned to our task, the hours flew by, filled with snippets of conversation, laughter, and the occasional heated debate about our findings. I found myself more drawn to Jude than ever, and in those fleeting moments, I almost forgot the turmoil swirling around us. But the undercurrent of danger was always there, lurking just beneath the surface.

Then, just as the sun dipped below the horizon, casting long shadows across the room, my phone buzzed ominously on the counter. The screen lit up with an unknown number, and a chill ran down my spine as I answered, my voice shaky.

"Hello?"

There was a pause, then a low voice echoed through the line, smooth yet laced with menace. "I hope you're enjoying your little investigation. Just know that some secrets are best kept hidden, and the truth is often more dangerous than you can imagine."

My heart pounded in my chest, the weight of his words hitting me like a blow. I glanced at Jude, who had tensed, the humor draining from his face as he leaned closer to listen.

"Who is this?" I demanded, trying to sound braver than I felt.

"Someone who knows what you're up against. Don't play games, or you might find yourself in over your head," the voice warned before the line went dead.

I stood frozen, the phone slipping from my fingers and clattering onto the countertop. "What was that?" Jude asked, his eyes wide with concern, reaching for my hand.

"I... I don't know," I stammered, trying to regain my composure. "Someone knows we're investigating."

"What did they say?" His voice was urgent, a hint of protectiveness in his tone that only fueled the fire inside me.

"They warned me to stop digging, that we might be in over our heads," I replied, my heart racing.

Jude's expression darkened, determination flooding his features. "We can't back down now. Whoever that was, they're scared of what we might find."

The resolve in his eyes ignited something deep within me, pushing aside the fear that threatened to swallow me whole. "You're right. We can't let them intimidate us. We have to figure this out."

But just as I felt a surge of confidence, the lights flickered ominously, plunging us into darkness. The soft hum of the shop's ambiance vanished, leaving a suffocating silence in its wake.

"What the hell?" Jude's voice was barely above a whisper, the shadows stretching like fingers across the room.

I fumbled for my phone, illuminating the space with a weak glow. "Maybe it's just a power outage."

"Or maybe it's more than that," he said, stepping closer to me, eyes scanning the darkness as if searching for unseen threats.

A distant crash echoed from the back of the shop, a sound that sent my heart racing. "Did you hear that?" I breathed, panic rising in my chest.

"Stay close," Jude murmured, his hand finding mine in the dark, anchoring me.

With our hearts pounding in tandem, we stepped cautiously toward the source of the noise, the air thick with dread. As we reached the back room, the shadows seemed to shift and sway, and just as we turned the corner, I caught a glimpse of movement—a figure slipping out the door at the back of the shop.

"Hey!" I shouted, adrenaline surging through me, but the figure was already gone, swallowed by the night.

"Did you see who it was?" Jude asked, breathless, urgency lacing his voice.

"No, but they were here! They must know something!" I replied, pulling away from him, ready to chase after the intruder.

But before I could move, the lights flickered back on, flooding the room with light. And there, on the floor where the figure had just vanished, lay a single, crumpled flower—a deep red rose, its petals darkening like a warning.

"What does this mean?" Jude whispered, bending to pick it up, his face a mask of confusion and concern.

In that moment, we both realized this was just the beginning. Riverview's secrets were unraveling faster than we could comprehend, and the tangled web we found ourselves in was about to ensnare us both. As I took a step back, heart racing, I could feel the looming danger close in around us, an unseen force that promised to change everything.

Chapter 6: The Bloom of Trust

The scent of lilacs and peonies wrapped around me like a cherished blanket, each delicate petal whispering secrets of the night as I delicately arranged them for the festival display. The soft glow of the moon filtered through the open windows of my shop, casting a silvery sheen across the worktable cluttered with stems and ribbons, while the distant hum of crickets created a rhythmic backdrop to my labor. With each snip of the shears, I poured not just flowers but fragments of my heart into the creation before me, envisioning the delight on the festival-goers' faces as they beheld my work. I could almost hear their praises echoing through the air, sweeter than the fragrance of the blooms.

Just as I was about to finish the final touches, an unexpected rustle caught my attention. I turned to see a folded piece of paper lying innocently on the edge of the counter. Frowning, I picked it up, the weight of its presence heavy in my palm. The ink was a deep black, the handwriting elegant yet urgent. My heart raced as I unfolded it, the words spilling out like a torrent of ice-cold water that splashed against my warmth, chilling me to the core.

"Beware of Jude. He's not what he seems. Look closely, and you will see the truth behind the flowers."

My breath hitched, my fingers trembling as I re-read the note, the accusations biting into my mind like thorns. Jude. The very name conjured images of the man who had slowly etched himself into the fabric of my life, whose laughter danced through the air like petals on a spring breeze. He had come into my world like a gentle summer rain, refreshing and invigorating, but now that rain felt ominous, threatening to flood my garden and drown the delicate flowers I had painstakingly nurtured.

I had always known Jude struggled. His flower shop had seen better days, the blooms he sold often underappreciated in the shadow of larger chains. Yet, I had admired his determination, the way he brought beauty to a world that often overlooked the subtleties of life. But now, this note forced me to question everything. Could he truly be hiding something darker beneath that charming smile?

Shoving the note deep into my pocket, I gathered my courage and headed outside. The moonlight bathed the garden in an ethereal glow, illuminating the blooms with a surreal beauty. Jude was at the far end, tending to his own flowers, his strong hands working the soil as if it were clay. The sight of him grounded me; his dedication was palpable, a tangible testament to his love for his craft.

"Jude?" My voice was steadier than I felt, but a tremor of doubt ran beneath it.

He looked up, his brow furrowing slightly, as if sensing the shift in the air. "Hey there, just finishing up. You're working late again?"

"Yeah, just... lost track of time." I stepped closer, the cool breeze carrying with it the scent of earth and blooms. "I found something tonight."

His expression changed, eyes narrowing as if he braced himself for impact. "What do you mean?"

I took a deep breath, the weight of the note pressing down on my shoulders. "An anonymous note. It mentioned you, Jude. Accused you of... things."

His reaction was immediate, an unsettling mix of hurt and confusion crossing his features. "What kind of things?"

"Things that could ruin your business," I said, my heart thudding heavily in my chest. "It hinted at something criminal."

He stepped closer, the moonlight glinting off his dark hair, making him appear almost otherworldly. "I can explain. Please, let me."

"Explain what? That you're involved in something illegal?" My voice was sharper than intended, and I hated myself for it.

"No! It's not like that!" He ran a hand through his hair, frustration mingling with desperation. "I've been struggling to keep the shop afloat. I've taken risks—maybe too many—but nothing that crosses the line."

The sincerity in his voice tugged at my heart, but doubt still gnawed at the edges of my mind. "What kind of risks?"

He hesitated, a shadow passing over his features. "Sometimes, I've accepted flowers from vendors who aren't exactly... legitimate. But they're the only ones willing to work with me at this point. I didn't want to let you down."

His words hung in the air, heavy and laden with vulnerability. In that moment, the animosity I felt began to ebb, replaced by a surge of empathy. This man—so passionate about his craft—was fighting against a world that seemed determined to drown him.

"Jude, I—" I started, but he interrupted, his voice thick with emotion.

"I never meant for you to find out like this. I wanted to keep the shop running so we could do this—together. You deserve the best, and I've only ever wanted to give that to you."

The moon bathed us in its silvery light, illuminating the turmoil on his face and the sincerity in his eyes. I felt the garden around us breathe, the flowers swaying gently as if encouraging me to take a leap of faith. In that moment, I realized trust was a fragile flower, needing care and attention to flourish.

With a sigh, I reached out, placing my hand over his. The warmth of his skin ignited something deep within me, a spark that spread through my veins. "I want to believe in you, Jude. But it's going to take time."

"Time," he echoed, a hint of relief breaking through the tension in his voice. "I can work with that."

In the moonlit garden, vulnerability began to bloom in the spaces between us, filling the air with the promise of something beautiful.

The cool evening air swirled around us, carrying the scent of jasmine and freshly watered earth, creating an intoxicating blend that felt both familiar and new. As I stood there, hand in hand with Jude, a delicate tension threaded between us, almost palpable like the threads of a spider's web glistening with dew. It was as if the world had faded away, leaving only the two of us entwined in this moment, vulnerable and exposed. Yet the shadows of uncertainty loomed overhead, and the truth hung in the air like a storm waiting to break.

"Are you sure you're ready for this?" Jude's voice was a low murmur, but the concern etched on his face cut through the night like a bolt of lightning. "I mean, trusting me again? After what you heard?"

I took a deep breath, allowing the crispness of the air to fill my lungs. "I don't know if I'm ready, but I want to be," I confessed, my voice steadier than I felt. "The flowers might not be the only thing I'm trying to cultivate here." The wry twist of my lips was an attempt to lighten the weight of our conversation, but deep down, I understood the gravity of what we were facing.

Jude's eyes sparkled with a mixture of gratitude and hope, a contrast to the shadows that had clouded them moments before. "Then let's start with honesty," he said, the sincerity in his tone cutting through the lingering tension. "I've been in some tricky situations lately. I didn't want you to see me as weak."

"Why would I see you as weak?" I raised an eyebrow, the challenge sparking a playful spark between us. "You're the one who lifts entire flowerbeds by yourself, Jude."

He chuckled, a sound that sent ripples of warmth through the cool air. "True, but those weights are a lot easier to handle than the pressure of running a business that feels like it's on the edge of a cliff."

"Maybe we can pull it back from the edge together," I suggested, the words spilling out before I could filter them. It was a risk, much like the kind he'd taken in the past.

"Together?" His gaze held mine, an intensity that made my stomach flip. "You really mean that?"

"Why not? We're already knee-deep in floral drama," I said, trying to keep the atmosphere light, but I could feel the weight of my sincerity hanging in the air. "What do you need me to do?"

"Let me show you," he replied, his smile breaking through the uncertainty like the sun peeking from behind the clouds. "Let's make this festival our turning point."

As he led me through the tangled rows of blooming flowers, each one a testament to our collective efforts, I felt the night shift. The moonlight danced over the petals, creating a shimmering effect that made the garden look alive, as if it were watching us with a knowing eye.

"I've had a couple of leads on new suppliers," Jude explained as we moved deeper into the garden. "Some might be a little unconventional, but I'm thinking of taking a chance on them. If we can get a few unique blooms for the festival, it might attract a different clientele."

"Unconventional how?" I asked, my curiosity piqued.

"Let's just say the source might involve a bit of floral... negotiation," he said, his eyes glinting mischievously.

I raised an eyebrow, intrigued despite myself. "Floral negotiation? Are we talking about flower mobsters now?"

"Maybe not mobsters, but let's just say they're not your average florists." Jude grinned, his charm sweeping me away like the scent of roses on a gentle breeze. "If I can get us a shipment of rare orchids, it could be a game-changer."

"Orchids? Those delicate beauties?" I was genuinely impressed. "But if they're rare, how do we get them without drawing too much attention?"

"We need to be discreet." Jude's expression turned serious again, the weight of the plan settling over him like a cloak. "I have a contact. They know how to operate under the radar."

"Why do I get the feeling this is going to be more complicated than you're letting on?" I asked, crossing my arms playfully.

"Because it probably will be," he admitted, a sheepish smile creeping onto his lips. "But I promise it'll be worth it. I just need you to trust me."

"Okay," I said, more resolutely than I felt. "Let's do this."

As the moonlight faded into the background, we discussed the finer details of our plan, excitement bubbling between us like the first sip of champagne. The trust I had hesitated to embrace began to bloom again, stronger this time, each word exchanged weaving a new thread into our connection.

Suddenly, the tranquil night was pierced by the ringing of my phone, startling us both. I fished it out of my pocket, frowning at the unknown number flashing on the screen. "Who could be calling me at this hour?"

"Could be an emergency," Jude suggested, his brow furrowing.

"Or a telemarketer." I answered the call, my voice tight with curiosity. "Hello?"

"Is this the florist?" a gravelly voice asked on the other end, sending a chill down my spine. "I have a proposition for you."

"Proposition? I'm not interested," I shot back, my heart racing as I glanced at Jude, whose expression mirrored my unease.

"Wait, wait. Just hear me out," the voice insisted, an edge of urgency threading through his tone. "I know about the orchids. You need to listen."

"Who are you?" I asked, my stomach churning with unease.

"I'm someone who can help you... but only if you're willing to make a deal." The line went silent, the weight of the unspoken hanging heavily between us. I felt Jude's eyes on me, the gravity of the moment undeniable.

"Why do I feel like we just stepped into a thriller?" I murmured, glancing at Jude's bewildered expression.

"Maybe because we did." He squeezed my hand tighter, the warmth spreading like wildfire between us, fueling an unexpected resolve.

"Okay, I'm listening," I said, leaning into the unknown as the night pressed closer, the thrill of danger tinged with an undeniable sense of adventure.

The gravelly voice on the phone pulsed through the air, laden with an intensity that sent shivers racing down my spine. "You're about to be offered an opportunity that could change everything for you and your friend. But it's not without its risks."

"Risks? Like what?" I shot back, my heart hammering in my chest. Jude leaned closer, his breath warm against my ear, urging me to listen. The air around us felt charged, alive with anticipation and the faint scent of impending danger.

"Meet me at the old bridge by the river, midnight. If you want the orchids, you'll need to come alone. There are things about Jude you don't know, and I can't say more over the phone."

"Why should I trust you?" I countered, my fingers curling tightly around the phone.

"Because he's running out of time, and so are you. The choice is yours, but you better decide fast." The call ended abruptly, leaving a hollow silence in its wake, the finality of it echoing around us like a bell tolling in the distance.

"Who was that?" Jude's voice cut through the thick fog of my thoughts, concern etched across his handsome features.

"A complete stranger," I said, my voice barely above a whisper. "They know about the orchids and... you."

His expression darkened, and a flicker of something dangerous passed through his eyes. "What did they say?"

"Just that I should meet them if I want the orchids and that you're running out of time." I swallowed hard, suddenly aware of how precarious our situation had become.

Jude ran a hand through his hair, frustration flaring in his blue eyes. "This isn't good. If they're involved, it could mean trouble."

"Trouble like you've never faced before?" I challenged, trying to keep my tone light despite the weight of my words. "I mean, if I'm going to wade into the deep end of your shady business dealings, I want to know what I'm getting into. Otherwise, I might just stick to flower arrangements and leave the intrigue to the professionals."

A small smile crept onto his lips, but it vanished as quickly as it appeared. "This isn't a joke, and I wouldn't blame you if you wanted to walk away. But if you don't, I can't let you go alone. We'll figure this out together."

"Together, huh?" I mused, my heart skipping at the notion but also heavy with apprehension. "I feel like we're both in over our heads. You're the one with the shady connections, remember?"

His gaze softened, and I caught the slightest hint of vulnerability in his posture. "Maybe I've taken too many risks, but I never wanted to drag you into it. You've made this place beautiful, and I won't let anything ruin that. We can't let fear dictate our actions."

"Agreed," I said, my resolve firming up despite the nagging doubt in my gut. "But we need a plan. You can't just go into the night without knowing what we're up against."

"We'll go to the bridge, and I'll talk to whoever it is," he replied, a hint of determination creeping back into his voice. "If they know something about me, we need to find out how deep this rabbit hole goes."

The clock on the wall ticked relentlessly, each second counting down to midnight. The tension between us thickened, the moonlight illuminating the uncertainty etched across our faces. We decided to meet at the bridge, but I couldn't shake the feeling that we were stepping into a trap, the kind laid with delicate care by those who thrived on secrets and shadows.

As the hour approached, I found myself pacing the small confines of my shop, nervous energy coursing through my veins like caffeine. Jude moved quietly behind me, his presence both a comfort and a reminder of how precarious our situation truly was. "Do you think this person has any real information?" I asked, the thought gnawing at my insides.

"Probably. If they're connected to the orchids, then they're connected to everything that's been happening," he replied, his tone grave. "But we need to be careful. This could turn dangerous very quickly."

"I get it," I said, glancing at the clock again. "But what if they're just trying to scare us?"

"Then we'll know they're scared of us, too," he shot back, a playful spark igniting in his eyes. "It's about time someone turned the tables, don't you think?"

I couldn't help but smile at his optimism, even if it felt like we were standing on the edge of a cliff, looking down into the abyss. "Okay, let's do this. But if we end up running for our lives, I'm holding you responsible."

"Fair enough," he said, the corners of his mouth curling into a smirk.

When the clock struck midnight, we slipped out into the night, the cool air wrapping around us like a shroud. The streets were eerily quiet, the only sound our footsteps echoing against the pavement. As we approached the bridge, a silhouette appeared against the backdrop of the river, illuminated by the soft glow of the moon.

"Who's there?" I called out, trying to sound braver than I felt.

The figure stepped closer, revealing a tall man clad in dark clothing, his features obscured by the shadows. "You made it," he said, his voice smooth yet unsettling. "I wasn't sure you would."

"Who are you?" Jude demanded, stepping protectively in front of me.

"Someone who knows what's at stake. I have information about the orchids, and I believe you'll want to hear it," the man replied, a sly grin spreading across his face. "But first, I need something from you both."

My heart raced, a sense of foreboding crashing over me like a wave. "What do you want?" I asked, unwilling to be drawn into whatever game this was without knowing the rules.

He leaned in closer, the moonlight revealing glinting eyes filled with mischief. "Trust," he said simply, and for a moment, the world around us seemed to freeze. "But know this: trust is a double-edged sword, and one wrong move could cut you deeper than you think."

Just then, a noise echoed from behind us, snapping the fragile tension. My heart plummeted as I turned, seeing shadows approaching—more figures, emerging from the darkness like phantoms.

"Looks like our meeting just got a little more complicated," Jude muttered under his breath, his stance shifting as he prepared for whatever was coming.

"Run!" I shouted, adrenaline surging as I turned to bolt away, the weight of uncertainty now fully realized. Behind us, the shadows converged, and I felt Jude's hand grasp mine, our bond igniting a flicker of hope as we sprinted into the night, the sound of pursuit echoing ominously in the dark.

Chapter 7: A Delicate Balance

Days turned into a blur of late-night brainstorming sessions, each more chaotic and electric than the last. Jude and I sprawled across the worn leather sofa in my cramped living room, surrounded by a haphazard collection of papers, coffee cups, and half-finished snacks. The air was thick with the scent of brewed coffee and something else—an unspoken tension that crackled between us. With each passing moment, the line that separated us began to fray, like the edges of a beloved book whose spine had been cracked open one too many times.

Jude had an uncanny ability to make even the most mundane aspects of our investigation feel like an adventure. His laughter was infectious, often spilling into the air like music, and his sharp wit kept me on my toes. Just the other night, while brainstorming theories about our elusive antagonist, he had leaned close, a teasing smile dancing on his lips, and whispered, "If this whole mystery thing doesn't pan out, I could always open a comedy club. The world needs more bad puns." I had laughed so hard I nearly snorted my coffee.

Yet, beneath the surface of our burgeoning camaraderie, a familiar chill crept in. I could feel the shadows drawing closer, looming like storm clouds ready to unleash their fury. There was a lurking sense of danger, the kind that wrapped around me like a heavy blanket, suffocating yet oddly familiar. It wasn't just the mystery we were trying to unravel; it was the sinister undertones that whispered of hidden eyes and unseen threats.

Each time Jude brushed against my arm or flashed a grin that sent my heart racing, I felt the heat of a connection that was both thrilling and terrifying. It was as if the universe conspired to blur the lines between desire and danger, leaving me vulnerable and confused. I wanted to lean into that warmth, to surrender to the chemistry crackling between us, but my instincts screamed caution. Trusting him felt like standing on the edge of a precipice, the ground beneath me unsteady and uncertain.

The night air was thick with the smell of impending rain as we sat outside on the rickety porch, piecing together fragments of clues that danced like fireflies in the twilight. The sun dipped low on the horizon, casting golden rays that flickered through the trees, and Jude's profile was framed by the warm glow, making my heart flutter against my ribs. His brows furrowed in concentration, and I found myself captivated by the way his mouth curved slightly when he was deep in thought.

"We've got to find out who else is involved," he said, breaking the spell. "The last thing we need is to get cornered by whoever's pulling the strings."

"Agreed," I replied, my voice softer than I intended. "But we need to be careful. I don't want to end up as collateral damage in some game we don't fully understand."

He turned to me, the warmth of his gaze settling like a comforting weight. "You're not collateral damage. You're the reason we'll figure this out."

My heart did a little somersault, and for a fleeting moment, I let myself bask in the glow of his words. But the reality of our situation clawed at the edges of my mind, dragging me back to the present. I couldn't ignore the feeling that someone was watching us, lurking in the shadows. The chill of paranoia crept in, and I scanned the dimly lit street beyond the porch. Every rustle of leaves, every distant sound, felt amplified, turning our serene setting into a precarious stage.

"Do you ever get the feeling that we're not alone?" I asked, my voice low, an uncharacteristic quiver threading through it.

Jude raised an eyebrow, the teasing grin faltering. "You mean besides the raccoon that lives in your trash?"

"Very funny." I rolled my eyes but couldn't suppress the unease that crept into my heart. "No, I mean it. Like, I don't know... like we're being watched."

"Okay, that's a little creepy." He leaned back, his posture relaxing again, but I noticed the way his eyes sharpened, scanning the surrounding darkness. "We could always set a trap. You know, lure them out with a fake clue or something."

I couldn't help but laugh, though it was tinged with a hint of anxiety. "You mean like bait? How very heroic of you."

"Hey, it's a classic tactic. Plus, it'd give me an excuse to keep you close." His smirk returned, mischief dancing in his eyes.

The warmth of his gaze sent shivers down my spine, igniting a flurry of butterflies that swarmed in my chest. "What if that close proximity turns dangerous?"

"Then we'll tackle it together," he said, his voice steady, reassuring. "You're not alone in this."

Yet, as much as I wanted to believe him, the worry gnawed at my insides. I was falling for him, deeper than I had ever anticipated, and with that came a vulnerability that made my stomach churn. The world around us could shift at any moment, and I couldn't shake the feeling that our laughter would soon be drowned out by chaos. As we resumed our discussion, my mind flickered between the magnetic pull of our chemistry and the lurking shadows that threatened to sever the fragile bond we had built.

Little did I know that the heart of our investigation was more complex than I could fathom, weaving a tangled web of deceit, desire, and danger that would soon test our resolve in ways I had never imagined.

The morning sun filtered through the leaves of the ancient oak outside my window, casting dappled patterns on the floor like a mosaic of light and shadow. It was a welcome distraction from the chaos in my head. I swung my legs over the side of the bed, the hardwood cool against my feet as I recalled the previous night's conversation. Jude had challenged me to a game of honesty, and while I had intended to stick to the facts, the moment his eyes locked onto mine, I found myself confessing not just about the mystery but about my lingering fears and desires.

"Do you ever think we're making this harder than it needs to be?" he had asked, leaning closer, that familiar teasing smile dancing on his lips.

"Of course! But who doesn't enjoy a little self-inflicted chaos?" I shot back, my heart racing. "It's practically a hobby at this point."

His laughter rang like music, momentarily sweeping away the unease that had clung to me for days. Yet as I prepared for another day of investigation, a dull knot of anxiety curled in my stomach. I needed to push past the nervous energy that thrummed in the air like an unseen current, and I could feel the weight of it settling over me like a fog.

A shower helped to wash away the remnants of sleep and doubt. The water poured over me in a comforting cascade, but as I stepped out, the chill of reality seeped back in. Today, we had planned to delve deeper into the murky waters of our investigation—an unassuming coffee shop across town would serve as our headquarters. I dressed carefully, wanting to feel both comfortable and confident; the snug sweater hugged my frame just right, while my favorite jeans added an air of casual nonchalance.

As I stepped outside, the crisp air filled my lungs, awakening my senses. I took a moment to savor the invigorating scent of autumn—the sweet decay of fallen leaves mixed with the promise of fresh beginnings. It was a bittersweet contrast to the tension knotting my stomach. The streets bustled with people, their lives weaving in and out of mine like a vibrant tapestry, yet I felt as if I were moving through a world apart, a spectator in my own life.

When I arrived at the café, the bell above the door jingled a cheerful greeting, but my heart sank as I spotted Jude already seated at a corner table, flipping through a stack of papers with an intensity that suggested a brewing storm. He looked up as I approached, his expression transforming from concentration to something warmer—a flicker of surprise followed by that familiar smirk that made my insides flutter.

"Didn't know I'd need a search party to find you," he quipped, motioning for me to sit. "What's the plan? Coffee first, or do we dive straight into the abyss?"

"Coffee first. The abyss can wait." I flashed a grin, trying to push the weight of our unspoken tension aside.

As I ordered, I caught sight of him tapping his fingers rhythmically against the table, an anxious habit that mirrored my own. I settled in, determined to keep our conversation light. "I think we should consider a more traditional approach to gathering information. You know, like interviewing suspects."

"Suspects?" He raised an eyebrow, a teasing glint in his eye. "I didn't realize we were doing this law and order style. I might need a badge."

I chuckled, my laughter mixing with the café's ambient sounds. "I think we'd both be better off without badges. We're not exactly cut out for the police force."

"Speak for yourself," he shot back, a mock-seriousness creeping into his voice. "I could rock the whole detective look. Picture me in a trench coat—very noir, don't you think?"

I could picture it all too clearly, and I felt my cheeks heat. "Only if you promise not to wear the hat. You'd look ridiculous."

The playful banter lifted my spirits, if only momentarily, until the feeling of being watched crept back in. I couldn't shake the nagging sensation that our little sanctuary was an illusion. As we sipped our coffees, I scanned the room, looking for anything that felt off. It was a quaint place, adorned with mismatched furniture and whimsical art, but every cheerful note seemed muted under the weight of my worries.

"So, what's our next move?" Jude asked, leaning back, his gaze searching mine. "We need to figure out who's been shadowing us—or at least, I need to figure out how to keep you safe."

"Why do you care so much?" I asked, surprised by the sudden edge to my voice. "You barely know me."

He met my gaze steadily. "I know enough to recognize that you're not just some girl who stumbled into this mess. You're smart, resourceful, and way too stubborn for your own good."

The sincerity in his words sent a thrill through me, but I quickly masked it with humor. "Stubborn? Who, me? I prefer to think of it as determination."

"Call it what you want, but I like it." His tone turned teasing again, but the undercurrent of seriousness remained. "And I don't want to see you get hurt."

Before I could respond, a shadow flitted across my peripheral vision. A figure lingered by the entrance, scanning the café with an intensity that sent prickles down my spine. I subtly tilted my head, my heart racing as the stranger's gaze landed on us, lingering longer than was comfortable before they turned abruptly and slipped out the door.

"Did you see that?" I whispered, my pulse quickening.

"See what?" Jude's brow furrowed as he followed my line of sight, but the figure had vanished.

"Someone was watching us. I swear I felt it."

He leaned in closer, concern etching his features. "Are you sure? Maybe it was just someone checking their phone or—"

"No," I interrupted, urgency coloring my voice. "I'm telling you, it felt deliberate. We need to figure out who it is before it's too late."

A flicker of understanding crossed his face, and he nodded, the playful banter falling away as we were pulled into the gravity of our situation. There was no denying it any longer—our investigation had drawn the attention of someone determined to keep us from the truth. The thrill of discovery now lay tangled with the fear of what might come next, each moment pushing us further into a game neither of us was fully prepared to play.

As we left the café, the weight of uncertainty hung in the air. The shadows were not just a backdrop but an ominous presence, intertwining with our every step. We were no longer simply investigating a mystery; we were standing at the precipice of something far more dangerous. And as I glanced at Jude, I could see it in his eyes—we were in this together, whether we liked it or not.

The days that followed felt like an intricate dance, with Jude and me moving in rhythm to the heartbeat of the mystery that consumed us. Each moment spent together pulled me deeper into a world I was both fascinated and terrified to navigate. The coffee shop had become our makeshift headquarters, a hub where laughter mingled with whispered fears. Yet beneath the playful banter and shared glances, I could feel the undercurrents of something more—a current of attraction tempered by uncertainty.

We had established a routine of sorts: I would arrive with fresh ideas and a hint of enthusiasm, and he would meet me with a mix of charm and earnestness. But today, the weight of the unspoken pressed down on my chest as I entered the café, my heart racing in anticipation of Jude's warm smile. Instead, I found him hunched over a table, scribbling furiously in a notebook, a frown marring his handsome features.

"What's up?" I asked, sliding into the chair across from him. The scent of coffee and baked goods surrounded us like a comforting cocoon, but Jude seemed distant, lost in whatever thoughts plagued him.

"Just trying to figure out a connection," he replied, glancing up briefly before returning his gaze to the page. "I think we might be missing something crucial about our shadowy friend."

A frown tugged at my lips. "Like what? A name? An address? A coffee order?" I attempted to lighten the mood, but his expression remained grave.

"I think it's bigger than that," he said, finally meeting my gaze with an intensity that sent a thrill of unease down my spine. "I'm starting to believe whoever is watching us might not be acting alone. There could be a whole network behind this."

A chill crept into the air, thickening the atmosphere between us. "You mean it's not just one person? There's a group?"

"Exactly." He leaned in, lowering his voice as if the walls themselves had ears. "If we're going to get to the bottom of this, we need to be smarter, more cautious."

"Right." I shifted in my seat, the weight of his words pressing down on me. "What's the plan then?"

"Let's dig deeper into anyone who might have a reason to keep us from figuring this out. Maybe a little research into local criminal activity, or even better, anyone who might have a grudge against us or our investigation."

The mention of "grudge" made my stomach twist. "You mean, like a vendetta? Great, that sounds fun. I was hoping for a relaxing weekend, but sure, let's dive into the criminal underbelly of the town."

Jude chuckled, the tension easing just a fraction. "You do know how to make even the worst situations sound entertaining."

"It's a talent," I said with a smirk. "Besides, I'm only half-joking. This is terrifying."

"Welcome to the club." His eyes sparkled with mischief. "But think of it this way: the more we learn, the better we can defend ourselves. Knowledge is power, right?"

"Knowledge is definitely a double-edged sword," I countered, still feeling the weight of dread. "But fine, let's uncover the secrets hiding in our little town. What's the worst that could happen?"

"Famous last words," he replied, his expression sobering. "Let's meet tonight and tackle the online research. We need a plan and a backup plan."

The sun dipped lower in the sky as we finished our coffees and gathered our things, the light casting elongated shadows across the café floor. My mind buzzed with possibilities as we stepped outside, the crisp air tinged with the scent of impending rain. The clouds had begun to gather ominously overhead, and I felt an eerie parallel between the brewing storm and the tumultuous atmosphere surrounding us.

We agreed to meet again later, but as I turned to walk away, a familiar figure loomed in my periphery. The sensation of being watched returned, prickling at the back of my neck. I glanced over my shoulder, but the street was simply filled with the usual hum of life: people rushing past, lost in their own worlds.

"Everything okay?" Jude asked, catching my unease.

"Yeah, I just—" I hesitated, unwilling to voice my fears. "I thought I saw someone."

"Like a shadow?" He studied my face, concern etched in his brow. "Maybe it's just nerves."

"Maybe." I forced a smile, but as I walked away, the feeling of unease lingered like a dark cloud, and it wasn't just the weather.

Later that evening, the rain poured down in heavy sheets, creating a rhythm on my window that felt both soothing and foreboding. I lit a few candles to ward off the gloom, the flickering flames casting dancing shadows that seemed to mock my apprehension. The atmosphere was heavy, saturated with the scent of wet earth and something indefinable that clawed at my gut.

As I reviewed the notes Jude and I had gathered, each paper felt like a breadcrumb leading us deeper into a forest of secrets. I lost track of time, my focus sharpening on the task at hand, when a knock at the door pulled me from my reverie.

Jude stood in the doorway, drenched and panting, his hair plastered to his forehead. "You might want to consider a better welcome," he joked, shaking the water off like a dog. "How about a towel next time?"

"Only if you bring the coffee," I shot back, my heart warming at his arrival.

We settled in quickly, the atmosphere shifting as the storm raged outside. We pored over our findings, tracing connections like threads through a tangled web. The clock ticked on the wall, each second echoing like a countdown to something inevitable. Laughter mingled with the rustle of papers, our camaraderie solidifying with every shared discovery.

As we dug deeper, however, an unsettling realization began to take shape. Each clue we unearthed only led to more questions, and the shadows outside seemed to deepen as the night wore on.

"We should take a break," I suggested, my voice barely above a whisper, the fatigue settling in my bones. "Maybe grab a snack?"

"Good idea," Jude replied, but as he stood, his expression shifted from playful to serious. "Wait... did you hear that?"

I froze, my heart skipping a beat. A soft thud echoed from outside, muffled by the rain. "What do you think it is?"

"Stay here." He moved toward the window, and I followed, peering through the glass just in time to see a figure darting across the street, cloaked in shadows.

"Who is that?" I whispered, dread pooling in my stomach.

"I don't know." Jude's voice was low, his gaze narrowing as he tried to discern the silhouette. "But it's not just our imaginations anymore."

Before I could respond, a loud crash broke through the quiet of the night, the sound reverberating against the walls of the house. I spun around, my heart pounding in my chest. The front door rattled violently, a shadow looming just beyond it, its presence felt like a weight pressing against the air itself.

"Get behind me," Jude commanded, his voice steady but urgent.

Fear surged through me as I felt the world tilt off balance. We were no longer just uncovering secrets; we were about to confront the very danger we had tried so hard to avoid. The shadows that had lingered in the corners of our lives were about to take center stage.

Chapter 8: Secrets Unveiled

The air buzzed with excitement as the annual Harvest Festival approached, its vibrant banners fluttering like butterflies in the crisp autumn breeze. I could almost taste the sweetness of candied apples and hear the laughter of children echoing through the town square. Yet, beneath the joyful façade lay an undercurrent of tension that had been growing steadily since Jude and I first discovered the sabotage of our flower shop's displays. Each morning, the sun would rise over our little town, illuminating the signs of our hard work marred by tampering—flowers wilted, petals torn, arrangements ruined. It felt personal, as if someone had taken a serrated knife to the heart of what we both loved.

Determination settled over me like a heavy quilt. I wasn't going to let some shadowy figure from a neighboring town snuff out our dreams. I found myself daydreaming about the festival, imagining our shop transformed into a vibrant oasis amidst the bustling crowd. Jude and I had always been competitive, but something deeper was stirring within me. Each fleeting glance, every shared joke about our eccentric customers, unraveled the threads of my former animosity towards him. Perhaps it was the way his eyes sparkled with mischief or how his laughter rolled out like the sound of wind chimes in a gentle breeze. I had to admit, my feelings had shifted from rivalry to something far more complex and delightful.

As we brewed plans over coffee, our conversations transformed from strategy sessions to flirtatious banter. I could feel my heart race when he leaned closer, his cologne mingling with the rich aroma of roasted beans. "What do you think? A grand unveiling of our floral creations at the festival?" he suggested, his eyes gleaming with enthusiasm. I couldn't help but smile at his earnestness. "Unless you plan to unleash a herd of goats to stomp on my daisies again, I'm in."

"Goats? A scandalous ploy indeed! But if you're willing to trust me, I might just surprise you," he replied, a playful smirk dancing across his lips.

The moments we spent together, plotting our victory, stitched a fabric of camaraderie that I hadn't anticipated. Each plan we concocted wove a deeper bond between us, something stronger than the competitive spirit that had originally defined our interactions. Yet, despite the burgeoning warmth in my chest, doubt niggled at the corners of my mind. Could I truly let my guard down? I had built walls to protect my heart, but with every shared laugh, every lingering touch, those walls threatened to crumble.

Our breakthrough came one evening while we were preparing our floral displays for the festival. I glanced up to find Jude intently inspecting a particularly rare bloom, his brow furrowed in concentration. "You know, this beauty is native to the coast. It's a wonder it thrives here," he mused, oblivious to the way his passion lit up his features.

"Maybe it thrives because it's surrounded by equally beautiful flowers," I replied, teasingly nudging him with my elbow. He looked up, caught off guard, and the air shifted, thick with unspoken words.

It was then that I noticed a flicker of doubt in his eyes, and I realized that we were both standing at the precipice of something extraordinary. "Do you think this sabotage is really just about flowers?" I asked softly, my voice almost lost in the rustle of leaves outside.

Jude sighed, running a hand through his tousled hair. "I thought it was. But what if it's more than that? What if someone wants to drive us apart?"

The possibility hit me like a gust of wind. Someone wanted to destroy our bond, our businesses, everything we had worked for. In that moment, I felt the fire of indignation ignite within me. "Then we need to show them we're not backing down. We'll confront this rival florist. Together."

The plan was risky, but we were driven by a shared purpose. We had both experienced loss—loss of our reputations, our businesses, and the sense of community that had drawn us together. That night, under the velvety blanket of stars, we made our way to the rival's shop, our hearts pounding with a mix of trepidation and anticipation.

"Just remember," Jude murmured as we approached the brightly lit storefront, "if they try anything, we stick together. Like a pair of roses."

I couldn't suppress a grin. "More like a thistle and a daisy, but I appreciate the sentiment."

As we stepped inside, the air thickened with the smell of flowers and rivalry. Rows of dazzling arrangements stretched before us, but the vibrant colors couldn't mask the tension coiling around us. The rival florist, a woman with sharp features and a sharper tongue, greeted us with an icy smile. "What brings you two here? Don't tell me you've come to admire the competition?"

Jude straightened, his demeanor shifting from warmth to resolve. "We're here to talk about the sabotage. It ends now."

Her laughter echoed, a sound devoid of warmth. "Oh, sweetheart, this is business. You shouldn't be so naive."

Before I could process her words, the air grew electric, a palpable shift swirling around us. Jude squeezed my hand, grounding me. In that instant, I knew we weren't just fighting for flowers; we were standing up for each other. What had begun as rivalry had blossomed into an unyielding partnership, one that was rooted in trust and budding affection.

"I refuse to let you undermine what we've built," I declared, my voice stronger than I felt. The energy in the room shifted as Jude and

I stood side by side, our hands intertwined, ready to face whatever came next.

The shop was abuzz with activity, the sweet scent of blooming flowers weaving through the air like a soft melody, drowning out the remnants of tension from our earlier confrontation. Jude moved gracefully among the arrangements, his hands deftly working to piece together a stunning bouquet that would steal the show at the festival. I admired the way his fingers danced over the petals, each touch imbued with a tenderness that reflected the passion he poured into his craft. It was hard not to be captivated by him, especially now that we were on the same team, united by our shared mission and blossoming feelings.

"Can you believe it? We actually stood up to her," I said, a mix of exhilaration and disbelief coursing through me. My heart was still racing from our confrontation, and I couldn't help but glance over at Jude, who was concentrating intently on his creation.

"Believe it," he replied, looking up with a grin that sent a jolt of warmth through my chest. "I could practically hear her ego deflating from here." He glanced toward the window, where the last rays of the sun dipped below the horizon, casting a golden glow over our little shop.

"Speaking of egos," I said, feigning a dramatic sigh, "I hope your flowers are ready to shine brighter than hers. We can't let her win this festival."

"Isn't that what we just did? Our glorious triumph over the floral villain?" Jude's laughter filled the room, and I couldn't help but join in, the sound echoing like a carefree promise amid the surrounding chaos of preparations.

As we worked side by side, an unspoken understanding blossomed between us, fueled by laughter and shared moments. Each arrangement we completed felt like a small victory, a step toward reclaiming what had been threatened. I could feel the excitement building, pulsing through the air like a lively tune that wouldn't let us stop moving.

"Okay, serious question," Jude said, suddenly pausing in his efforts. He wiped a bead of sweat from his brow and looked at me with an intensity that made my stomach flutter. "If we pull this off and win the festival, what's the first thing you're going to do?"

I thought for a moment, glancing around the shop that felt like a second home. "Probably scream," I admitted, unable to suppress a grin. "And then throw a massive celebration. I mean, we've earned it, right? With the sabotage and all that drama."

He chuckled, leaning against the counter, his expression softening. "I can't wait to see that. You know, I always thought you were more of a quiet, reserved type. But you've got some fire in you, and I like it."

"Fire? Please," I said, waving my hand dismissively, though my heart raced at the compliment. "I'm basically a walking flower pot with feelings."

"Exactly! A lovely, fiery flower pot," he countered, stepping closer, the air between us charged with something palpable. His gaze held mine, a mix of challenge and warmth, and I suddenly felt vulnerable yet exhilarated, like I was teetering on the edge of a thrilling ride.

Before I could respond, a loud crash interrupted our moment, and we turned to see a tray of vases teetering precariously before toppling to the ground in a spectacular shower of glass. "What the—" I exclaimed, rushing to help clean up the mess.

"Seriously? That's not how we want to start the festival," Jude grumbled, his tone playful despite the chaos. "You think they'll give us extra points for dramatic flair?"

I couldn't help but laugh as we knelt to pick up the shards. "Only if they appreciate a good glass-shattering performance."

As we worked, I felt a growing sense of camaraderie, an understanding that we were in this together, ready to face whatever challenges awaited us. The day of the festival dawned bright and clear, a stunning backdrop to the colorful celebration of harvest and community. I arrived at the town square early, my heart racing with anticipation. The vibrant stalls were adorned with pumpkins, corn stalks, and a rainbow of flowers, each one vying for attention. I could already see the rival florist's booth, an intimidating fortress of extravagant floral arrangements that seemed to shout, "Look at me!"

"Stay close," Jude whispered, his hand brushing against mine as we approached our stall, which was draped in white linens and overflowing with blooms that radiated warmth and cheer.

"You think they'll notice if we make our booth more appealing?" I joked, attempting to defuse the tension coiling in my stomach.

"Only if we start throwing petals," he replied with a smirk, and in that moment, my worries felt just a little lighter.

The festival began with laughter and music filling the air, and people drifted through the stalls, marveling at the displays. I felt the thrill of competition mixed with excitement, knowing we had fought against the odds to be here. As the day progressed, our booth attracted attention, the sun casting golden light on our carefully crafted arrangements. The colors seemed to dance, drawing people in like moths to a flame.

But just as we were beginning to feel the thrill of success, a figure approached our booth—tall, elegant, and exuding an air of confidence that could silence a room. It was the rival florist, her eyes glinting with a mix of disdain and determination.

"Nice attempt," she said, her voice dripping with sarcasm as she surveyed our arrangements with a critical eye. "But I don't think your little display can compete with my flowers."

I felt the tension spike as Jude stepped forward, a protective instinct flaring within him. "We're not here to compete. We're here to celebrate our craft. If you've forgotten that, then maybe you shouldn't be here at all."

Her laughter rang out, sharp and bitter. "Oh, sweetie, you think this is about artistry? It's business, plain and simple. I'll do whatever it takes to come out on top."

The air thickened with unspoken challenges, a battle of wills unfolding before us. I felt a rush of adrenaline. "So, sabotage is just a part of business now? Is that what you're saying?"

Her smile was unsettling, like a cat who had cornered its prey. "It's called strategy, darling. You should try it sometime."

I exchanged a glance with Jude, his eyes darkened with resolve. "We're not afraid of you," he declared, a firm hand resting on the table. "You may have tried to undermine us, but we're still here, stronger than ever."

As the crowd began to gather, drawn by the escalating tension, I could feel the weight of the moment pressing down on us. This was more than a festival; it was a chance to stand our ground, to prove that we wouldn't be pushed around. I squeezed Jude's hand beneath the table, a silent promise that together, we were ready to face whatever storm awaited us.

The atmosphere in the town square pulsed with energy, a vivid tapestry of colors and laughter weaving through the air as festivalgoers milled about, indulging in the delights of autumn. Our booth, adorned with a riot of flowers, stood proudly against the backdrop of competing stalls, each vying for attention. I could feel the electric buzz of anticipation mingling with the rich scent of blooming marigolds and dahlias. As the crowd swelled, a sense of hope bloomed within me, but so did the knot of anxiety that twisted in my stomach when I noticed the rival florist lingering nearby, her gaze sharp and predatory.

"Look at her, trying to steal the spotlight," I whispered to Jude, who was busy arranging a bouquet of sunflowers that seemed to burst with energy.

He glanced up, the corners of his mouth turning up in a slight smirk. "Let her try. Our flowers can outshine any wilted blooms she's got. Just watch."

His confidence was infectious, and for a moment, I felt invincible. I was about to respond when a commotion erupted from the other end of the square. A cluster of children had gathered around a small puppet show, their delighted shrieks piercing through the buzz of conversation.

"Perfect distraction," I murmured, and Jude chuckled, his attention shifting toward the crowd. "I think we should capitalize on this. Let's offer free flower samples to the kids. You know, win over the parents."

"Brilliant idea!" he replied, his enthusiasm contagious. "I'll grab some tiny arrangements."

As he dashed off to prepare, I took a moment to soak in the festival atmosphere. Laughter floated through the air like petals on the wind, and the golden sun bathed everything in warmth. I watched as families moved from stall to stall, their arms laden with treats and trinkets. This was what I had dreamed of—an event that brought our community together, showcasing the beauty of our hard work.

But just as I was about to dive into my task, the rival florist strutted over, a fake smile plastered on her face. "How quaint," she said, her tone dripping with sarcasm. "Are you really going to give away your precious flowers to children? Such a charitable gesture, really."

"Charity starts at home, doesn't it?" I replied, meeting her gaze with a steady determination. "You know, some people find joy in sharing."

Her laughter rang out like a bell, sharp and cutting. "Joy? Or desperation?"

Jude returned just in time, a handful of small bouquets in his arms. "What's this? A verbal sparring match?" He shot me a look of support, his presence a comforting shield.

"Nothing I can't handle," I said, but I appreciated his arrival.

"Oh, I was just explaining how your little booth can't possibly compete with my arrangements," the rival florist said, feigning innocence.

"You mean your arrangements that are covered in last week's dust?" Jude shot back, his eyes glinting with playful mischief.

I stifled a laugh, unable to contain the growing bond between us that was blossoming into something more. "What's the point of trying to undermine each other? We should be supporting our community, not tearing it apart."

"Support?" She scoffed. "This is business. And if you can't handle the competition, perhaps you should step aside."

With every word, I could feel the tension escalate, thickening the air around us. Yet, instead of crumbling under the weight of her insults, I felt an urge to rise above. "You're welcome to think that way. But I believe in what we're doing here, and I won't back down."

The festival continued around us, oblivious to our clash, and the crowd swelled with anticipation. I could feel the adrenaline coursing through my veins, propelling me forward. "Let's show everyone that kindness can win out over rivalry," I said, turning my back on the florist and focusing on our booth, where families were starting to gather, drawn by the promise of colorful flowers.

Jude grabbed my hand, a gesture that sent a rush of warmth through me. "You're right. Let's make this festival ours. After all, they're here to enjoy what we love."

As the hours flew by, laughter and excitement enveloped us, the children giggling as they clutched their tiny bouquets, parents smiling in delight. I could feel the tide turning in our favor, and with each passing moment, my confidence grew. We were making a name for ourselves, one flower at a time.

Then, just as the festival hit its peak, an unexpected twist sent shockwaves through the crowd. A commotion erupted from the other end of the square, drawing everyone's attention. I squinted against the sun, trying to see what was happening. My heart raced as I noticed people gathering in a tight circle, their faces pale and anxious.

"Something's wrong," I said, gripping Jude's arm.

"I'll check it out," he replied, his voice steady as he moved toward the crowd. I followed closely, adrenaline kicking in as we pushed our way through.

When we reached the center, the scene unfolded before us—a young girl was crying, clutching a small toy that had fallen into the muddy puddle beside the fountain. Panic bubbled in my chest, and I instinctively knelt down. "Hey there, it's okay," I said gently, my voice soothing. "We can get it for you."

As I reached for the toy, I heard Jude speaking with the girl's mother, assuring her that everything would be alright. But just as I grasped the toy, a low rumble echoed from behind me, causing everyone to turn in unison.

A massive shadow loomed over the square, and I felt the ground vibrate beneath my feet. My heart raced as I glanced up, my breath hitching in my throat. There, towering over us, was a large truck emblazoned with the rival florist's logo, careening toward our booth with alarming speed, flowers spilling from the back like confetti.

"Jude!" I screamed, the world around me blurring as the reality of the situation hit me like a wave. I lunged toward him, but time seemed to stretch and slow as panic engulfed the scene. The truck careened, the driver oblivious to the chaos that was about to ensue, and in that heartbeat, everything shifted.

As the crowd gasped in horror, I felt the ground beneath my feet tremble with uncertainty, and I knew that our hard-won victory was hanging by a thread.

Chapter 9: Whispers in the Dark

As the festival approached, my quaint little shop brimmed with vibrant blooms, each petal a splash of color against the ever-deepening twilight. The air was perfumed with the sweet scent of jasmine and honeysuckle, their fragrances intertwining like whispers shared between close friends. I arranged the flowers meticulously, but despite the cheerful surroundings, an unsettling undercurrent tinged the air, like a storm brewing just out of sight.

The hum of activity from the street outside drifted in, a chorus of laughter and chatter, the townsfolk buzzing with anticipation for the festival. Yet, the joyous sounds felt muffled, overshadowed by a sense of dread that had nestled itself deep in my gut. It had been a few days since Jude and I discovered the subtle sabotage plaguing the event preparations, and though we had vowed to keep our eyes peeled, I felt as though a storm was on the horizon—a storm I wasn't prepared for.

That night, the shop was dimly lit, the shadows dancing in the corners as I clipped stems and arranged blooms. The rhythmic sound of snipping scissors filled the silence, a meditative practice that usually calmed my restless thoughts. But tonight, the atmosphere felt charged, electric with an energy I couldn't quite place. A shiver ran down my spine, and I couldn't shake the feeling that I was being watched.

Just as I placed the final sprig of rosemary into the arrangement, an unexpected sound broke through my concentration—a faint rustling outside, as if the shadows themselves were shifting. My heart raced, the peaceful ambiance shattered by a rising tide of anxiety. I set down my shears, gripping the edge of the counter as I steeled myself for whatever lay beyond the door. Curiosity wrestled with caution, and after a moment's hesitation, I tiptoed to the window, my pulse echoing in my ears.

Peering out into the night, I squinted against the soft glow of the streetlamp. The festival lights twinkled in the distance, a stark contrast to the encroaching darkness that cloaked my shop. That's when I saw it—a figure, half-hidden in the shadows, standing still as if waiting for something. My breath caught in my throat. Was it a prankster? A misguided soul drawn by the allure of the festival? Or was it something far more sinister?

The figure shifted slightly, and my breath hitched as I realized it was a man. He seemed familiar, yet the deeper shadows obscured his features. I instinctively stepped back, my heart pounding against my ribcage like a caged bird desperate to escape. The feeling of being observed tightened around me like a vice. I couldn't ignore the chill creeping into my bones. I needed to know who this person was and what he wanted, but dread pulled me back.

With trembling hands, I reached for my phone, my lifeline in moments like this. I contemplated calling Jude, but a rush of apprehension washed over me. What if this was connected to the sabotage? What if I was drawing Jude into something dangerous? I could already hear his voice—both soothing and firm, like the strong arms I imagined would hold me against the chaos of the world. "You need to be careful, Amelia." The words echoed in my mind as I weighed my options.

Suddenly, the figure turned, catching the light just enough for me to see a glimmer of recognition in his eyes. My heart dropped. It was Leo, the artist who had come to town for the festival and whose mural was supposed to be a centerpiece of the celebrations. But why was he lurking outside my shop in the dead of night?

Adrenaline surged through me, pushing me to action. I swung the door open, stepping out into the cool night air. "Leo! What are you doing out here?" My voice was steady, though I felt anything but. The uncertainty etched across my features must have been apparent, for Leo's expression shifted from surprise to concern.

"I didn't want to interrupt," he said, his voice low and cautious, almost conspiratorial. "I saw you working late, and I thought..." He trailed off, glancing nervously over his shoulder. The tension hung thick in the air, wrapping around us like a fog that refused to dissipate.

I stepped closer, the flickering light from the streetlamp casting shadows that played tricks on my mind. "Thought what? That you could just stand out here and watch me without saying anything?" I tried to inject a bit of humor into my words, but it fell flat. My instincts told me there was more to this encounter than met the eye.

"I thought you might like to know what I overheard," he said, glancing around again, his voice barely above a whisper. "There are people in town who don't want the festival to happen. They're planning something, Amelia, something that could ruin everything."

My stomach sank as I absorbed his words. The very whispers I had sensed earlier were manifesting right before me, an unsettling premonition that what I feared was not merely in my head. I felt a chill wash over me, merging with the cool night air. "What do you mean? Who?"

Leo hesitated, his eyes darting again to the shadows that seemed to pulse with secrets. "I can't say just yet. But if you're serious about helping Jude and the others, you need to be careful. They're watching you, too."

The weight of his words settled heavily on my shoulders, igniting a fire of determination within me. I had no intention of being pushed aside by shadows or threats, no matter how sinister they seemed. "I can handle myself, Leo. But if we're going to figure this out, I need you to be honest with me. No more secrets."

He nodded, the tension in his shoulders easing slightly. "Alright. Just promise me you'll be cautious. I don't want anything to happen to you."

His concern caught me off guard. Here we were, two unlikely allies standing on the cusp of something much bigger than either of us had anticipated. “And I don’t want to lose my chance at a festival that could bring this town back to life,” I replied, my voice firm.

As we stood there, shadows flickering around us like the uninvited guests to a party, I felt a strange sense of camaraderie forming between us. Together, we would unravel the mystery lurking in the dark corners of our town, but I couldn’t shake the feeling that the deeper I delved into this world of whispers and secrets, the more perilous the path would become.

The night wrapped itself around me like a shroud as I stared at Leo, his expression a mix of apprehension and urgency. The streetlamp flickered, casting erratic shadows that danced around us, creating a backdrop more fitting for a suspenseful thriller than a peaceful festival preparation. I could feel the tension crackling in the air, thick enough to cut with a knife, and despite my resolve to face whatever dark forces lurked in the shadows, I couldn’t help but feel a flutter of fear.

“Why are you so sure they’re watching me?” I asked, trying to project confidence even as uncertainty gnawed at my insides. “What exactly did you overhear?”

Leo glanced over his shoulder again, as if the very act of speaking might summon an unseen threat. “I was sketching near the old oak by the river,” he explained, his voice low and urgent. “Some locals were talking about how they couldn’t let the festival happen, how it would expose their secrets. They mentioned sabotage and distractions, ways to draw attention away from whatever they’re planning.”

A chill ran through me, a sinister echo of the sabotage Jude and I had encountered. “Do you think they’re connected to what happened with the flowers?” My voice wavered as I struggled to connect the dots.

"Maybe. But it's more than just petty sabotage. It feels... bigger. They want to send a message, and you've become part of that message."

I shuddered at the implication. "You're saying I'm a target? For what? Because I care about the festival?"

His eyes narrowed, and he nodded gravely. "Because you're a threat to their plans. People don't like change, especially in a small town where everyone knows everyone else's business. You're shaking things up, and they don't take kindly to outsiders stirring the pot."

Outsider. The word hung heavy between us, invoking the very feeling I'd tried to shake off since moving here. My connection to this place felt tenuous, like a thread stretched thin. Yet, I couldn't just walk away. The festival was more than just a celebration; it was a chance for the town to come alive again, to rekindle lost friendships and breathe life back into old traditions. I had invested too much of myself to let it all unravel.

"Then we have to do something," I declared, my determination hardening like the petals of the roses I loved to arrange. "We can't let them win."

Leo's gaze softened, but I caught a flicker of uncertainty in his eyes. "What do you suggest? It's not just about confronting them; it's about being smart."

"I'll talk to Jude," I decided, the thought sparking a flicker of hope within me. "He'll know what to do. If we can gather more information, figure out who's behind this... we might have a chance."

Leo nodded slowly, but I could see he still harbored doubts. "Just promise me you'll be careful. These people aren't playing games."

With the weight of his warning lingering in my mind, I turned to head back inside the shop, only to be halted by a sudden rustling in the bushes nearby. My heart leapt to my throat, and I grabbed Leo's arm instinctively. "Did you hear that?"

"Yes," he replied, his eyes widening. "Let's not stick around to find out."

We retreated into the shop, locking the door behind us. As I flicked on the overhead lights, the warm glow washed over the flowers, and for a brief moment, the world felt safe again. The walls, filled with the calming scent of fresh blooms, felt like a fortress against the chaos outside.

"Are you alright?" Leo asked, concern threading through his voice as he leaned against the counter, his arms crossed tightly over his chest. "You look pale."

"I'm fine," I lied, though the tremor in my hands betrayed me. "Just a little rattled, I suppose."

The quiet moment stretched between us, charged with unsaid words and lingering tension. I could feel a bond forming, an understanding forged in the fires of shared danger. "You really think I'm a threat to them?" I asked, seeking validation in his gaze.

"Absolutely," he said, his tone firm. "You care about this town. That passion makes you dangerous to people who want to keep everything just as it is."

A soft laugh escaped me, surprising us both. "Dangerous, huh? Maybe I should add that to my résumé: florist by day, town liberator by night."

Leo grinned, and for a fleeting moment, the tension eased. "Well, if you're a liberator, I'm definitely the sidekick. No capes, just paintbrushes and flowers."

We exchanged a lighthearted glance, but the gravity of our situation hung heavily in the air. I couldn't help but admire the way Leo's passion for art and this town mirrored my own, intertwining our fates in a way I hadn't anticipated. Yet, the playful banter felt like a fragile shield against the shadows creeping ever closer.

"Let's go talk to Jude," I finally said, gathering my resolve. "If there's a threat, we need to confront it together."

Leo nodded, the humor fading from his face as he straightened, the weight of reality settling back on his shoulders. "Right. But remember, if things go sideways, we need an escape plan."

As we stepped into the cool night air, I took a moment to breathe deeply, allowing the scents of blooming flowers and the crispness of autumn to fill my lungs. The festival was on the verge of becoming something magical, but now, it felt more like a battleground—a place where hidden agendas lay in wait, ready to strike.

The streets were quiet, the excitement of the festival still a distant hum in the background. As we walked, I could feel the pulse of the town beneath our feet, the heartbeat of a place filled with history and hopes yet to be realized. But the whispers of danger danced just at the edge of my senses, and I couldn't shake the feeling that we were being watched.

"Do you think it's the same people from the sabotage?" I asked, breaking the silence as we approached the small coffee shop where Jude often worked late into the night.

"Could be," Leo replied, his eyes scanning the dark corners of the street. "But we can't jump to conclusions without evidence. We need to gather intel first."

As we reached the door, a sudden thought struck me. "What if we're walking into a trap?" I whispered, the weight of possibility hanging heavy in the air.

"Then we'll outsmart them," Leo said, determination lining his features. "Together."

With one last glance at the shadows lingering around us, I pushed open the door, the familiar bell chiming cheerfully as we entered the warm embrace of the coffee shop. The scent of freshly brewed coffee wrapped around us like a comforting hug, a stark contrast to the uncertainty lurking just outside. I spotted Jude at the counter, his back turned as he meticulously arranged pastries.

"Hey, Jude!" I called, trying to mask my anxiety beneath a layer of enthusiasm. "Can we talk?"

He turned, surprise flickering across his face as he noticed Leo beside me. "Sure, everything alright?"

"Not exactly," I replied, pulling him aside, my voice dropping to a conspiratorial whisper. "We need to talk about the festival... and the people who don't want it to happen."

Jude's expression shifted, concern etching itself into his features as he leaned closer, listening intently as I began to unveil the tangled web of whispers, secrets, and threats that had begun to shroud our festival in darkness.

Jude's brow furrowed deeper as I shared what Leo had overheard, his focus sharpened with each detail. The coffee shop buzzed around us, the hum of conversation and the clattering of cups creating a background melody that felt both comforting and disconcerting. I could see the gears turning in his mind, assessing the implications of our conversation like a strategist plotting a course through enemy territory.

"So you're telling me that someone is actively working against the festival?" he asked, leaning in closer. His voice was steady, but I could sense the tension in his posture.

"Exactly. And they're not just being petty; they want to destroy it," I replied, glancing over my shoulder as if the lurking figure might suddenly appear behind us. "Leo overheard them talking about sabotage and making sure we fail."

"Why would anyone want to ruin something that brings the town together?" Jude's voice held a mix of disbelief and anger. "There's something deeper going on here."

"Yeah, and that's what we need to find out. This isn't just about the festival anymore. It's about the heart of this town," I said, feeling the weight of our mission settle onto my shoulders. "We have to gather more information. We can't let this go unchecked."

Jude nodded, determination replacing the initial shock on his face. "We'll need a plan. If these people are as dangerous as Leo says, we can't just confront them recklessly."

"Right," I agreed. "But how do we figure out who they are?"

"Let's start by talking to the vendors and anyone else involved in the festival preparations. They might have noticed something suspicious or heard something." Jude's voice steadied, his earlier concern transforming into purpose.

As we plotted our next steps, Leo stood slightly apart, his gaze flitting between us. "I can help," he offered, his tone earnest. "I've been talking to some of the local artists. They might have seen or heard things."

"Great! The more eyes we have, the better," I encouraged, a flicker of hope igniting within me. "We'll work together to gather intel, but we need to stay cautious. If we're right, these people won't hesitate to protect their interests."

"I'll reach out to some of the artists tomorrow," Leo said, a determined glint in his eye. "In the meantime, let's keep our heads low. I'll come by the shop later, and we can regroup."

With a plan forming between us, we wrapped up our conversation, the air thick with the promise of impending action. Jude made a quick call to some vendors, reassuring them about the festival despite the uncertainty lurking beneath the surface. I busied myself with tidying the shop, though my mind raced with thoughts of what lay ahead.

As the day slipped into evening, the quiet of the shop felt almost comforting. I rearranged the flowers, their vibrant colors a stark contrast to the murky threats that hovered just outside. The soft glow of the shop lights created an inviting atmosphere, but even the beauty around me couldn't entirely dispel the unease gnawing at my insides.

Hours later, as the last of the sunlight faded and the streetlamps flickered to life, Leo returned, his demeanor more serious than before. "I talked to a few vendors, and you were right. There's definitely a vibe of tension among some of them. A few even mentioned feeling watched," he said, his voice low.

"Watched?" I echoed, my heart racing again. "Did they see anyone suspicious?"

"Not exactly. Just a feeling, you know? Like someone was lurking around, listening. It's unsettling." He shifted uncomfortably, his hands shoved deep in his pockets.

"We have to dig deeper," I said, feeling the urgency of our mission tightening around me. "What if we set up a few listening posts? We could overhear conversations when they don't realize we're there."

"Good idea," Jude chimed in. "We could hide in plain sight, act like we're just enjoying the festival while keeping our eyes peeled for anything unusual."

"Let's scout the area tomorrow," Leo suggested, a spark of excitement illuminating his features. "We'll blend in, and if we notice anything strange, we'll follow up."

Our plan solidified, we ventured into the night, the cool air crisp against my skin as we stepped outside the shop. I glanced around, half-expecting to see the shadowy figure again, but the street lay still, a deceptive calm enveloping us.

We split up after agreeing to meet back at the shop later. As I strolled through the quiet streets, I took in the familiar sights—the quaint little homes, the local shops that lined the roads, and the large oak tree that stood sentinel in the town square. The warmth of the festival was palpable in the air, despite the danger lurking just beneath the surface.

As I passed the old theater, I caught a glimpse of movement in the shadows. My heart quickened. There it was again—the unsettling feeling that I wasn't alone. I paused, straining to hear any sounds that might indicate who or what was hiding in the darkness.

"Hello?" I called out, my voice echoing slightly in the stillness. The darkness seemed to hold its breath, and I waited, heart racing, for a response.

"Is someone there?" I pressed, my pulse racing as the silence stretched, thick and suffocating.

Suddenly, a figure stepped out from behind the theater's entrance. My breath caught as I recognized him—the very man I had seen lurking outside my shop. The shadows obscured his features, but I could make out his intense gaze, locking onto mine with a chilling clarity.

"You shouldn't be out here alone," he said, his voice smooth yet laced with an underlying menace that sent shivers down my spine.

"Who are you?" I managed to ask, each word a challenge, even as I felt the weight of fear creeping back into my bones.

He stepped closer, the faint light illuminating a smirk that sent a jolt of anxiety through me. "Just someone who knows things, Amelia. Things about the festival, about you, and what you're trying to do."

The world around me faded into a blur, the vibrant colors of the festival losing their charm in the face of his ominous presence. My heart pounded in my chest, and instinct kicked in. I had to get away.

"Stay back!" I shouted, backing away, but he merely chuckled, the sound dark and low.

"Running won't help you," he said, advancing slowly. "You're already in over your head, and it's only going to get messier from here."

With adrenaline coursing through my veins, I turned on my heel and sprinted down the street, my mind racing as I thought of how to warn Jude and Leo. I couldn't let fear paralyze me, not now. I had to stay one step ahead of whatever danger was waiting in the dark.

But as I ran, the chilling realization settled over me: the shadows were alive, and they were closing in fast.

Chapter 10: Shadows of Doubt

The air was thick with tension, a kind of charged silence that crackled like static before a storm. As I sat across from Jude in our favorite corner of the café, the dim lighting cast soft shadows on his face, accentuating the sharp lines of his jaw and the furrow in his brow. The scent of freshly brewed coffee mingled with the sweet, buttery aroma of pastries, but I barely registered it. My heart raced, not from the usual buzz of caffeine, but from the swirling storm of emotions within me.

"I'm telling you, we can't just ignore what's happening," I insisted, my voice low yet fervent. I leaned forward, trying to bridge the distance that felt as vast as the ocean between us. "Our rival isn't just trying to scare us off. There's something more at play here, and you know it."

Jude's gaze flickered, a momentary crack in his otherwise stoic demeanor. "Look, I get that you're worried, but we can't let fear dictate our actions. If we react to every shadow lurking around, we'll never move forward." His words were laced with a frustration that mirrored my own, but beneath it all, I sensed an undercurrent of something deeper—an unwillingness to confront the looming storm that threatened to engulf us both.

"Maybe it's not fear," I countered, my voice steady despite the tremors in my gut. "Maybe it's instinct. We can't just brush off our opponent's tactics as mere intimidation. They're playing a game, and we need to be ready for their next move." My frustration simmered, bubbling just beneath the surface. I wanted him to understand, to see the complexities I felt intertwining with my very thoughts. But instead, it felt like I was shouting into a void.

Jude leaned back in his chair, crossing his arms defensively. The movement seemed to shield him from my words, as if he were bracing for a storm that I could already feel gathering. "And what do you propose we do? Start digging into shadows that might not even exist? You can't let paranoia lead you down a rabbit hole." His tone was sharp, cutting through the fragile space we'd created between us.

I recoiled slightly, the bite of his words striking a chord deep within me. "I'm not being paranoid, Jude. I'm being cautious. There's a difference." My mind raced, searching for the right words to peel back the layers of his stubbornness, to show him that my concerns weren't mere figments of my imagination but rather the embodiment of an instinct honed by years of navigating the unpredictable terrain of our world. "You don't know what's going on behind the scenes. We're risking too much by ignoring it."

Jude's lips pressed into a thin line, and I could see the tension in his shoulders, a tightness that spoke volumes. "You know, sometimes it feels like you're not even listening to me," he said, his voice low, almost as if he were afraid to raise it. "I'm trying to keep us focused, to stay on course."

A wave of anger coursed through me, a sudden fire igniting as I replied, "And it feels like you're dismissing my concerns as if they don't matter." I leaned in closer, lowering my voice to keep our conversation intimate. "You think I'm not aware of the stakes? You think I'm here for the drama? I've invested everything into this, and it terrifies me that you seem more focused on maintaining some ideal of strength rather than facing the reality."

Jude's expression shifted, a flicker of vulnerability breaking through the armor he wore so confidently. "I'm not trying to undermine you. I just... I don't want to see you hurt," he admitted, his tone softening. The shift in his demeanor brought a wave of relief that mingled with the storm of frustration still swirling between us.

"Then let me in," I urged, my voice almost pleading. "Don't push me away. We're stronger together, but only if we're honest with each other." The sincerity of my plea hung in the air, a fragile thread that could either bind us closer or snap beneath the strain.

For a moment, silence enveloped us, wrapping us in an uncertain embrace. I could feel the tension in the air shift, morphing into something palpable—a fragile truce forged in the crucible of shared fears and dreams. But just as I thought we were on the verge of bridging that emotional chasm, Jude glanced away, his eyes distant, searching for something beyond the walls of the café.

"I need time," he murmured, his voice barely above a whisper. The words struck me like a physical blow, leaving me reeling. I had opened up, laid my heart bare, and now he was retreating once again. It felt like standing on the edge of a cliff, the abyss yawning below me, ready to swallow me whole.

As I watched him, my heart twisted painfully. I understood his need for space, but my instincts screamed that he was harboring secrets, shadows of doubt that lingered just out of reach. My mind raced, churning with a desperate need to unearth whatever lay hidden in his heart. "Jude," I began, but he held up a hand, the gesture silencing me.

"I'll come to you when I'm ready," he said, his eyes resolute yet distant. "But for now, we need to focus on the work. The project is what matters." With that, he turned his attention to the chaos of the café, the laughter and chatter swirling around us like a whirlwind of normalcy, so starkly contrasting with the turmoil brewing between us.

I sat there, feeling small and insignificant amidst the bustling crowd, as if I were watching our world unravel through a thick glass wall. The warmth of the coffee cup in my hands felt like a cruel reminder of the distance between us. I fought the urge to let my insecurities take root, pushing them down like weeds in a garden, but the fear of losing him loomed larger than ever.

With each passing moment, I could feel the shadows gathering, an inescapable truth settling in my gut. This was not merely a disagreement; it was a fracture in our fragile alliance, and I needed to know the truth before it consumed us both. A rush of determination surged through me, fueling my resolve. I would dig deeper, even if it meant wandering into the very shadows Jude wanted to avoid. The secrets swirling in the dark were waiting to be uncovered, and I was ready to face them head-on.

The moment I stepped out of the café, the brisk evening air wrapped around me like a cold, unwelcome embrace, shaking off the remnants of our heated conversation. My mind was a tumultuous sea, waves of frustration crashing against the rocks of doubt that had begun to build between Jude and me. As I walked through the dimly lit streets, the glow of streetlamps flickered overhead, their light casting elongated shadows that danced along the pavement, mirroring the conflict inside me.

I needed clarity, a break from the emotional whirlpool that threatened to pull me under. My feet carried me toward the park, a familiar refuge where the sounds of the city faded, replaced by the soft rustling of leaves and the distant chirping of crickets. It was a small sanctuary, but tonight it felt more like a confining cage, the darkness creeping in too closely for comfort. I settled onto a weathered bench, the wood cool against my skin, and inhaled deeply, attempting to ground myself in the moment.

The serenity of the park was almost mocking. My mind spun with memories of Jude's words, his stubbornness like a brick wall, immovable and frustratingly high. I pulled out my phone, staring at the screen as if it held the answers I desperately sought. Messages flickered from friends and acquaintances, mundane updates that seemed trivial in light of our looming rivalry. A pang of envy shot through me as I read about parties, escapades, and effortless connections. I longed for that simplicity, that easy laughter and companionship, instead of the tangled web I found myself ensnared in with Jude.

A sudden sound broke the tranquility—a soft crunch of leaves underfoot. I turned to see a figure approaching, the dim light revealing a familiar silhouette. It was Mia, my best friend, a whirlwind of energy wrapped in a coat that seemed too large for her petite frame. She spotted me, her face lighting up with a mix of concern and curiosity.

"There you are! I thought you were lost in the coffee shop abyss," she teased, plopping down beside me. Her cheerful demeanor contrasted sharply with my dark thoughts, and for a moment, I couldn't help but smile at her exuberance.

"More like lost in a philosophical debate with Jude," I replied, rolling my eyes. "You'd think we were arguing about the meaning of life rather than how to handle a rival."

Mia's expression shifted from playful to serious in an instant. "What's going on? You look like you've just survived a hurricane."

"Jude doesn't take this seriously," I sighed, frustration bubbling to the surface again. "I'm convinced our rival is up to something. It's like he can't see the bigger picture."

Mia nodded thoughtfully, her brow furrowing. "Men can be dense sometimes. Not that I would know anything about that." She gave a mock glare in the direction of an unsuspecting jogger passing by. "But seriously, if he's not listening to your instincts, that's a problem."

I glanced sideways at her, the warmth of her friendship washing over me like a comforting blanket. "It's like he wants to brush it off, to pretend everything's fine when clearly it's not. I can feel the tension rising, and it's not just about our project anymore. It's personal."

"Have you told him that?" she asked, her tone earnest. "Because I can't imagine that it's easy for him either, dealing with all this pressure."

"Trust me, I've tried," I replied, the edge in my voice betraying my irritation. "But he's so fixated on being strong and in control. Sometimes, I wonder if he thinks I'm just a distraction."

Mia leaned in closer, her eyes searching mine. "You're not a distraction. You're his partner. If he can't see that, then he's the one who needs to wake up. But maybe you need to approach him differently? Find a way to reach him that doesn't feel like an accusation."

Her words hung in the air, a lifeline I hadn't expected but desperately needed. "You might be right. Maybe I should find a way to show him that my concerns come from a place of care, not just anxiety."

The thought settled in me like a soothing balm, easing some of the tumult within. "I just want us to be on the same team, you know? It feels like we're playing for different sides, and that terrifies me."

Mia nodded, her expression softening. "You have to remind him that you're in this together. It's not just about strategy; it's about trust. And if there's no trust, what's the point?"

Her words resonated, stirring a determination within me that I hadn't realized was buried beneath the weight of our argument. I would approach Jude differently. I would find a way to break through his walls without igniting the fire of his defensiveness.

"Thanks, Mia. You always know how to help me see things clearer," I said, my heart feeling a little lighter. "Let's get back to the café. I think I need to confront him."

Mia grinned, her spirit infectious. "That's the spirit! Let's storm the castle, shall we?"

As we walked back, the shadows began to recede, the flickering streetlamps illuminating our path. The atmosphere felt different, charged with the promise of change, and I clung to that hope like a lifeline. I would confront Jude, but this time it would be with understanding rather than accusation.

Upon reaching the café, the warm glow from within spilled out onto the sidewalk, enveloping us in a cocoon of comfort. I took a deep breath, steadying my nerves. This wasn't merely about confronting Jude; it was about reclaiming my place beside him, about reestablishing the partnership that had begun to fray at the edges.

Pushing through the door, the familiar scent of coffee and pastries wrapped around me, a comforting reminder of countless shared moments. The café buzzed with life, laughter and chatter mingling in the air. But my focus narrowed, my gaze landing on Jude at our usual table, a frown etched on his face as he scrolled through his phone.

With newfound resolve, I strode over, my heart pounding in my chest like a war drum. As I approached, Jude looked up, surprise flickering across his features. "Hey, I didn't expect to see you so soon," he said, a hint of wariness in his voice.

"Good, because I'm here to talk," I replied, my tone firm yet inviting. "We need to sort this out, Jude. I don't want to keep going around in circles."

His brow furrowed, and for a moment, I feared he would retreat behind those same walls he had erected earlier. But then he nodded slowly, the tension in his shoulders easing just a fraction. "Alright. Let's talk."

With that simple agreement, we settled into our seats, the noise of the café fading into a backdrop as the real conversation began to unfold.

The moment of silence hung between us, heavy with the weight of unspoken words and unresolved tension. I could see the flicker of something behind Jude's dark eyes—an emotion he was desperately trying to hide. My heart raced, caught between the urge to push him for more and the fear of breaking whatever fragile bond we still had.

"Let's lay it all out on the table, Jude," I said, my voice steady despite the nerves prickling at the back of my mind. "You're holding something back, and I can feel it. If we're going to navigate this rivalry, I need to know everything."

Jude leaned back in his chair, crossing his arms tightly over his chest, as if trying to shield himself from my scrutiny. "You think I'm hiding something? Why would I do that?" The defensiveness in his tone was palpable, and I could see the tension snapping at the edges of his patience.

"Because you're acting like a classic boy in a standoff," I shot back, my frustration bubbling to the surface. "Denying everything and dodging the real issues doesn't help us. What's the worst that could happen if you let me in?"

He hesitated, the flicker of conflict passing across his features. "What if I'm trying to protect you? Maybe I don't want to drag you into this mess." His words hung in the air, a double-edged sword that cut through the tension, leaving a raw ache in its wake.

"Protect me from what?" I pressed, leaning forward, desperate to break through the barrier he had built. "I can handle myself, Jude. I've been doing it for a long time. You can't just decide what's best for me without involving me in the decision."

The soft thrum of conversation around us faded as the focus narrowed to our table. It felt like the world had fallen away, leaving just us and the jagged truths waiting to be uncovered. Jude opened his mouth to respond, but the moment was interrupted by the sudden arrival of an old acquaintance—Daniel, our rival's right-hand man. His presence felt like ice water thrown over a flame, extinguishing the heat of our argument in an instant.

"Look who it is," he said, a smirk curling at the corners of his mouth. "The dynamic duo, plotting your next big move, I see." He slid into the booth across from us, his casual demeanor masking a predatory glint in his eyes. "Should I be worried? Because last I checked, you two were playing it pretty close to the vest."

Jude stiffened, the moment of vulnerability slipping away like sand through my fingers. "What do you want, Daniel?" he asked, his voice now edged with irritation.

"Just checking in. Heard some interesting things about your little project. Rumor has it you're in over your heads." He leaned back, his gaze shifting from Jude to me. "And it seems like you might be the weak link in this operation." His taunt stung, and I could feel heat rising to my cheeks, the pressure of his words thrumming in my chest.

"I'm not a weak link," I shot back, anger igniting within me. "You'd be surprised at how much I can handle."

"Easy there, tiger," Daniel replied with a condescending chuckle. "I'm just saying, it's a tough game out there. You might want to keep a closer eye on your partner. I hear there are sharks in these waters, and they're hungry." With that, he rose, the lingering smirk still plastered on his face. "Good luck. You'll need it."

As he walked away, the air between Jude and me turned icy. I could feel the weight of his gaze on me, an unspoken tension brewing like a storm on the horizon. "What was that about?" I asked, crossing my arms defensively.

"Nothing to worry about," Jude replied, but his tone was evasive, the usual confidence fading from his voice.

"Nothing? Are you kidding me?" My frustration bubbled over again, the remnants of our earlier conversation returning with renewed force. "He's trying to intimidate us, Jude! He knows something—something that could put us at risk. Why aren't you taking this seriously?"

"I'm trying to focus on our strategy, not get caught up in their games," he replied, his tone clipped, a veneer of calm barely concealing the turmoil beneath. "We can't let them rattle us."

"Rattle us? You're the one acting like a deer in the headlights!" I shot back, anger surging. "You can't ignore the threat. It's not just about strategy anymore; it's about our safety."

Jude ran a hand through his hair, a gesture of frustration that only fueled my determination. "You think I don't see the risks? I do! But we can't let Daniel's words get under our skin. If we do, we're already lost."

A heavy silence settled between us, thick and suffocating. I could feel the tension rising, threatening to crack our already fragile alliance. "I need you to trust me, Jude," I said, my voice softer now, a hint of desperation creeping in. "This isn't just about being strong; it's about being smart. We need to investigate, to understand what's really going on."

Jude's expression shifted, the hardness in his eyes softening slightly. "I do trust you," he murmured, though his voice was laced with uncertainty. "But trust goes both ways. I can't help you if you're constantly second-guessing me."

I sighed, the weight of our argument pressing down on me like a heavy blanket. "I'm not second-guessing you. I'm trying to be proactive. We need to confront this before it gets out of hand."

Before he could respond, a loud crash echoed from the back of the café, cutting through the charged atmosphere. I turned instinctively, adrenaline spiking as I saw a figure tumble through the door, breathing heavily. It was Mia, her expression a mix of panic and urgency.

"There you are!" she exclaimed, rushing toward us, her eyes wide. "You won't believe what I just heard."

"What is it?" I asked, the tension from earlier forgotten in an instant.

"There's been a breach. Someone's been digging into our project—like, really deep," she said, her voice breathless. "I overheard it at the bar down the street. They're planning something, and it's not just talk. They're moving fast, and they're targeting you both!"

A cold wave of dread washed over me, the implications crashing down like a tidal wave. "Targeting us? Why?"

Mia leaned closer, her voice low and urgent. "Because they think you're weak, and they're ready to pounce. They've got plans, and it's all centered around you two."

Jude's expression turned grave, the weight of Mia's words hanging in the air like an executioner's blade. I felt my heart race, the urgency of the moment spiraling into something palpable and terrifying. "We need to do something," I saïd, adrenaline coursing through my veins.

Mia nodded, her gaze darting around the café, as if the walls themselves were closing in. "We can't wait. They're making moves, and we need to counteract them—fast."

The gravity of the situation settled heavily in the pit of my stomach, every instinct screaming for action. "What's the plan?" I asked, my voice firm, ready to face whatever shadows lay ahead.

As we began to strategize, the café's ambiance shifted, the laughter and chatter fading into the background. Shadows crept in around us, ominous and threatening, swirling with uncertainty. A chill raced down my spine as I realized the stakes had never been higher.

Just as we were ready to formulate a plan, the door swung open violently, and a figure cloaked in darkness stepped inside, his features obscured. A jolt of fear shot through me. The air became electric, charged with impending confrontation. "I've come to deliver a message," the figure announced, his voice low and foreboding.

My breath caught in my throat as I exchanged a glance with Jude, the weight of unspoken dread heavy between us. In that instant, I knew we were no longer just players in a game—we were pawns on the brink of a much larger chessboard, one where the stakes were life and death.

Chapter 11: Blooming Betrayals

The festival surged around me, a vibrant tapestry of colors, sounds, and scents that enveloped Cedar Ridge. The air buzzed with laughter and chatter, punctuated by the distant sound of live music drifting from the main stage. I stood behind my booth, adorned with an array of floral arrangements that I had crafted with care over the past weeks. Petals of soft pinks and vibrant yellows danced in the breeze, their delicate fragrances mingling, creating an olfactory symphony that pulled in passersby like moths to a flame. Yet beneath this lively exterior lay an undercurrent of tension that twisted like a vine around my heart.

"Can you believe the turnout?" I asked Jude, my trusted friend and fellow florist, as I arranged a cluster of peonies. His eyes sparkled, but there was something in his gaze that suggested he was not entirely present.

"Yeah, it's incredible," he replied, adjusting the collar of his shirt, a nervous gesture that didn't escape my notice. I caught a hint of uncertainty in his voice, like the sudden dampness of a storm cloud darkening a sunny sky. His charm had always had a way of disarming me, but today, it felt overshadowed by a creeping anxiety that I couldn't ignore.

As the afternoon wore on, the booth became a whirlwind of activity. Customers flowed in and out, their faces bright with excitement as they browsed the flowers and inhaled their scents. Each sale was a small victory, a testament to my hard work and dedication. But my heart was heavy. Something felt off, and every laugh from the crowd was a reminder that beneath the surface of joy, shadows lurked.

When I stepped back to catch my breath, my eyes swept over the arrangements. That's when I noticed it—a bouquet, once pristine, now sat askew, the flowers deliberately rearranged. A sickening twist of suspicion churned in my stomach. Who would dare? A clenching sense of betrayal crawled up my spine, urging me to scrutinize the faces around me. Could someone among my friends be behind this? The thought felt like ice water coursing through my veins.

"Jude," I called, trying to keep my tone light, masking the unease swirling inside me. He looked up from his own booth across the way, where he was juggling customers with his usual ease. I gestured toward the altered bouquet, hoping to catch his eye, but his expression shifted—an uncharacteristic look of concern crossed his face.

"I'll be right there," he replied, but just as I expected him to join me, his phone rang, its sharp tone slicing through the cheerful atmosphere. He frowned, glanced at the caller ID, and excused himself, stepping away to answer it. The fleeting moment of eye contact we shared was laced with unspoken questions, and an inexplicable pang of jealousy stabbed at my heart. What could be so important that it required him to abandon me in this moment of chaos?

I busied myself rearranging flowers, but my mind raced. The festival, which had once seemed like a platform for my dreams, now felt like a stage set for betrayal. I didn't just feel alone; I felt abandoned. My thoughts spiraled into dark territories, wondering if Jude had been hiding something all along, his flirty banter merely a mask for deeper secrets.

"Hey! You're not going to believe the deals I just snagged on artisanal bread!" my friend Jess chirped as she bounced over, her arms laden with baked goods. The smell wafted toward me, warm and enticing, but it only served to deepen my sense of disarray.

"That's great," I said, forcing a smile that felt more like a grimace. "How's the festival treating you?"

"Busy as ever! But I noticed your booth is swamped," she said, her eyes glancing at the line of eager customers. "Isn't it exciting?"

"Yeah, but..." I hesitated, torn between the weight of my worries and the need to keep my tone upbeat. "I think someone's been messing with my flowers."

"What?" Jess leaned in closer, her brows furrowing in concern. "Are you serious?"

"Yeah. I just saw a bouquet that was completely rearranged. I can't shake the feeling that someone's trying to sabotage me."

Her face turned serious, reflecting my own anxiety. "Do you think it could be someone from the festival? Maybe another vendor?"

I shrugged, feeling a lump form in my throat. "I don't know. But I can't shake the feeling that I'm being watched." Just as I said the words, I caught a glimpse of a figure lingering at the edge of the crowd—a woman with dark hair and an enigmatic smile that sent a shiver down my spine. She was staring right at me, her gaze unwavering.

"Who is that?" Jess asked, following my line of sight.

"I have no idea," I whispered, my heart racing as the woman's expression morphed from intrigue to something more sinister. The festival felt suddenly small and suffocating, the laughter and music fading into a distant hum. I turned back to my flowers, willing myself to focus on the beauty I had crafted, but the weight of unease pressed heavily against my chest.

Jude returned, his expression strained. "Sorry about that. Just a work thing," he said, but I noticed how he avoided my eyes, as if there were words lingering on the tip of his tongue that he dared not speak. The tension hung in the air, thick and palpable, and I felt the chasm between us widen, gnawing at the connection we had begun to forge.

"Everything okay?" I asked, my voice barely a whisper.

"Yeah, just... just a little unexpected news," he replied, glancing around as if seeking an escape. The fleeting look of vulnerability in his eyes tugged at my heart, and I desperately wanted to reach out to him, but the swirling chaos around us felt like an insurmountable barrier.

I stood at my booth, surrounded by vibrant flowers and the laughter of festival-goers, yet I felt like a stranger in my own world. The once-familiar faces of friends and customers began to blur, their cheerful chatter morphing into whispers of doubt. Each passing moment heightened my resolve to uncover the truth, to unravel the threads of deceit that threatened to bind me in their sinister grip. But as the sun dipped lower in the sky, casting long shadows that danced across the ground, I couldn't shake the feeling that the real storm was yet to come.

The sun dipped low on the horizon, casting a golden hue across the festival, but the warmth that once felt inviting now seemed to amplify my anxiety. Customers jostled for my attention, their laughter ringing in my ears, but I felt like a ghost drifting among them, disconnected from the revelry. As I arranged the last of my blossoms—a riot of color that should have brought joy—I couldn't shake the unease coiling within me.

"Hey! What's got you looking like someone stole your last cookie?" Jess reappeared, a plate of mini pastries in hand, her voice a bright spark in the growing twilight. The sugary treats were a distraction, the kind of indulgence that could momentarily lift spirits. "Try one of these! They're practically magic."

"Magic or not, I'm pretty sure I just need a miracle," I replied, forcing a smile. She handed me a pastry, and I took a small bite, its sweetness juxtaposing the bitterness swirling in my heart. "I think someone's sabotaging my booth."

Jess's eyes widened, a hint of mischief flickering across her face. "Are we talking drama here? Like, a rival florist trying to steal your thunder?"

“More like a backstabber with a vendetta.” I glanced around, ensuring no one was listening. “Someone messed with my arrangements. And now, Jude’s gone off on some mysterious phone call. It’s all feeling a bit too... shady.”

“Shady is my least favorite shade,” Jess replied, glancing around as if trying to spot the enemy in the crowd. “Do you want me to help you investigate? I have a nose for trouble—just ask my last boyfriend.”

“Trouble does seem to follow you,” I said with a smirk. “But honestly, I don’t know if I can handle more right now.”

As I turned to survey my booth, I caught sight of a familiar figure weaving through the crowd. Lydia, the reigning queen of the local florist scene, strode past, her designer heels clicking authoritatively against the pavement. She was the kind of woman whose very presence demanded attention, and not just because of her striking auburn hair that cascaded down her back like a waterfall. It was her piercing gaze, sharp enough to slice through the fluff of any festival atmosphere, that always made me squirm.

“Is it just me, or is she plotting something?” I muttered under my breath, eyeing Lydia as she stopped to inspect the booth of a competitor.

“Definitely plotting,” Jess agreed, her tone light but her expression serious. “And if you’re a target, she’s not above using dirty tricks to take you down. I mean, she can’t stand that you’re stealing her limelight. You’re like a cute little sunflower blooming in her rose garden.”

“Great analogy, but I’d rather be a sunflower without the thorns,” I sighed, watching as Lydia leaned in close to the other vendor, whispering conspiratorially. “It’s just not right. I work hard for my customers, and then... this?”

Jess patted my shoulder, her grip warm and reassuring. "You're a fighter, and I'm right here with you. If Lydia is up to no good, we'll figure it out."

Just then, Jude returned, his expression oddly strained, as if he'd just sprinted a marathon. "Sorry about that," he said, running a hand through his hair, which had started to stick up at odd angles. "Work stuff."

"Work stuff, huh?" I shot him a look, my skepticism evident. "Is it the same work stuff that makes you look like you've seen a ghost?"

"Let's just say it's been a long day," he said, avoiding my gaze. "What's the verdict? Are we winning the flower wars?"

"Depends on who you ask," I muttered, my voice laced with sarcasm. "If you ask Lydia, I'm sure she'd say I'm losing miserably."

Jude frowned, the tension in the air palpable. "You think she's behind this?"

I shrugged, frustration bubbling beneath the surface. "It would fit her MO. I just wish I could prove it. And then there's this whole phone call mystery you've got going on."

Before he could respond, a sharp scream pierced the festive atmosphere, slicing through the laughter and music. The crowd froze, eyes darting toward the source of the noise. A young girl, no older than eight, stood by the face painting booth, her hands trembling as she pointed toward something—or someone—behind me.

"What happened?" I asked, heart racing as I turned to see what had captured everyone's attention.

Jude and Jess followed my gaze, and we all stood frozen as we spotted Lydia, her pristine blouse smeared with vibrant paint, standing next to the face painting booth. Her expression was one of utter shock, a stark contrast to her usual confidence. I had to admit, it was rather satisfying to see her flustered.

"Somebody should check on her," Jess said, her lips twitching as she struggled to suppress laughter. "I bet the face painter just got a little too... enthusiastic."

Just then, a burst of laughter erupted from the crowd as Lydia tried to regain her composure, her hand moving to wipe the paint from her cheek, only to smear it further across her face.

I glanced at Jude, and a flicker of understanding passed between us. "What if this was part of someone's plan? Distract her, embarrass her?"

"Or it could just be an accident," Jude replied, though I sensed a hint of doubt in his voice.

I couldn't help but smile at the chaos unfolding before us. "You've got to admit, it's a bit poetic. She's always trying to one-up everyone else. Maybe karma's finally catching up with her."

But as Lydia stormed off, her face a canvas of humiliation, I felt a twinge of guilt. Was it wrong to relish in her misfortune? After all, I wasn't without my own faults.

"Let's not dwell on her," Jude said, nudging me gently. "You've got customers to attend to, and this festival isn't going to run itself."

As I turned back to the booth, the energy shifted again, this time with a renewed sense of purpose. I was determined not to let anyone—or anything—get the better of me. I poured myself into my work, weaving together arrangements with a fervor I hadn't felt before. The flowers transformed under my fingers, blooming into stunning creations that would catch anyone's eye.

With every arrangement I crafted, I could feel the chaotic energy of the festival merging with my own. The festival might be filled with uncertainty, but I was resolute. I would protect my work, my booth, and whatever flickering remnants of hope I still held close to my heart. Even if betrayal lurked in the shadows, I refused to be a mere victim in this flower-filled drama. I would bloom in spite of the chaos.

With a new surge of determination, I dove back into my work, hands moving rhythmically as I crafted each arrangement. The colors of the blooms pulsed with life, bright oranges and vivid blues creating a kaleidoscope that stood in stark contrast to the dark clouds gathering in my mind. Each flower felt like a protest against the chaos swirling around me, a defiance that was more than mere decoration; it was my declaration of independence in a world that seemed intent on tearing me down.

"Is it just me, or is the drama here thicker than a fruitcake?" Jess leaned over the booth, a half-eaten pastry in her hand, her eyes sparkling with mischief. She watched the festival's unfolding chaos with the fascination of a spectator at a car crash—unable to look away, yet thrilled by the spectacle.

"Thicker, and slightly more disheartening," I replied, brushing a stray petal from my cheek, the floral essence of my labor mingling with the hint of sugar from her pastry. "I'm trying to focus on making sales, but the sabotage angle is really putting a damper on my flower power."

"Flower power, indeed," she chuckled, eyeing the arrangements with the analytical gaze of a true friend. "You've got a killer setup here. Just look at those sunflowers—they're practically dancing!"

"Thank you. But the real question is, who's behind the mischief? It's like I'm starring in my own personal soap opera." I gestured dramatically, a playful flare that belied the anxiety simmering beneath.

Before Jess could respond, the crowd shifted as a gust of wind rustled through the fair, and in that moment, I caught sight of Lydia again. She stood nearby, talking to a group of fellow vendors, her expression one of simmering anger masked by a veneer of forced politeness. My heart raced. Did she know something I didn't? Was she part of the conspiracy?

"Jess, keep an eye on her for me, would you? I have a feeling she might be plotting something," I whispered, my voice low as I maneuvered to grab another bundle of fresh flowers from under the table.

"Consider it done," she winked, taking a sip from her coffee, her gaze fixed on Lydia as if she were a hawk watching its prey.

I turned back to my booth, focusing on arranging a display of daisies and delphiniums, but my mind was elsewhere. The clamor of the festival faded into background noise as I lost myself in thought. What did Jude really know? I replayed his earlier expression in my mind, the fleeting hint of worry that hadn't been there before. Maybe my imagination was running wild, but I felt certain he was holding something back.

Just then, Jude returned, his earlier tension replaced by a forced smile that made my stomach twist. "Hey, sorry for the interruption. You'd think people would know not to call me during a festival," he said lightly, but the edge to his voice betrayed him.

"Sure, because who doesn't love a little festival fun?" I replied, trying to match his energy but failing. "You know, like sabotage and secrets. All the things that really get the blood pumping."

He raised an eyebrow, a flash of concern crossing his face. "What do you mean?"

"Just the usual—arrangements being tampered with, strange phone calls, the works," I said, folding my arms and leaning back slightly. "You wouldn't happen to know anything about that, would you?"

"I'm not involved in whatever's happening with your flowers," he said, his voice firm but his eyes darting away. The dissonance between his words and actions sent alarm bells ringing in my head.

"Right. Because that's reassuring." I tried to keep my tone light, but the anxiety in my chest felt like a weight pressing down on me. “Just thought we were supposed to have each other’s backs, you know?”

He opened his mouth to respond, but the sudden sound of laughter from the crowd interrupted us. We both turned to see a group of children chasing a colorful parade of balloons, their joy infectious. The moment pulled me back momentarily, reminding me of the festival’s charm, but I couldn’t shake the undercurrent of suspicion swirling between us.

“Maybe we need to take a break, clear our heads?” Jude suggested, and I could hear the urgency behind his words.

“Break? During the busiest time of the festival?” I asked, raising an eyebrow, a smile creeping onto my lips despite the tension. “What do you have in mind? A quiet stroll down the flower aisle?”

“More like a few minutes by the fountain. I think we need to talk.” His eyes bore into mine, an intensity that made my heart skip.

“Okay, but if this is about your phone call...”

“Let’s not get into that right now.” He ran a hand through his hair again, a gesture that was becoming all too familiar.

With a reluctant nod, I agreed, curiosity piqued. I wasn’t going to solve the mystery of the tampered flowers in the booth, and perhaps a little distance from the chaos would help. As we made our way through the festival, the vibrant energy around us faded into a hushed backdrop, the laughter and music blending into a distant hum.

We reached the fountain, a lovely centerpiece bubbling with life, surrounded by intricately carved stone and blooming azaleas. Jude leaned against the rim, the water shimmering in the fading sunlight, casting fleeting shadows that danced around us.

“Okay, spill it,” I said, crossing my arms as I leaned closer, ready to dissect whatever was swirling beneath his surface. “What’s going on?”

He hesitated, gaze fixed on the water as if it held the answers. "It's just... things have been complicated. I'm trying to figure out how to explain everything without making it worse."

"Worse? Jude, that sounds ominous." My heart raced with a mix of apprehension and intrigue. "Just tell me, please."

He sighed, the weight of the moment heavy between us. "I got a call about a job offer—one that could mean big changes. I didn't want to bring it up here, not when you're trying to make this festival work."

I opened my mouth to respond, but the words got stuck in my throat. A job offer? My mind whirled, processing the implications. Was this why he had been acting strange? Was he planning to leave?

"Jude, I—"

Before I could finish, a shout erupted from behind us, breaking the fragile bubble we had created. We turned to see Lydia storming toward us, her face a mask of fury and embarrassment.

"You two think you can just stand there while I'm made a fool of?" she spat, eyes blazing like the very sun setting behind her. "This is ridiculous!"

"Lydia, we're not—" Jude started, but she cut him off.

"Save it! This is your fault! Everyone is talking about how you sabotaged my display!"

My stomach dropped. "What are you talking about?"

"Don't act innocent! I know you're behind the whispers! Just because you can't handle the competition doesn't mean you can drag me down with you!"

"I didn't sabotage anything!" I shouted back, my voice trembling with a mix of anger and disbelief. "I'm just trying to run my booth here!"

"Then how do you explain your flowers being tampered with? Or maybe you're just so desperate for attention that you had to resort to this!" Lydia's words sliced through the air, sharp and cutting.

Jude stepped forward, his hands raised in a placating gesture. "Lydia, it doesn't have to be like this—"

"Stay out of this!" she barked, her voice rising as she pointed a finger at him. "This is between me and her! You think you can just waltz in and take what's mine?"

A crowd began to gather, drawn by the escalating confrontation, their whispers merging into a cacophony of speculation.

"I'm not taking anything from you!" I snapped, adrenaline surging through me. "Maybe you should take a look in the mirror before you start pointing fingers!"

Lydia's eyes narrowed, and in that instant, I realized the depth of her rage. This wasn't just about the flowers; this was about pride, reputation, and the cutthroat nature of competition.

As she turned to leave, her silhouette framed against the sinking sun, I felt a new wave of determination rise within me. I wouldn't let her walk away unchallenged.

"Lydia!" I called, my voice steady. "If you really think I'd sabotage you, then maybe it's time we face the truth together. Because I'm done playing games."

The tension crackled in the air, charged and electric, leaving everyone in a breathless pause. Just then, Jude placed a hand on my arm, his eyes wide, as if sensing that something was about to unravel, something far bigger than either of us could anticipate.

Before Lydia could respond, the ground beneath us trembled slightly, a low rumble echoing from somewhere deep in the festival grounds. The people around us gasped, the laughter and chatter dying down as uncertainty washed over the crowd.

"What the hell was that?" I breathed, looking around in panic.

As if in answer, a piercing shriek tore through the evening air, sending chills racing down my spine. The ground shook again, and I realized this was no ordinary festival.

Something was about to change, and I wasn't sure if it would shatter everything I had worked for or bring to light the hidden truths lurking in the shadows.

Chapter 12: The Enemy Within

The scent of fresh blooms filled the air, wrapping around me like a comforting shawl, yet it did little to alleviate the growing knot in my stomach. I stood in my shop, Blossom & Vine, its walls lined with colorful arrangements that should have brought joy. Instead, they felt like a masquerade, a façade masking the chaos brewing beneath. I had always prided myself on the charm and warmth of my little florist, where love stories blossomed and fragrant dreams took root. But now, the very essence of that sanctuary felt tainted by whispers of deceit and betrayal.

It was just another Tuesday morning when the door swung open with a chime, and she stepped inside—a figure cloaked in uncertainty. Her name was Lila, a name I barely remembered from my early days in the industry. A former employee of Petal Pushers, the rival florist down the street, Lila had left that world behind, but today, she stood in my shop with an urgency that electrified the air between us. Her hands trembled as she clutched a bouquet of daisies, their bright yellow faces stark against the pallor of her skin.

"Can we talk?" Her voice wavered, barely above a whisper, but the weight behind her words was palpable. I nodded, guiding her to a cozy nook near the window where sunlight streamed in, illuminating the delicate petals surrounding us.

"What's going on, Lila?" I asked, my heart racing. The tremor in her hands sent alarm bells ringing in my mind. "You look like you've seen a ghost."

"I... I can't stay long," she stammered, her gaze darting around the shop as if expecting shadows to spring from the vibrant floral arrangements. "But I needed you to know. There's something sinister happening, and it's bigger than just you and me."

Her confession hung in the air like a heavy fog, obscuring the bright colors around us. I leaned closer, urging her to continue, the sunlight suddenly feeling too bright, too revealing. "What do you mean? What's happening?"

Lila took a deep breath, her eyes shimmering with unshed tears. "I saw things at Petal Pushers—transactions that weren't just about flowers. There were threats, intimidation... I thought it was just the pressure of business competition, but now I realize..." She faltered, her voice trembling. "It's more than that. There's someone pulling the strings, and they won't stop until they get what they want."

The reality of her words sank in like a stone thrown into still waters, rippling outward into the corners of my mind. I had always known that rivalries in the floral industry could get competitive, but this—this was something altogether different. The notion that our quaint little town was steeped in darker dealings sent chills racing down my spine. "What kind of threats? What did you see?"

Lila glanced over her shoulder again, paranoia etched into her features. "I'm not sure I can say it all, but I've seen people come in and out of the shop late at night. Transactions happening in the back room—money exchanging hands in hushed tones. I overheard a couple of conversations... about you."

"About me?" My stomach twisted further, the realization that I had unwittingly become a pawn in some twisted game overwhelming. "What were they saying?"

"They know about your shop and how well you're doing. They see you as a threat, and they're not going to let you stay in business without a fight. I thought if I left, I'd be safe. But now..." Her voice cracked, revealing the raw edge of fear beneath her composure. "I had to warn you. They've been watching you."

The pieces of the puzzle began to fit together in a grotesque picture that made my skin crawl. This wasn't just about flowers; it was about power, control, and whatever it took to maintain dominance. My rival florist wasn't simply competing; they were preparing for war, and I was an unsuspecting target.

As Lila spoke, my mind wandered to Jude, my partner and confidant, who had always been by my side. Trust felt like a delicate porcelain figure, one wrong move, and it could shatter into irreparable pieces. Was he involved in this mess? Could I truly trust anyone anymore? The thought sent tendrils of doubt creeping into my heart.

"Lila," I said, my voice steadying, "if what you're saying is true, we need to take action. I can't let them intimidate me or ruin everything I've built. I won't go down without a fight."

Her eyes widened in surprise, but there was a flicker of determination in them, too. "You're braver than I ever was, and I respect that. But be careful. They won't hesitate to use whatever means necessary. Just promise me you'll watch your back."

"I promise," I replied, a resolve settling within me like a fierce flame. "But you need to be careful too. They might come after you if they realize you've spoken out."

With a heavy heart, Lila nodded, and as she rose to leave, a weight hung between us, a connection forged in the flames of fear and determination. We were both caught in a web spun by a predator lurking in the shadows, and I was no longer just a florist; I was now a player in a game where the stakes had grown perilously high.

As she stepped out of Blossom & Vine, I felt the chill of uncertainty wrap around me like a cloak. The sun, once a source of warmth and comfort, now cast long shadows that danced ominously across the floor. The cheerful blooms around me took on a new significance, symbols of resilience and beauty amidst a brewing storm. I would fight to protect my shop, my dreams, and the people I cared about. But first, I needed to uncover the truth.

The door swung closed behind Lila, leaving a suffocating silence in her wake. I stood amidst the fragrant blooms, the cheerful daisies and vibrant roses now feeling like a mockery of the chaos swirling in my mind. The shop that had always been my sanctuary was becoming a battleground, and I was painfully aware that the enemy was not just a faceless rival florist; it was something darker and more insidious lurking just beneath the surface.

I glanced at the clock, its hands ticking steadily, mocking my unease. The afternoon sun poured through the windows, casting warm pools of light that contrasted sharply with the cold dread pooling in my stomach. It was time to act. I couldn't wait for the enemy to strike; I needed to gather my forces, even if those forces were just me and my trembling resolve.

Picking up my phone, I dialed Jude's number, my heart racing with the decision to involve him. Would he be a willing ally, or had he been playing a part in this elaborate ruse all along? The line rang, each tone echoing my rising anxiety, until he finally picked up, his voice warm and familiar.

"Hey there, flower queen. How's my favorite florist?"

I hesitated, caught in a web of affection and suspicion. "Jude, we need to talk. Can you come by the shop?"

His tone shifted slightly, curiosity piquing. "Sure thing. Is everything okay?"

I opened my mouth to respond, but words failed me. The uncertainty hung heavy between us like an uninvited guest. "Just... just come as soon as you can."

Moments later, the door chimed again, and Jude stepped in, his tall frame filling the space with an easy confidence. His tousled hair caught the light, and for a brief moment, I was reminded of all the reasons I cared for him. He approached with a smile that faltered slightly when he noticed my tense posture.

"Okay, what's going on? You look like you've seen a ghost," he said, glancing around as if expecting to find one lurking among the petals.

"Worse," I muttered, leading him toward the back of the shop where the sweet fragrance of blooming lilacs hung in the air. "I've just had a talk with Lila, and it seems Petal Pushers isn't just your average rival. There's something much more sinister happening, and I'm afraid it's targeting me."

Jude's brow furrowed, his easy demeanor shifting to concern. "What do you mean? What kind of targeting?"

I recounted Lila's revelations, my voice steadying as I poured out the details of the shady transactions and threats she had witnessed. As I spoke, Jude's expression darkened, and the easy banter that usually flowed between us was replaced by a weighty silence.

"Lila's been through a lot," he finally said, his voice low. "But do you really think she's trustworthy? I mean, she could be exaggerating."

"Maybe," I conceded, a pang of doubt creeping in. "But what if she's not? This could be bigger than us, Jude. I can't just sit back and wait for them to make their move."

He rubbed the back of his neck, an endearing gesture of frustration. "Okay, so what's our game plan? We can't just storm into Petal Pushers and start throwing accusations around. That could blow up in our faces."

"You're right," I sighed, feeling the weight of my predicament settle deeper in my chest. "But we can't ignore it either. I need to know who I can trust, and if Lila's right, then the threats could escalate."

Jude's eyes met mine, a flicker of determination sparking within their depths. "Let's start by gathering some intel. We can do a little reconnaissance. Maybe find out what's really happening behind the scenes at Petal Pushers."

A smile tugged at the corners of my mouth despite the gravity of the situation. "I love it when you talk spy tactics. You should have been in the movies."

"Right? I'm like a florist-turned-bond villain," he said with a smirk, but the lighthearted banter was short-lived, the reality of our task looming large.

As we plotted our next steps, I felt a flicker of hope amidst the chaos. Perhaps together, we could uncover the truth and protect what I had worked so hard to build. We spent the next hour preparing, assembling a plan that was equal parts strategic and daring, punctuated by our witty banter that felt like a lifeline amidst the turmoil.

Before I knew it, the sun began to dip lower in the sky, casting long shadows across the shop. "We should head over there now," I suggested, glancing at the clock again. "The sooner we get this over with, the better."

"Let me grab my jacket," Jude said, stepping out for a moment. I took a deep breath, gathering my thoughts as I prepared to face whatever awaited us.

When he returned, a determined look crossed his face. "Ready?"

I nodded, the adrenaline coursing through my veins as we stepped outside into the cool evening air. The walk to Petal Pushers felt like a journey into the unknown, the familiar streets morphing into a treacherous landscape fraught with danger. Each step echoed in my mind, a reminder of what was at stake.

As we neared the shop, the bright lights and cheerful displays contrasted sharply with the unease settling in my stomach. The vibrant blooms, usually a source of joy, now seemed to mock my apprehension. The familiar sounds of customers chatting and cash registers ringing filled the air, but it felt like a façade, a veneer covering something much darker.

"Let's hang back for a moment," Jude suggested, glancing around to assess the scene. "See if we can catch a glimpse of anything unusual."

I nodded, scanning the area as we stood just outside the shop's entrance. My heart raced as I watched employees bustling about, their faces painted with forced smiles that felt eerily hollow. Then I noticed a figure lingering by the back entrance—someone I recognized, someone who had been part of the floral scene for years.

"Isn't that Miranda?" I whispered, my heart pounding. "She used to work at Petal Pushers."

Jude squinted, studying the woman's tense posture. "Looks like she's in deep conversation with someone. Should we go closer?"

"Absolutely," I replied, curiosity mingling with the need to uncover the truth. We edged closer, hearts racing with the thrill of the chase, ready to unravel the mystery that lay before us.

The tension between Jude and me crackled like static in the air as we observed Miranda, her usually confident demeanor now replaced by a shifty uncertainty. She stood at the edge of the back entrance, her eyes darting nervously. The low hum of the floral shop's bustle faded into the background, leaving only the sound of my heartbeat thudding in my ears.

"She looks like she's about to make a deal with the devil," Jude murmured, the corner of his mouth quirking up in that charming way of his, though his eyes remained serious.

"More like a deal with the competition," I shot back, a nervous laugh escaping me. It was easier to hide behind humor than to confront the anxiety clawing at my insides. "Should we approach her?"

"Let's play it smart for now. We need to hear what she's saying first." Jude gestured subtly, his brow furrowed in concentration.

We edged closer, hiding behind a nearby display of vibrant tulips. The colors blurred together as my mind raced, plotting a course of action while I strained to catch snippets of the conversation unfolding just a few feet away.

"I told you, I can't keep doing this," Miranda's voice trembled, the desperation palpable even from where we stood. "If they find out..."

"They won't find out if you just keep your mouth shut," a gravelly voice responded, one I didn't recognize. "You think they care about you? You're just another pawn in this game. So either keep feeding us information, or you can find out what it's like to be on the receiving end of their threats."

My stomach twisted at the implication. This was worse than I'd imagined—an actual threat to Miranda's safety. I glanced at Jude, whose expression mirrored my alarm.

"Should we intervene?" he whispered, his eyes scanning the scene.

I shook my head. "Not yet. Let's see how this plays out."

Miranda shifted uncomfortably, her eyes darting to the door as if weighing her options. "I just need more time. I didn't sign up for this."

"That's not how this works," the stranger hissed. "You either play your part, or you'll regret it. You know what happened to the last person who got cold feet."

A chill ran down my spine at the mention of regret. The air grew heavy, thick with the weight of Miranda's fear. It was evident she was caught in something far darker than petty rivalry.

Just then, the door to Petal Pushers swung open, and the warm light spilled onto the pavement. I instinctively pulled back into the shadows, holding my breath as a group of customers spilled out, laughing and chatting.

"Do you think she knows?" Jude's voice was barely above a whisper.

"No way," I said, but doubt crept into my mind. If Miranda was involved in this web of deceit, what did that mean for me? For my shop? "We need to confront her. She can't go back in there without knowing we're watching her."

As the laughter faded into the distance, I stepped out of the shadows, determination taking root. "Let's go."

Before I could take more than two steps, Miranda turned sharply, her eyes locking onto mine. The color drained from her face, and for a moment, I thought she might bolt. But instead, her expression softened, a mix of fear and relief washing over her.

"Emily! What are you doing here?" she gasped, her voice a low whisper.

"We need to talk," I said, my heart racing. "That conversation you just had... it sounded serious."

Miranda looked over her shoulder, panic rising. "I can't. They'll know if I say anything."

I stepped closer, my voice steady and calm despite the storm swirling in my chest. "They already know you're in trouble. We can help you, but you need to tell us everything."

Jude joined me, his presence reassuring. "You're not alone in this, Miranda. Let's figure out how to get you out safely."

Her shoulders slumped, the fight draining from her. "They're dangerous, Emily. You don't understand. If they find out I've talked, they'll come after me... and you."

"That's a risk I'm willing to take," I insisted, my resolve hardening. "I'm not going to stand by while they threaten you—or me."

She hesitated, biting her lip as if weighing the danger against her desire to confide in us. Finally, she whispered, "I've been feeding them information about your shop—what's selling, who's buying, everything. They said they'd make sure I was safe as long as I complied."

"Feeding them information?" I echoed, feeling a fresh wave of betrayal wash over me. "What do they want with my shop?"

"They think you're a threat. Your success has drawn their attention, and they're willing to do anything to keep you from competing with them. They don't just want to push you out; they want to eliminate you."

The words hit me like a punch to the gut. The stakes had risen far beyond anything I had anticipated. I glanced at Jude, whose expression had shifted from concern to an intense focus, his mind racing with the implications of Miranda's admission.

"We need to come up with a plan," he said, his voice low and steady. "If they're watching you, Miranda, you'll need to lay low. We can figure out a way to turn the tables."

"I don't want to drag you into this," she said, tears glistening in her eyes. "It's my mess, not yours."

"Too late for that," I replied, my heart swelling with determination. "You're in this with us now, and we won't leave you behind."

The night air felt charged as we stood there, a trio united by the threat looming over us. But as I caught sight of a shadow shifting at the edge of the alley, my breath caught in my throat.

"Get down!" I hissed, instinctively pulling Miranda behind me as a figure emerged from the darkness, the glint of a blade catching the light of the nearby streetlamp.

"Thought you could play both sides, did you?" The stranger's voice was cold, dripping with menace. "You've made a big mistake, and now it's time to pay the price."

The threat hung heavy in the air, and I could feel the fear radiating off Miranda, the reality of our situation crashing down around us. My heart pounded furiously as I took a step back, adrenaline surging through my veins. This was no longer just about flowers and rivalries; it was about survival, and the enemy had just made their move.

Chapter 13: A Dangerous Gamble

The vibrant hues of the festival enveloped me like a warm embrace, a stark contrast to the simmering tension that crackled in the air. Colorful banners fluttered against a backdrop of blue sky, while the sweet scent of candied apples wafted through the throngs of festival-goers. Laughter mixed with the sound of live music, creating a symphony of joy that masked the underlying storm brewing in our midst. But here I was, amidst the joyous celebration, cloaked in an aura of clandestine purpose. I could hardly believe that Jude and I were about to embark on a mission that could shake the very foundations of our small town.

With each step we took, the thrill of our secret plan surged through me, yet it was Jude's proximity that set my heart racing even more than the impending confrontation. His presence was magnetic, drawing me closer, igniting a fire within that I didn't know I was capable of feeling. Dressed in casual clothes—a simple T-shirt and jeans—he seemed to effortlessly blend into the festival crowd, but to me, he stood out like a beacon in the night. The way his dark hair tousled slightly in the breeze made him seem boyish and carefree, even as a serious determination flickered in his deep-set eyes.

"Remember," he whispered, leaning closer, the warmth of his breath brushing against my ear, sending shivers cascading down my spine. "We're here to gather information, not to engage in a floral duel."

I smirked, shaking off the enchantment of his closeness. "Right, because the last thing we need is to get caught up in some epic battle of blooms. Though I'm not sure my geraniums would stand a chance against those monstrosities they sell at Willow Grove."

Jude chuckled, his laughter rich and genuine. "I think your geraniums are more than capable. They just need a little pep talk."

We navigated the festival stalls, weaving through families and groups of friends, each lost in their merriment. The air buzzed with excitement, children darting about, their faces painted with delight and candy smudged across their cheeks. I could hear the distant laughter of a group playing games, and the low hum of people chatting, all underscored by the playful notes of a band strumming nearby. Despite the festive atmosphere, my mind was a whirlpool of worry, the stakes of our plan echoing in my ears like the distant drumbeats.

We approached the corner booth where the rival florist, Celeste, reigned supreme. Her stand was a cacophony of colors—overly bright flowers that seemed to scream for attention, drawing eyes like moths to a flame. Sunflowers, daisies, and an absurd number of hybrid roses vied for dominance. It was as if she had orchestrated a floral pageant, one where my quiet little flower shop was the wallflower in the corner. I cringed at the thought, but Jude's hand brushed against mine, grounding me.

"Focus," he murmured, his voice low but filled with the urgency of our task. "We need to blend in, keep our heads down."

I nodded, taking a deep breath as I adjusted the scarf around my neck—a makeshift disguise to shield my identity. "Let's just see what she's up to," I whispered, stepping closer to the booth while trying to keep my demeanor casual.

The booth was bustling with customers, and I couldn't help but notice how Celeste's charm seemed as manufactured as the plastic flowers hanging from her display. She twirled her hair absentmindedly, her laughter too bright, almost rehearsed. It was as if she were performing, and we were the reluctant audience.

"Ten percent off all arrangements today!" she chirped, her voice projecting over the crowd, luring customers like a siren's call. "Only for this festival!"

I exchanged glances with Jude, who rolled his eyes. "Discounts don't make it good. It just makes it cheap."

I chuckled, appreciating the fire in his spirit. He was right; Celeste's offerings lacked the soul that imbued every bloom I sold. My flowers were more than mere products; they were crafted with love and care.

As we stood there, my heart pounded not just with the thrill of our covert mission but with the growing attraction I felt toward Jude. The way his brow furrowed in concentration as he surveyed the scene made my heart flutter in a way I had never experienced before. Each stolen glance between us felt charged with an electricity that I couldn't ignore. I could feel the weight of his gaze, and it made me yearn for something deeper than our current predicament.

Suddenly, Celeste's voice sliced through my thoughts, drawing our attention. "Oh, darling, do come closer! You won't want to miss this!" She gestured toward a spectacular arrangement that seemed to sparkle under the afternoon sun.

Jude leaned closer, his breath brushing against my cheek. "We need to get closer to hear her."

With a nod, we edged forward, pretending to examine her flowers while straining to catch snippets of conversation. I could feel the tension rising, not just from our proximity to the rival florist but from the undeniable connection building between Jude and me.

I glanced at him, and our eyes locked for a heartbeat longer than necessary. The world around us faded, the sounds of the festival dimmed, and all that remained was the intensity of that moment, the realization that whatever this was between us could evolve into something far more complicated than a simple alliance against a common enemy.

But then, as if the universe had decided to shatter our fragile peace, a figure emerged from the crowd—someone I never expected to see here, someone who threatened to blow our cover wide open.

The figure pushing through the crowd was unmistakable—Celeste's assistant, Lily. Her sharp eyes roamed the festival as if hunting for a target, and she wasn't just any assistant; she was a loyal watchdog, known for her fierce loyalty to Celeste. My heart sank, a cold wave of panic washing over me. If she recognized us, our secret mission would be as good as over.

"Isn't she adorable?" Jude whispered, his voice laced with a teasing tone that made me momentarily forget my anxiety. "She looks like a vulture in a floral paradise."

I couldn't help but snicker, but I quickly stifled my laughter. "Not the best comparison if we want to remain under the radar, don't you think?"

He shrugged, that devil-may-care grin spreading across his face. "Desperate times call for desperate humor."

Lily paused, her gaze briefly landing on us, and I held my breath. I willed myself to blend into the colorful chaos, focusing on the nearby booths and the vibrant floral displays instead of the looming threat just a few feet away. Her expression seemed to soften for a moment, as if she were recalling the friendly rivalry we shared in our floral arrangements. Just as quickly, though, her frown deepened, and she swept away, continuing her search for something—or someone—specific.

"Do you think she's onto us?" I murmured, attempting to ease the tightness in my chest.

Jude, ever the optimist, shook his head. "If she were, we wouldn't be standing here. Besides, she's not exactly the brightest bulb in the bunch."

"Yeah, a bulb that can bite," I shot back, my nerves dancing like fireflies. "We need to act natural."

"Right. Because nothing says 'natural' like two people lurking in the flower section at a festival. So, what's the plan? We simply stroll up and ask Celeste about her suspicious dealings?"

"Subtlety is key," I said, struggling to maintain my composure. "We need to keep our eyes peeled for anything unusual. Look for customers who seem out of place or anyone acting too... enthusiastic."

Jude raised an eyebrow, his gaze scanning the crowd. "And what exactly constitutes 'too enthusiastic' in a place like this?"

"Maybe someone trying too hard to impress Celeste, or—"

My sentence was cut short when a sudden commotion erupted at the rival booth. A large man, clad in a ridiculous flower-patterned shirt that should have been relegated to the depths of fashion hell, had decided that now was the time to make a scene. His voice boomed, drowning out the cheerful melodies around us.

"I demand to speak to your manager!" he bellowed, pointing an accusatory finger at Celeste, who stood behind her floral fortress looking simultaneously flustered and amused.

"Maybe we should take notes," Jude whispered, amusement dancing in his eyes. "This is how you don't sell flowers."

"Trust me, I'll keep my day job," I replied, already envisioning the awkwardness of getting involved in an explosive argument that had nothing to do with us.

As the spectacle unfolded, I noticed a small cluster of spectators gathering, eager to witness the drama. I leaned closer to Jude, trying to catch snippets of the exchange.

"Your flowers are wilted! I'm not paying for this rubbish," the man shouted, gesturing wildly toward a bouquet that was—admittedly—looking a little worse for wear.

Celeste maintained her composure, a practiced smile plastered on her face as she responded. "Sir, flowers are living things, and they require proper care. I can offer you a replacement—free of charge."

The man crossed his arms, still simmering with indignation. "And I can offer you a piece of my mind if you think I'm leaving here with a wilted bouquet!"

In the midst of this floral showdown, I turned to Jude, eyes wide. "This is our chance! While everyone is distracted, we can check out her supply crates in the back."

"Lead the way, my stealthy partner." He winked, making the butterflies in my stomach flutter.

We slipped away from the chaos, edging around the booth and making our way to a narrow alley that led to the back of the vendor area. My heart raced, not just from the thrill of our mission but from the unspoken chemistry building between us. The world behind us faded as we darted deeper into the shadows, determined to uncover Celeste's secrets.

The back of her booth was cluttered with cardboard boxes and crates, each overflowing with floral supplies and tools. It felt like stepping into a forgotten realm, where creativity thrived but deceit lingered just beneath the surface. I felt a rush of exhilaration, the sense that we were intruding into something forbidden.

"Okay, keep watch," I said, my voice barely a whisper, and Jude nodded, his attention on the alleyway as I crouched beside a box marked with Celeste's logo. My fingers brushed against the cardboard, and I felt the thrill of the unknown course through me.

"What are we looking for?" he asked, glancing over his shoulder.

"Anything that seems... off. She could be using cheap materials or cutting corners. If she's endangering her customers, we need to know."

"Or if she's hiding something altogether," he added, his brow furrowing with determination.

I pried open the box, the flaps creaking under the strain. Inside, I found an array of vibrant flower seeds, all pristine and packaged neatly. I held one up, admiring the bright colors, but my excitement faded when I noticed a faded label at the bottom—"imported from unverified sources."

"Jude, look at this," I breathed, pulling out the seed packet. "If these aren't regulated, she could be risking her business and her customers' health."

"Right," he said, leaning closer to examine the packet. "That's definitely something we can use against her."

As we shared a glance, a wave of adrenaline surged between us, and in that moment, the world outside faded entirely. The air was thick with tension and possibility, and I could feel the thrill of our impending confrontation pulling us closer together.

Just then, a rustle in the distance interrupted our clandestine operation. My heart dropped. I shot Jude a panicked look. "Someone's coming! We have to go—now!"

We scrambled to close the box, shoving the seed packet back inside just as footsteps echoed ominously through the alley. I grabbed Jude's hand, yanking him toward the far end, our breaths quickening as we navigated the clutter.

"Just act natural!" he hissed, but as we dashed toward the exit, it felt anything but.

We stepped out into the festival just as the sun dipped lower in the sky, casting long shadows across the ground. The chaos resumed around us, laughter and music flowing like a tide, but the urgency of our mission gripped me tighter than before. I could feel the adrenaline pulsing through my veins, and as we weaved through the crowd, the realization of what we had just uncovered sent my mind racing. The evening promised twists yet to come, and the festival, a backdrop to our secret battle, buzzed with an energy that matched my own tumultuous feelings toward Jude.

As we rejoined the throng, I felt the gravity of our actions weighing heavily on my shoulders. We were playing a dangerous game, one that could unravel everything I held dear. But somehow, in the midst of it all, I couldn't shake the feeling that the stakes had never been higher, nor the connection between us more electrifying.

The rhythm of the festival pulsed around us, a cacophony of laughter, music, and the tantalizing aroma of street food. Yet, as Jude and I melded into the throng of vibrant bodies, the world outside our secret mission faded into insignificance. Each step we took seemed to draw us closer, our shared purpose intertwining like the blooms we both adored. The festive atmosphere couldn't overshadow the tension brewing between us; every glance felt charged, every accidental touch a spark igniting a flame that I was both exhilarated and terrified to explore.

"Do you think she's still arguing with that man?" I whispered, scanning the area where Celeste had held court just moments before.

"Probably. Her flower stand seems to attract all sorts—drama included." Jude leaned casually against a booth, pretending to browse a nearby display of sunflowers, but his eyes were locked on me. "I mean, those petals can really bring out the inner diva, can't they?"

I couldn't help but laugh, my nerves temporarily eased by his playful banter. "If I had a nickel for every diva I've encountered in this town, I'd have enough to open a boutique flower shop, complete with its own reality show."

"'Flower Wars: Battle of the Blooms.' I can already see the ratings skyrocketing," he quipped, his eyes glinting with mischief.

Just as we shared a moment of lightness, I caught sight of Lily reemerging, her gaze darting around the festival. Panic seized my heart again. "We should get moving. If she spots us, this whole thing could blow up in our faces."

"Right. Let's fade into the flowers." Jude smirked as we both slipped into a more secluded pathway that wound behind the booths, littered with discarded napkins and the remnants of half-eaten pretzels.

The alley was quieter, but the excitement buzzing between us hadn't diminished. I stole a glance at Jude as we walked, the way the sunlight danced off his tousled hair, and the intensity in his gaze made me wonder if he could sense the shift in our dynamic as much as I did. With every brush of our shoulders, my heart beat faster, making it impossible to focus on anything other than him.

"Do you think we'll actually find something worth exposing?" he asked, his tone suddenly serious, pulling me from my thoughts.

I nodded, the conviction settling into my voice. "If Celeste is using those unverified seeds, it's not just about the quality of her flowers. It could jeopardize her business, and worse, put customers at risk. We have to do this."

He nodded in agreement, the gravity of our mission hanging heavy in the air. "Okay, then let's dig a little deeper."

We continued down the alley, now mostly shrouded in shadows, away from the festive chaos. The vibrant colors of the festival faded to muted tones, the sound of laughter becoming a distant echo. I felt the thrill of adrenaline coursing through my veins as we reached the back of Celeste's booth, where an unguarded storage shed loomed.

"This looks promising," Jude said, gesturing to the door slightly ajar. "What do you think we'll find inside?"

"Only one way to find out," I replied, pushing the door open just enough to peek inside. A faint musty smell greeted us, mixing with the fragrant remnants of flowers. The dim light revealed crates piled high with supplies, and at the far end, I spotted a small desk cluttered with papers.

"Let's split up," Jude suggested. "I'll check out the desk, and you can see what's in those crates."

I hesitated, the idea of separating making me uneasy. "What if something goes wrong? I don't want to be caught alone."

He stepped closer, a reassuring smile playing at the corners of his mouth. "I'll be right here. Just yell if you need me. I promise I won't let anything happen to you."

His words settled my nerves, though I wasn't entirely sure they were grounded in reality. I took a deep breath, steeling myself for what lay ahead, and nodded. "Okay. Let's do this."

As I moved toward the crates, I felt his gaze linger on me, an anchor amidst the uncertainty. The first crate I opened revealed a mix of flower pots, soil bags, and a few wilting blooms. Nothing seemed out of the ordinary, but I could sense something lurking beneath the surface. I pushed aside the pots, looking for hidden surprises or anything suspicious.

Meanwhile, Jude rifled through papers at the desk, muttering under his breath. "Come on, Celeste, what are you hiding?"

The intensity of the moment was palpable, and I couldn't help but steal glances at him. The way he focused, brow furrowed, made him look almost heroic—a knight determined to uncover the truth. I smiled at the thought, the warmth spreading through me as I returned to my task.

"Any luck?" I called over my shoulder, fingers brushing against the rough wood of the crates.

"Some contracts and receipts," he replied, his voice tinged with disappointment. "Nothing alarming yet, but it all feels... off. Like she's trying to hide something big."

Just then, I felt a surge of excitement as I unearthed a hidden compartment beneath one of the crates. My heart raced as I pried it open, revealing a small stash of neatly packed seed packets. The labeling was strange—no brand names, just an odd mixture of names I'd never seen before.

"Jude! Come look at this!" I called, urgency creeping into my voice.

He quickly moved to my side, eyes widening as he scanned the packets. "What are they? Are they similar to the ones we found before?"

"Even worse," I replied, lifting one to examine closely. "These are marked 'experimental.' No details, no warnings. If these seeds are what I think they are, it could be a serious risk to anyone buying her arrangements."

His jaw clenched. "This is it. This is what we need to confront her with."

As we huddled together, a sudden noise from outside jolted us. The unmistakable sound of laughter and chatter, but it was accompanied by a raucous cheer, one that sent chills racing up my spine.

"Someone's coming!" Jude hissed, pushing the crate closed with a rush. "We need to hide!"

Before I could react, he grabbed my hand and pulled me behind the desk just as the door swung open, revealing a tall figure silhouetted against the dim light of the festival. My breath caught in my throat, panic surging through me as I pressed against Jude, feeling his warmth envelop me.

"Are you sure you want to do this, Celeste?" The voice was low, gravelly, and familiar—my stomach dropped as I recognized it. It was Frank, Celeste's business partner, his tone dripping with a mix of anger and desperation.

The tension in the room escalated, and I exchanged a worried glance with Jude. "What's happening?" I whispered, my heart pounding.

"We can't keep hiding this from the public," Frank continued, his frustration palpable. "We've built this business, and I won't let you ruin it over some petty rivalry."

Celeste's voice floated back, sharp and defensive. "You don't understand. I'm doing this for us. If we can get ahead, no one will ever question our practices again. We'll be unstoppable."

The words hung in the air like a storm cloud, darkening the atmosphere. I felt my pulse quicken, realizing the weight of their conversation. They were discussing more than just flowers; this was about manipulation and deception.

"We need to get out of here," Jude murmured, his expression serious.

But just as we began to make our escape, the unmistakable sound of footsteps echoed in the corridor outside, followed by a sudden flash of light. My heart raced as the door swung open again, and a pair of eyes pierced through the gloom.

"Thought you could sneak around without anyone noticing?" The voice dripped with disdain. It was Lily, standing in the doorway, her presence blocking our only exit.

Trapped and cornered, the weight of the situation crashed down around us, the festival's vibrant chaos suddenly feeling worlds away. The tension in the air crackled as we stood frozen, caught between the allure of uncovering a dark secret and the fear of what lay ahead.

Chapter 14: Heart of Thorns

The festival was a kaleidoscope of color and sound, vibrant booths lining the narrow streets of the small town, their hues bright enough to rival the sun itself. As laughter and music blended into a joyous cacophony, I felt an odd juxtaposition within me—my heart was a tempest, while the world around me danced in celebration. I moved through the crowd, dodging cheerful families and frantically waving vendors, searching for my rival, Mia, who had made it her mission to dismantle everything I had fought for.

When I finally found her, she stood at the edge of a flickering bonfire, shadows twisting around her like dark tendrils. Her smirk was wicked, a flicker of triumph in her eyes. "There you are, Lily. Thought you could hide behind all this festivity?" she taunted, her voice smooth like silk, but laced with poison.

The heat from the fire washed over me, but it could not melt the ice that had settled in my chest. "Mia, this isn't the place for whatever game you think you're playing," I shot back, trying to sound braver than I felt.

"Oh, but it is, darling. A perfect backdrop for secrets and revelations, wouldn't you say?" She stepped closer, her confidence radiating like the firelight. I couldn't help but notice how the glow accentuated the sharp angles of her face, giving her an almost ethereal beauty that was deceptive in its allure.

With the festival swirling around us, I braced myself for what was to come. The air buzzed with anticipation, a quiet hum beneath the surface, like the first stirrings of a storm. Just as I was about to retort, she struck. "Did you know about Jude's past? The one he's kept hidden under layers of charm and smiles?"

I stiffened, an icy grip tightening around my heart. Jude, the boy who had captivated me with his laughter and warmth, was suddenly a stranger. "What are you talking about?" I demanded, my voice shaky.

"Oh, come on, Lily. Don't pretend you're unaware. Jude was involved in some serious dealings back when he was living in the city. Drugs, theft... you name it." The words poured from her lips like venom, each one puncturing my defenses, and the world around me blurred into insignificance.

Shock washed over me, an electric jolt that sent my thoughts spiraling into chaos. I wanted to deny it, to scream that Mia was lying, but the flicker of doubt ignited a firestorm in my chest. "That's not true. He wouldn't..."

"Wouldn't he? I have proof, you know." She leaned closer, her voice dropping to a conspiratorial whisper, the very essence of a seductress. "A man like him doesn't just change overnight, Lily. You're playing with fire, and one day, you'll get burned."

As I searched Mia's expression for any hint of deceit, I felt as if I were trapped in a nightmare from which I could not awaken. My mind raced back through the moments I had spent with Jude—his laughter, the way he always seemed to understand me. Had it all been an act? My heart shattered like fragile glass, pieces slicing through the tender flesh of my soul, and the wound was deep.

Before I could respond, Jude appeared, the warmth of his presence somehow both soothing and terrifying. "Lily! There you are." His voice was bright, but I saw the concern etch itself onto his features as he registered the tension.

"Mia was just telling me about your 'past,'" I spat, the words tasting bitter as they slipped from my tongue.

His face paled, the smile slipping away as quickly as it had come. "What did she say?"

"Enough to make me question everything," I replied, the accusation hanging heavy between us.

"Lily, please, let me explain." Jude reached for my hand, but I recoiled as if burned, shockwaves of hurt reverberating through me. The sound of the festival faded into a distant hum, replaced by the pounding of my heart.

"Explain what, Jude? How you've been lying to me this entire time?" I felt like a wounded animal, raw and exposed, the scent of betrayal thick in the air.

Mia's laughter cut through the silence, sharp and mocking. "You see, Jude? You can't hide behind your charm forever. You'll always be that boy from the city, and one day, it'll all catch up to you."

Jude's eyes narrowed, anger flashing beneath the surface, but I could sense his desperation. "It's not what you think, Lily. I left that life behind. I swear. I was trying to protect you, to keep you safe from my past."

The sincerity in his voice sent another jolt of confusion through me. "Safe? You think I'd be safer without knowing the truth?"

"I did what I thought was right," he shot back, frustration leaking into his tone. "I didn't want you to see me as someone unworthy of your trust."

"Trust? It's too late for that now," I whispered, the hurt twisting like a dagger in my chest.

The silence that followed was deafening, each breath I took heavy with the weight of our shattered connection. The world around us continued to celebrate, the laughter and music a cruel reminder of the joy we once shared. Jude's expression softened, desperation mingling with regret as he took a step closer, searching my face for something—an understanding, a forgiveness I wasn't sure I could give.

"Lily, please," he said softly, his voice a fragile thread in the chaos. "Let me show you that I'm not that person anymore."

As the flickering light of the bonfire danced in his eyes, I felt the last remnants of trust slip through my fingers, like grains of sand in an hourglass. A choice loomed ahead, and the stakes had never been higher. Would I let the echoes of my heart guide me back to him, or would I let the thorns of betrayal draw blood and keep me at bay? The festival swirled around us, but within me, a tempest raged, and I was left teetering on the precipice of love and loss.

Mia's mocking laughter echoed in my ears, a sharp reminder that the words exchanged between us were not just idle threats but were laced with genuine malice. The festival, with its radiant colors and boisterous laughter, felt like a twisted joke against the backdrop of my spiraling emotions. As I stood there, my heart racing and my mind whirling, the celebratory atmosphere dulled into a haze. It was a painful contrast to the revelation I had just endured, and it was becoming harder to breathe, as if the very air around me had thickened with dread.

"Lily!" Jude's voice cut through my turmoil, and I could see him stepping closer, his brow furrowed with concern. His attempts to reach out to me only added fuel to the fire of my anger. "You have to understand—"

"Understand what?" I snapped, my voice sharper than I intended. "That you've been lying to me? That everything you said was just a pretty façade?"

The hurt in his eyes stung more than I anticipated, yet I felt no sympathy. It was as if we were standing on opposite shores of a raging river, and I couldn't see how I could ever bridge the divide. "Lily, I did it to protect you! I thought... I thought you would be safer not knowing the truth!" His voice trembled, and for a fleeting moment, I saw the boy I had fallen for—the one who made me laugh, who understood my dreams and fears.

"Safer? You think ignorance is safety?" I threw back, incredulous. "It's not just my safety at stake here. It's everything we've built together, Jude. I can't just pretend this doesn't exist!"

Mia's presence loomed like a storm cloud, her smirk still firmly in place. "And here I thought you were the one with the dream, Lily. You're just another pawn in his game."

"Shut up, Mia!" Jude's voice boomed, surprising both of us. I could see the shift in him, a hint of the protective fire that had drawn me to him in the first place. But the warmth I had once felt was smothered beneath layers of betrayal and anger.

I took a step back, the distance between us a chasm I couldn't navigate. The laughter from the festival seemed to grow distant, replaced by the throbbing silence that wrapped around us like a shroud. "What did you do, Jude? What did you get yourself into?" My voice cracked, the tremor betraying my attempt at composure.

"Lily, please," he said, desperation clawing at his tone. "It was years ago. I made mistakes. I was a stupid kid trying to survive. But I'm not that person anymore. You have to believe me."

The sincerity in his eyes pierced through my defenses, a flicker of light in an otherwise bleak landscape. Yet, the shadows of doubt clung to me, refusing to let go. I wanted to believe him. I wanted to trust the boy who had made me feel more alive than I had in years, but the truth was a heavy burden to bear.

"Believe you?" I whispered, the vulnerability spilling from my heart like ink on a page. "How can I believe you when you've kept this from me? How can I trust anything you say?"

"I'll prove it to you," Jude insisted, stepping forward again. "Let me show you. Just give me a chance to make it right."

Before I could respond, the festival erupted with a sudden cheer, fireworks painting the sky in a dazzling array of colors. The crowd erupted into applause, momentarily drowning out the storm brewing between us. I caught a glimpse of families, lovers, and friends lost in the beauty of the moment, a stark contrast to the turmoil gnawing at my insides.

Mia, however, seemed unfazed by the spectacle. She leaned closer, her voice a conspiratorial whisper that carried more weight than it should. "What if I told you that Jude's past isn't the only secret lurking in the shadows? What if the real danger lies in who he's still connected to?"

I turned my gaze back to Jude, the warmth of his presence now cold and unwelcoming. "What does she mean?" I asked, my voice barely above a whisper, laced with trepidation.

"Lily, it's not—" Jude began, but the frantic look in his eyes cut him off.

"She's just trying to manipulate you," he continued, frustration surfacing. "I told you I cut ties with my past. I'm not the same person I used to be."

"Are you sure?" Mia interjected, a glint of triumph in her eyes as she pressed the advantage. "Because it sounds like you're still connected to some pretty unsavory characters. You don't just walk away from that life without consequences, do you?"

"I don't have connections like that anymore!" Jude's voice rose again, a desperate plea. "I was a kid; I made mistakes. But I'm trying to be better. Please, believe me!"

"Why should I?" I challenged, crossing my arms defensively.

"Because I love you," he said, the confession hanging in the air, heavy and unyielding.

For a moment, time froze, and the cacophony of the festival faded to nothingness. Those three words ricocheted in my mind, spinning around like a whirlwind. Love. A word that once held such sweetness was now a bitter reminder of trust broken and futures uncertain.

Mia, sensing the shift, stepped back, the predator retreating momentarily from her prey. "Think about it, Lily. Do you really want to be with someone who could drag you down with him?"

I hesitated, uncertainty swirling within me like the colors exploding overhead. The vibrant fireworks burst into the night sky, but all I could see was the darkness that threatened to engulf me.

"What if he is still tied to his past?" Mia's voice slipped back in, silk wrapped around barbs. "What if you're the one who ends up hurt?"

"Enough!" Jude exploded, his frustration spilling over into anger. "You don't know what you're talking about, Mia. You don't know anything about me!"

"Maybe I know more than you think," she shot back, her confidence unwavering. "You think you can just sweep your past under the rug? It doesn't work like that."

I felt the pull of their words, like currents in a river threatening to drag me under. Jude's declaration of love felt simultaneously beautiful and terrifying, a lighthouse in the storm but also a warning of rocky shores. What if love wasn't enough? What if I was stepping into a world where I'd only end up drowning?

"Lily," Jude's voice softened, and his expression transformed from one of desperation to earnestness. "I'm asking you to trust me. Just this once. Let me prove that I can be better, that I can be the person you deserve."

As I stared into his eyes, the chaos around us faded into a muted blur. I was faced with a choice—one that could alter the course of my life. The festival glowed with laughter and light, a sharp contrast to the shadows pooling in my heart. I needed to decide if I would step forward into the light with Jude or retreat into the safety of the darkness that had begun to envelop us.

Jude's gaze bore into mine, a mix of vulnerability and desperation that tugged at my heartstrings, even as the storm inside me raged on. The cheers and laughter of the festival echoed around us like a cruel reminder of the happiness that felt a world away. How could everything seem so bright while I was drowning in shadows?

"Just... think about what you're saying," he implored, his voice strained. "I want to be someone you can trust. But I can't do that if you shut me out."

"Trust is built on honesty, Jude," I replied, my voice steadier than I felt. "And you've been hiding something monumental."

His expression shifted, pain flickering across his face like lightning in a darkened sky. "I was trying to protect you. I never wanted you to find out like this."

"Right, because the best way to protect someone is to keep them in the dark about who you really are." I was aware of how sharp my words sounded, but the bitter truth was hard to swallow. "What did you expect would happen? That I'd happily skip through the fields of daisies with you while you hid a piece of your past like a dirty little secret?"

"You think I wanted this?" he shot back, frustration breaking the calm façade he had maintained. "Do you think I ever wanted to be that guy? I've worked hard to distance myself from that life. Every day is a struggle to be better."

"Better? Or just better at lying?" I spat, feeling the weight of the world pressing down on my shoulders.

Mia took a step forward, clearly reveling in the drama unfolding before her. "How poetic, really. The prince turned pauper trying to prove his worth to the princess. But how can you be a prince when your castle is built on lies?"

"Enough, Mia!" Jude's voice reverberated with authority, but it only seemed to embolden her further.

I watched as the tension escalated, the fireworks above bursting with colors that felt hollow against the chaos of our confrontation. The warmth of the festival faded, replaced by a chill that seeped into my bones. "I need to know the truth, Jude. I can't stand here wondering if every smile was a mask, every laugh a performance."

"Please, just give me a moment," he pleaded, eyes searching mine for a sign that I might still be with him. "Let me explain everything."

Before I could respond, the atmosphere shifted. The laughter and music from the festival grew louder, almost mocking the seriousness of our situation. In that moment of distraction, a figure brushed past me, the jostle unexpected and unsettling. I turned just in time to catch a glimpse of someone slipping into the darkness beyond the fairgrounds—a shadowy form moving with purpose.

"What was that?" I pointed toward the direction the figure had gone, heart racing with an adrenaline I hadn't expected.

"Lily, focus," Jude urged, stepping between me and the direction of the shadow. "We need to talk about this."

"I don't care about talking right now!" I shot back, feeling an urgency rising within me. "Someone just went that way."

Mia's eyes glinted with a predatory light, and for a moment, I felt as if she were the true threat lurking in the shadows. "Do you really want to chase after a ghost, Lily? Or do you want to face the man in front of you?"

But I couldn't shake the feeling that what I had seen was important. "I think we should check it out," I insisted, my instincts pushing me forward.

"Lily, it could be dangerous," Jude cautioned, concern etched in his features.

"That's rich coming from you," I snapped, but I couldn't ignore the flutter of anxiety that flickered beneath my bravado. The darkness beyond the festival seemed to stretch endlessly, filled with secrets waiting to be uncovered.

"I'm not letting you go alone," Jude insisted, determination setting his jaw.

"You think you can protect me?" I retorted, feeling the tension between us shift again. "Maybe you're the one who needs protecting,

Jude. You've built your life on deceit, and I don't even know if you can be trusted."

"Then let me prove it to you," he replied, his voice low and earnest.

With a glance back at Mia, who stood watching us with a mix of amusement and intrigue, I finally relented. "Fine. But we need to keep our eyes open. We don't know who—or what—we're dealing with."

Jude nodded, the urgency of the moment washing over us. Together, we moved toward the darkened edge of the festival, where the bright lights flickered like stars swallowed by an approaching storm. My heart raced with every step, the thrill of the unknown mingling with the dread of what we might discover.

As we stepped beyond the illuminated tents, the world fell into an eerie silence. The sounds of the festival faded into the background, replaced by the rustling of leaves and the distant murmur of the river flowing nearby. The moon hung low in the sky, casting an ethereal glow that illuminated our path, but shadows lurked just beyond the reach of its light.

"Do you see anything?" Jude whispered, his voice barely breaking the stillness.

"No," I admitted, straining my eyes to pierce the darkness. "But I can feel it. Someone was here."

The tension between us was palpable, a fragile thread binding us together as we edged deeper into the shadows. Suddenly, a branch snapped behind us, sharp and loud, sending us both into a defensive stance.

"Who's there?" Jude called out, voice steady but with an undercurrent of fear.

No answer came, only the sound of the wind rustling through the trees, as if the forest itself was holding its breath.

"Maybe we should turn back," I suggested, unease creeping along my spine.

But before we could retreat, a figure emerged from the darkness—tall, cloaked in shadows, and stepping forward with a confidence that made my skin crawl.

"Looking for something?" the figure asked, voice smooth and dripping with condescension, as if they had been waiting for us all along.

I exchanged a glance with Jude, panic surging through me like a tidal wave. The figure was uncomfortably familiar, the silhouette igniting a spark of recognition that sent chills racing down my spine.

"What do you want?" Jude demanded, but I could see the uncertainty flickering behind his bravado.

"Just a little chat," the figure replied, stepping into the light cast by the fading festival. My breath caught in my throat as recognition struck with the force of a sledgehammer.

And with that revelation, the ground beneath us felt like it was shifting, the world tilting on its axis, and I realized that everything we had known was about to change irrevocably.

Chapter 15: In the Wake of Shadows

The soft chime of the bell above the door barely broke the silence as I sat in my shop, cocooned by the heady scent of wilting roses and the warm earthiness of freshly cut stems. Sunlight streamed through the large window, creating patterns of light that danced on the polished wood floor. But despite the beauty that surrounded me, a heavy shroud of melancholy clung to my heart, each petal I touched feeling like a reminder of the betrayal I had endured.

Jude's words echoed in my mind like a broken record, haunting me even in this sanctuary I had created. "I did it to protect you," he had said, but all I could hear was the sharpness of his confession, the way it sliced through the fabric of our friendship, unraveling the threads of trust I had woven so carefully. The very foundation of our bond felt compromised, and I didn't know how to rebuild it.

Outside, the town buzzed with life, children laughing and playing, the faint sound of music drifting from the nearby café. I could almost hear my friends calling out to me, their voices laced with concern. They had tried to check in, offering comfort and encouragement, but I had retreated into a fortress of my own making. I wasn't ready to face their worry or the pitiful looks in their eyes. I buried myself in work, meticulously arranging blooms, attempting to drown out the chaos of my emotions. Yet, with each flower I handled, the weight of my sorrow seemed to grow heavier, as if each arrangement was a tribute to what I had lost.

And then, there it was. The crisp sound of paper against wood, an unexpected intrusion that broke through my reverie. I glanced up, my heart racing, as I spotted the familiar folded note slipped under the door. It had become a routine I hadn't asked for—these ominous letters that sent chills racing down my spine. I took a breath, steadying my shaking hands before bending to retrieve it. My gut twisted with foreboding as I unfolded the paper, the sunlight catching the edge, illuminating the stark, black letters that scrawled across the page.

"You think you're safe, don't you? Just wait. Your pretty little shop will be nothing but ashes if you don't close up. Consider this a warning."

My stomach dropped, a wave of nausea crashing over me as I reread the words. The threats weren't just targeted at my business—they hinted at something more personal, something insidious that made my skin crawl. I was no stranger to fear, but this was a different kind of terror; it seeped into my bones, curling around my heart and squeezing until I could hardly breathe.

Panic swirled within me, bubbling up like a toxic brew. I needed help, someone who could stand by me, someone who understood the nuances of my life, my fears. Despite my anger and heartache, there was one person who still had a place in my heart—Jude. The thought of reaching out made my chest ache, but I knew I couldn't fight this battle alone. I needed him, even if it felt like my soul was caught in a tug-of-war between love and betrayal.

I grabbed my phone, fingers trembling as I scrolled through my contacts. Jude's name stared back at me, a bittersweet reminder of what we had been. After a long moment, I took a deep breath and hit dial, the familiar tone ringing in my ear. Each ring felt like a heartbeat, steady and relentless, and when his voice finally came through, I was nearly paralyzed with emotion.

"Hello?"

"Jude," I managed to say, my voice cracking under the weight of unspoken words.

"Hey, is everything okay?" he asked, his tone brightening, but it faltered when he heard my silence.

"I— I need you," I said, the admission hanging between us like a fragile thread.

The tension was palpable as he paused, perhaps weighing the significance of my words. "I'll be right there."

Hanging up, I felt a surge of both relief and anxiety. I wiped my damp palms on my apron, forcing myself to focus on the task at hand, arranging the remaining flowers in a burst of color. I needed to stay busy, to create something beautiful even when everything else felt like it was crumbling around me.

When the bell jingled again, I spun around to face the door, my heart racing at the sight of him. Jude stood there, looking worn yet undeniably handsome, a little disheveled as if he had rushed over. His blue eyes locked onto mine, and in that moment, I saw a flicker of concern shadowing his features, a reminder of the connection we still shared.

"Hey," he said softly, stepping inside as the door closed behind him.

"Hey," I replied, my heart pounding.

"I got your message," he said, taking a step closer. "What's going on?"

I took a deep breath, feeling the air thick with tension and unresolved feelings. "I got another note," I said, the words spilling out before I could censor myself. "It's a threat—aimed at me and the shop."

His expression darkened, and he closed the distance between us, taking my hands in his. "What did it say?"

I handed him the note, watching as his jaw tightened with each line he read. "This is serious," he muttered, a deep frown forming on his lips. "You shouldn't be alone right now."

"I know," I said, my voice barely above a whisper. "But I don't know who to trust. I thought I could handle this on my own."

"Don't do this to yourself," he urged, his grip tightening around my fingers. "You're not alone in this fight. You never have to be."

His words sent a shiver down my spine, stirring something deep within me—an ember of hope amid the darkness. In that moment, the past felt far away, and I could almost believe that maybe, just maybe, we could mend what was broken between us.

Jude's grip around my hands anchored me, a small island of warmth in the sea of uncertainty that surrounded us. The air between us was thick with unspoken words, and I could see the flicker of resolve in his eyes, an unyielding determination to protect me despite everything that had come between us.

"Let's figure this out," he said, his voice steady but laced with urgency. "Do you have any idea who might be behind this?"

I shook my head, the weight of dread settling heavily in my chest. "No one specific. It could be anyone. I've made enemies in this town, Jude. With every flower arrangement I send out, there's a chance someone could feel slighted. Business can be cutthroat in ways I never imagined."

"Then let's take it seriously," he insisted, stepping back to create space, though his eyes lingered on mine, seeking a flicker of trust I wasn't ready to give. "We'll look through your records, talk to anyone who might have a grudge. You shouldn't have to shoulder this alone."

I could only nod, caught in the crosshairs of my fear and the flicker of hope his presence ignited. The very thought of involving him in my troubles sent a shiver down my spine—how could I drag him into the chaos I had created? But I knew I needed to unravel this knot before it tightened further around us both.

As we moved through the shop, I forced myself to focus, pushing aside the memories of that fateful night when everything spiraled out of control. I showed him the various floral arrangements, each telling its own story of love, loss, and sometimes even betrayal. Jude listened, his eyes scanning my work with genuine appreciation, as if seeing the colors and textures of the flowers revealed hidden layers of my soul.

"What about your clients?" he asked, gesturing toward the guest book that lay on the counter, its pages filled with names scrawled in neat cursive. "Anyone unusual?"

I flipped through it, my fingers grazing the familiar names. There were brides-to-be, mothers planning birthdays, and a smattering of funeral arrangements that brought with them echoes of sadness. But one name caught my attention, an entry that had been hastily scribbled, the penmanship frantic.

"Wait. This one," I said, my finger landing on the page. "Claire Hawthorne. She ordered a bouquet last month, but I remember it being strange. She kept insisting on a specific shade of purple—said it meant something significant. I thought she was just eccentric, but now..."

"Now it looks suspicious," Jude interjected, his brow furrowing as he leaned closer. "What do you know about her?"

I hesitated, a knot forming in my throat. Claire had always been a whirlwind of energy, with wild stories about her life in the city and a penchant for drama that often overshadowed her requests. But there was a particular intensity in her gaze that unsettled me. "She seemed obsessed with perfection. If something didn't match her vision, she would lash out. I thought it was just her personality."

"And now it's a potential motive," Jude said, his voice steady as he took a step back. "Let's pay her a visit. If she's behind these notes, we need to know why."

A wave of trepidation washed over me. The idea of confronting Claire filled me with a mix of apprehension and anger. But I also felt a surge of defiance—the kind of spark that reminded me I was more than a victim in this situation. I was a florist, a fighter, and I would reclaim my narrative.

"Let's go," I said, surprising even myself with my resolve.

Jude nodded, his expression shifting from concern to determination as he grabbed his jacket. We stepped into the daylight, the sun warm against my skin, yet the shadows of my fear trailed closely behind. The streets were alive with the buzz of weekend activity—children chasing each other, couples enjoying leisurely strolls, and the distant sound of laughter blending with the hum of conversation. But the vibrancy of the day felt distant, muted by the growing anxiety coiling in my stomach.

Arriving at Claire's quaint cottage, I couldn't help but admire the vibrant garden that flourished in front of her home. It was a cacophony of colors, a stark contrast to the turmoil swirling within me. I knocked hesitantly on the door, my heart racing as I waited for her to answer.

"Claire, it's me, it's—I mean, it's Sarah," I called out, the weight of her name feeling heavy on my tongue.

The door creaked open, revealing Claire in a flowing floral dress that seemed to blend seamlessly with her surroundings. "Sarah! How lovely to see you! What brings you here?"

Her voice dripped with sweetness, but I couldn't shake the feeling that her smile was a mask, concealing something darker.

"I wanted to talk to you about the arrangement you ordered last month," I said, forcing the words out. "You seemed pretty passionate about it. I thought maybe we could—"

"Oh, I don't want to talk about that old thing," she interrupted, waving her hand dismissively. "It's all in the past. Let's have tea instead! I just baked some lavender scones. You must try them."

Jude shifted beside me, his eyes narrowing at Claire's sudden change of subject. "Actually, we need to discuss the recent notes I received, Claire," I said, my voice firm despite the quiver of uncertainty within.

Her expression darkened momentarily, and I caught the flash of something cold behind her eyes. "Oh? Notes? How fascinating," she replied, her tone shifting from bubbly to icy in a heartbeat. "What sort of notes?"

"Threatening notes," Jude said, stepping forward. "We believe they might be linked to you."

"Me? How absurd!" Claire laughed, though the sound was sharp, devoid of humor. "I would never waste my time on such nonsense. But if you're feeling threatened, perhaps you should consider moving away from this quaint little town. It can be... unfriendly."

The air thickened with tension, and I could see the defiance in her eyes, like a storm brewing on the horizon. I had stepped into a trap of my own making, and the realization stung like a thorn embedded in my skin.

"Is that a threat, Claire?" I asked, my voice steady despite the fear thrumming through me.

"Threats? My dear, I only wish you well," she said, her voice dripping with saccharine sweetness that felt like poison. "I wouldn't want anything to happen to your precious shop—or to you."

The layers of deception unfurled around us like a wilting flower, and suddenly, I understood. This wasn't just about floral arrangements or a personal vendetta; it was about power and control, and Claire had it in spades. I felt Jude tense beside me, ready to protect me from whatever storm Claire had brewing.

"We're leaving," he said firmly, grasping my elbow gently but decisively.

As we turned to leave, I felt Claire's gaze boring into my back, a warning etched in the air between us. The encounter had shaken me to my core, but as we stepped back into the sunlight, the heat of the day infused me with a renewed determination. I would not be bullied; I would not let fear dictate my life.

And as we walked away from the charming facade of Claire's home, I felt the tight grip of dread loosen, replaced by the stirring of a plan. I wasn't just going to defend my shop; I was going to take control of my life, even if it meant walking through the shadows.

The air buzzed with an electric tension as we stepped away from Claire's cottage, the door clicking shut behind us with a finality that sent a shiver down my spine. The vibrant garden, once a riot of color, now felt like a facade, hiding the malice lurking just beneath the surface. Jude walked beside me, his presence both a comfort and a reminder of the precariousness of our situation. I could feel his concern radiating off him like heat, but beneath it lay a shared determination, a bond strengthened by the shared threat we faced.

"Do you think she's behind the notes?" Jude asked, his voice low but edged with urgency.

"I don't know. She's certainly unpredictable enough," I replied, my fingers trembling as I tucked a loose strand of hair behind my ear. "But if she is, she's playing a dangerous game. Threatening me is one thing, but involving my shop... that's crossing a line."

"Then we need to go on the offensive," he said, glancing around as if the shadows might be listening. "What if we set a trap? Catch her in the act?"

I turned to him, my heart racing at the thought. "A trap? Like, bait her with a flower delivery or something? It sounds a bit like a bad movie plot, doesn't it?"

"Bad movies can be entertaining," Jude replied, a hint of a grin breaking through the tension. "And sometimes they're the only way to get what you want. Let's be smart about this. We can figure out a way to catch her off guard."

The idea felt both thrilling and terrifying, but there was a spark of hope igniting within me. I wasn't going to let fear dictate my life any longer. I was tired of being a pawn in someone else's game. Together, we could reclaim control. "Okay, let's do it," I said, my resolve hardening. "But how do we lure her out?"

Jude thought for a moment, his brow furrowed. "What if we announce a special arrangement? Something extravagant that would pique her interest? Maybe something she can't resist."

"A grand reopening special?" I suggested, the gears in my mind starting to turn. "We could use social media to create buzz. Offer a deal that's too good to pass up."

"Exactly. And if she's watching, she won't be able to resist trying to get a piece of it," he replied, the excitement in his voice palpable.

As we brainstormed ideas, my mind began to race with possibilities. We decided to create a limited-edition bouquet, something unique that would showcase the beauty of my work while enticing Claire to make a move. The plan felt daring, reckless even, but in that moment, I couldn't ignore the thrill of taking action.

That evening, we gathered supplies and spent hours crafting the arrangement. Flowers in shades of deep purple and fiery red intertwined, their fragrances mingling in the air like a secret shared only between us. Each petal and stem felt like a message, a declaration that I wouldn't be silenced by fear or betrayal.

"I can't believe we're actually doing this," I said, stepping back to admire our creation. "This feels... empowering."

"See? You've got this," Jude said, a proud smile gracing his lips. "And if Claire shows up, we'll be ready. Just don't let her charm you too much."

"Oh, please," I scoffed, a grin spreading across my face. "I have a better chance of falling for a cactus."

We shared a laugh, and for the first time in what felt like ages, I felt lighter, as though a weight was being lifted. But the moment of levity was fleeting, a reminder that lurking beneath the surface was a current of danger that wouldn't simply fade away.

The next morning, I posted about the special arrangement, detailing its limited availability and the breathtaking design that would be the centerpiece of my shop's grand reopening. The response was immediate—likes, shares, comments buzzing in faster than I could keep up. But deep down, a thread of anxiety tightened in my chest. What if Claire didn't take the bait? What if the note was simply the work of a random troublemaker, and I had let paranoia lead me down a path of confrontation?

As the day wore on, customers began to trickle in, drawn by the promise of something special. I engaged with them, exchanging smiles and laughter, feeling a semblance of normalcy return. But just as the sun began to dip low in the sky, casting a golden hue across the shop, the bell above the door chimed, and my heart lurched.

Claire walked in, her expression deceptively calm, as though she were a friendly neighbor rather than the potential source of my fears. She wore a bright yellow sundress that matched the flowers surrounding her, yet the air crackled with unspoken tension, a storm brewing just beneath her cheerful facade.

"Sarah! What a delightful surprise!" she chirped, her voice too sweet to be genuine. "I couldn't resist coming to see this magnificent arrangement for myself!"

"Glad you could make it," I replied, forcing a smile that didn't quite reach my eyes.

"I must say, the colors are stunning. How clever of you to incorporate such rich shades. They really pop!" Her gaze flicked over the arrangement, her fingers twitching as if she yearned to reach out and touch it.

"Thank you," I replied, crossing my arms defensively. "It's one of a kind. Only a few are available."

"Ah, a rarity!" she exclaimed, her enthusiasm oddly over-the-top. "I simply must have one. It would brighten up my home so beautifully."

"Unfortunately, they're going fast," I said, my heart pounding as I wondered whether she could sense the undertones of warning woven into my words. "But I can put you on a waiting list."

Her smile faltered for just a moment, and I caught a flash of something in her eyes—a flicker of frustration before she masked it with a bright laugh. "Oh, darling, don't be coy. We both know how to play this game."

Jude stood at the back of the shop, watching the exchange with an intensity that made my stomach flutter. He wasn't just my ally in this endeavor; he was also a source of strength, reminding me that I wasn't alone. I shot him a glance, hoping for reassurance.

"Game?" I echoed, feigning ignorance.

"Let's not pretend we're not both aware of what's at stake here." She stepped closer, her voice dropping to a conspiratorial whisper. "Your little notes and threats. They're charming, but I assure you, they're misguided."

My heart raced as I processed her words, the tension in the air palpable. "You think this is some kind of game? Because I assure you, it's anything but."

Claire's expression shifted, a smirk curving her lips. "Then you've got more to worry about than just floral arrangements, my dear. You might want to reconsider your strategy."

With that, she turned on her heel, striding toward the door with a confidence that left me reeling. I felt a wave of dizziness wash over me, the ground beneath me shifting as I struggled to understand what had just transpired.

"Wait!" I called after her, desperation creeping into my voice.

But she simply waved her hand over her shoulder, the door closing with a soft click that felt like a final nail in my coffin. I turned to Jude, my heart pounding. "What does she know?"

"I don't know," he said, his voice low and serious. "But we need to figure it out fast. This isn't just about your shop anymore."

Suddenly, the bell above the door jingled again, and I felt my heart drop as I turned to see another figure stepping inside, a shadow falling across the threshold. This time, it was someone I never expected to see.

"Sarah, I need to talk to you," said a voice that sent a chill racing down my spine, and I froze, fear flooding my senses.

It was someone from my past, someone who shouldn't be here, and my mind raced with the implications of their sudden appearance.

Chapter 16: The Power of Petals

I reached out to Jude, my heart pounding with uncertainty. The air was thick with unspoken words as he entered the flower shop, the bell above the door tinkling like a hesitant chime signaling the start of a new chapter. Sunlight streamed through the large windows, illuminating the vibrant blooms that lined the shelves, their colors dancing against the backdrop of a fading afternoon. The sweet fragrance of roses mixed with the sharpness of freshly cut stems, filling the room with a sensory bouquet that almost made me forget the storm brewing outside, a storm that threatened not just my livelihood but the fragile peace between us.

Jude stood there, his silhouette framed by the soft golden light. There was a flicker of hope in his eyes, though it battled fiercely with the weight of our shared past. We needed to set aside our differences, to cast aside the bitterness that had grown like weeds in a neglected garden, and join forces to confront the shadow lurking at the edges of our lives. "We can't let this person tear us apart," I said, my voice trembling slightly, betraying the confidence I tried to project. "If we want to protect our businesses, we need to work together."

He nodded, a hint of reluctance still evident in the way he crossed his arms. "I never wanted things to come to this. I thought we were beyond it." His voice was low, almost gravelly, as if the words were dragged out from somewhere deep within him. The tension in the room thickened, wrapping around us like a suffocating vine, but I could see something shifting in his expression, a glimmer of understanding peeking through the clouds of regret.

"Then let's move forward," I replied, surprising myself with the steadiness in my tone. "We can't let whoever's behind this win." The shop, once a haven filled with my dreams and aspirations, transformed into our makeshift command center, cluttered with sketches of flowers, notes scribbled in haste, and the remnants of our shared animosity. Together, we devised a plan—a framework of ideas and strategies laid out like petals on a delicate bloom, each one contributing to a greater whole.

As we worked side by side, the air between us shifted. The anger that had once boiled over, fueled by misunderstandings and past grievances, was replaced by something more constructive—understanding. I could see the genuine remorse in Jude's eyes as he recounted his own struggles, the way the burdens he carried had clouded his judgment. We had both faced shadows in our lives; perhaps, together, we could emerge into the light.

"Remember when we used to compete in the flower shows?" I ventured, a small smile tugging at my lips as nostalgia wrapped around us like a warm blanket. "You always insisted on showcasing those gaudy sunflowers that looked like they had been doused in neon paint."

He chuckled, the sound a deep rumble that reverberated through the shop, momentarily easing the tension. "Hey, those sunflowers were a bold statement! But I get it—you and your delicate lilies, always trying to win over the judges with elegance." He smirked, his eyes sparkling with mischief.

"Elegance is timeless, Jude. Something you wouldn't understand with those oversized monstrosities." My playful jab hung in the air like a fragile petal, a reminder of a time when laughter had been the glue holding us together instead of sharp words and accusations.

"Alright, alright, I see your point. Maybe we can find a balance," he conceded, the corners of his mouth quirking up in a reluctant grin. The room felt lighter, the shadows of our past battles receding for a moment as we found common ground in our shared love for flowers, the very essence of beauty and fragility.

We mapped out our next steps on a large sheet of butcher paper, the sprawling lines and sketches taking on a life of their own. "We'll start by reaching out to our suppliers," I suggested, my brow furrowing in concentration. "If we can establish a network of communication, we might uncover who's been sabotaging our orders."

Jude nodded, his focus sharpening. "And I'll talk to my contacts in the local market. If anyone knows something, it'll be them." There was a determination in his voice that I hadn't heard in a long time, and it ignited a spark of hope within me. "We need to be careful, though. This person is watching us, and we can't afford to show any weakness."

"Agreed," I said, my heart racing at the thought. The idea that someone was lurking in the shadows, plotting against us, sent a shiver down my spine. "We'll keep this under wraps. No one else needs to know."

We worked late into the evening, the light outside fading to twilight. The gentle glow from the overhead bulbs cast a warm halo over our workspace, creating a cocoon of safety in which we could share ideas freely, without the weight of our past hanging over us. With each idea we exchanged, I felt the distance between us shrink. It was as if we were knitting together the frayed edges of our history, carefully mending the fabric of our relationship with every plan we devised.

As we continued to brainstorm, a comfortable silence enveloped us, punctuated by the occasional chuckle or teasing remark. I caught him stealing glances at the bouquet on the counter—a vibrant arrangement of lilies, daisies, and an extravagant peony. "Are you going to keep that monstrosity in your shop?" he teased, pointing at the peony with mock disdain.

"Excuse me, that 'monstrosity' happens to be the centerpiece of my best-selling arrangement," I shot back, playfully swatting his arm. The banter felt like a breath of fresh air, a release from the tension that had built up over the months. I could see the storm clouds parting, and with each exchange, the warmth between us grew, blooming like the flowers surrounding us.

In that moment, surrounded by the scent of blossoms and the flickering glow of candlelight, I realized that beneath the layers of hurt and misunderstanding, there was still a connection—a bond forged through shared memories and unspoken dreams. Perhaps together, we could weather this storm and cultivate something beautiful from the chaos.

The day wore on, the last remnants of sunlight slipping behind the horizon, casting long shadows across the flower shop's polished wooden floors. The mingling scents of fresh blooms began to mingle with the crispness of evening, creating an atmosphere that was both comforting and charged with a sense of urgency. Jude and I leaned over the butcher paper, our heads close together, the tension morphing into something more like camaraderie with each passing moment.

"What if we set a trap?" Jude suggested, his brows knitting together in concentration. "Something to draw this person out into the open."

I looked up, intrigued. "You mean like a lure? I'm not sure if it's a great idea to bait a possible lunatic." I shot him a teasing smile, the spark of banter rekindling between us. "But then again, when has my sanity ever been an issue?"

His lips quirked up at the corners. "You're right. We've definitely both lost our marbles somewhere along the way." He gestured toward the flowers, and I could see the fire in his eyes as he continued, "How about we host an open house? A big event, something to draw attention to our businesses and show that we're united."

I paused, contemplating the implications. "An open house could work. It would attract customers and maybe this person too, thinking they could rattle us. But it also risks drawing unwanted attention."

"True, but it could also make them overconfident. Maybe they think we're too fractured to stand together," he replied, his voice dropping to a conspiratorial whisper, as if saying the words aloud would somehow summon our adversary. "Plus, I'm pretty sure my donuts will lure anyone out."

"Your donuts are a powerful weapon," I chuckled, the warmth between us expanding. "Let's do it. An open house it is."

With renewed determination, we spent the next few hours planning every detail, the excitement building in the air. We meticulously crafted invitations that blended our businesses—my floral artistry and his bakery. "How about we incorporate a 'bloom and bake' theme?" I suggested, twirling a pen in my fingers. "Guests can pick a flower while sampling your treats."

"Now you're talking. I'll whip up some floral-infused pastries—think lavender lemon tarts and rose petal macarons." His eyes gleamed as he leaned back in his chair, hands clasped behind his head. "I'm sure the entire town will want to attend, especially if I put out a sign that says 'free donuts.'"

"You're incorrigible," I said, shaking my head in mock disapproval. "But I think it might just work."

As we plotted the day away, the air grew thick with laughter and playful jabs, the remnants of our past grievances fading into the background like an afterthought. It was strange how quickly we fell back into our rhythm, as if the universe had conspired to remind us of the ease we once shared.

But just as the conversation turned lighthearted, my phone buzzed on the counter, a harsh jolt back to reality. I glanced at the screen and felt my stomach drop. A message from my supplier, notifying me of yet another canceled shipment due to a "suspicious circumstance." My heart raced; the ominous words echoed in my mind like the tolling of a bell.

"Jude," I said, my voice trembling slightly as I shared the news. "It's happening again. Our orders are getting canceled."

He shot up from his seat, the camaraderie evaporating in an instant. "We have to act fast. Whoever this is won't stop until they've destroyed us both."

We turned back to our plans, tension radiating from every inch of the room. My fingers tapped nervously on the counter, the once vibrant atmosphere now suffocating under the weight of uncertainty. Jude caught my eye, his expression serious, almost fierce. "We'll figure this out. We can't let them intimidate us."

"I just... I don't want to lose everything," I admitted, my voice small. The words hung between us like a fragile bloom, vulnerable and beautiful yet easily crushed.

"Hey." Jude stepped closer, the warmth of his presence grounding me. "You won't lose anything. We'll stand strong, together. Remember that."

His sincerity ignited a flicker of hope within me, a reminder of the strength we both possessed. "You're right. We need to remain vigilant. But what if they strike again before the open house?"

"Then we do what we do best," he replied, an earnest glint in his eye. "We adapt. We pivot. We're not just flower and sugar, you know. We're fighters."

I couldn't help but smile, feeling the embers of determination rekindle within me. "Then let's gather our resources and prepare for this open house. We'll put everything we have into it, making it impossible for them to ignore us."

The next few days were a blur of activity. The shop transformed into a bustling hive of creativity. Flowers bloomed vibrantly in every corner, and Jude's bakery began producing the most exquisite treats that carried hints of floral notes. The invitation design morphed into a work of art—a pastel-hued card adorned with hand-painted flowers and whimsical lettering that beckoned everyone in the town to join us for a day of sweetness and beauty.

As we worked side by side, a sense of anticipation crackled in the air. Yet, beneath the surface, the tension simmered, reminding us both that our adversary was still out there, watching, waiting.

On the day of the open house, the shop was alive with laughter and chatter, the scent of fresh flowers mingling with the sweet aroma of baked goods. Customers flowed in, their faces lighting up with delight as they sampled Jude's creations while I guided them through the floral arrangements, sharing stories about each bloom.

"Are you trying to steal all my customers?" Jude teased as I guided a couple to the tray of lavender-infused cupcakes.

"Please, they're just here for the flowers. You're merely the icing on the cake."

"Funny. I was thinking of you as the icing—sweet on the outside but a little nutty on the inside."

I rolled my eyes but couldn't help the laughter bubbling up inside me. Our playful banter eased the tension, a welcome distraction from the shadows that loomed just outside our window.

As the afternoon wore on, the shop bustled with activity. Just as we began to feel a sense of triumph, a figure appeared in the doorway—a tall, dark silhouette that immediately stilled the laughter in the room. My heart sank as I recognized the unmistakable aura of trouble that surrounded them.

The atmosphere shifted, and I exchanged a quick glance with Jude, his expression matching my own concern. The evening was far from over, and with it, the weight of uncertainty settled back into the pit of my stomach.

The figure in the doorway stepped into the soft glow of the shop, and my breath caught in my throat. It was a tall woman with sharp features and a piercing gaze that seemed to cut through the cheerful atmosphere like a knife. She wore a crisp black blazer, too formal for the whimsical vibe of the open house, and her hair, slicked back into a tight bun, accentuated the seriousness of her demeanor. I felt Jude tense beside me, his eyes narrowing as he instinctively positioned himself slightly in front of me, a subtle gesture of protection that sent a flutter of warmth through my chest.

"Can I help you?" I asked, forcing a smile that felt too strained. The joy in the room faded as guests shifted their attention to the newcomer, curiosity mingling with apprehension.

"I'm here for the flower shop," she stated, her voice cold and authoritative, cutting through the lighthearted chatter like a winter breeze. "You're the owner, I presume?"

"Yes, I am." I straightened my back, trying to project confidence despite the unease settling over me. "And you are?"

"I'm Claire Reynolds," she replied, her gaze piercing through me as if assessing my worth in a single glance. "I represent the Downtown Business Council."

The words hung heavy in the air. "Oh, um, nice to meet you." My enthusiasm faltered. "Is there something we can help you with?"

She glanced around, her lips curling into a barely concealed smirk. "I came to see how you're managing with all the recent... disruptions in the area. Quite a bold move to hold an open house with everything that's been happening, don't you think?"

"Disruptions?" I echoed, feigning innocence while my heart raced. "You mean the canceled orders?"

She tilted her head, her expression inscrutable. "Yes, those. And the reports of vandalism at several local businesses. One might wonder if you're a target."

I could feel the tension creeping back into the room, the guests now quietly observing the interaction, the atmosphere charged with a sense of impending doom. "We're aware of the situation, and we're doing everything we can to—"

"Are you?" she interrupted, her voice laced with skepticism. "Because it looks to me like you're trying to hide behind flowers and baked goods instead of addressing the real issue. Ignorance is not a strategy."

Jude stepped forward, his tone assertive. "We're not hiding from anything. We're standing our ground. If you have concerns, you should bring them to us directly instead of casting aspersions."

Claire narrowed her eyes, assessing Jude as if deciding whether to engage further. "Then perhaps I should recommend that you strengthen your security measures. There are rumors circulating that someone is watching, waiting for the right moment to strike."

A chill ran down my spine. I exchanged a glance with Jude, the unspoken worry mirrored in his eyes. "We're doing our best," I managed, my voice steadying as I regained some semblance of control. "And we'll take your advice into consideration."

"Good," she said, her tone softening slightly. "Just know that the Council is concerned for the safety of all businesses in this community. You're not alone in this." With that, she turned on her heel and strode back toward the door, leaving a trail of uncertainty in her wake.

As she exited, the buzz of conversation resumed, but the lively energy had dimmed, replaced by a heavy blanket of unease. Jude and I exchanged glances again, and I could see the question hanging in the air: What did she know?

"Should we be worried?" I whispered, my pulse quickening as I took in the room's atmosphere, which had shifted from celebration to caution.

"Definitely," Jude replied, running a hand through his hair, an action that seemed to denote a mix of frustration and concern. "But let's not panic. We have people here, and we can't let them see us falter."

"Right," I agreed, forcing myself to smile as I stepped back into the fray, but the vibrant conversations felt muted now, the laughter less genuine. I grabbed a tray of lavender lemon tarts and offered them to a couple nearby, forcing a chipper tone. "Would you like to try these? They're a delightful combination of sweet and floral!"

The couple took a tart each, their smiles sincere but tinged with concern as they glanced at Jude, who was speaking with another guest. I could see the worry etched into the lines of his face, a reflection of the rising tension that seemed to envelop us both.

As the afternoon wore on, I found it increasingly difficult to focus on the task at hand. My thoughts swirled around Claire's ominous warning, the echoes of her words mixing with my own rising anxiety. It was hard to shake the feeling that we were being watched, that our efforts to stand united might be futile against an unseen enemy.

"I need to step outside for a moment," I said to Jude, who was busy directing guests toward the floral arrangements. "I'll be back."

"Everything okay?" he asked, concern etched on his features.

"Just a breath of fresh air." I forced a smile, though it didn't quite reach my eyes. The weight of the open house felt heavier than ever, as if the walls themselves were closing in.

I stepped outside, grateful for the cool evening breeze that wrapped around me, offering a momentary reprieve. The sun was dipping low in the sky, casting a warm golden hue over the street as I took a deep breath, inhaling the fragrance of the blooming flowers mingled with the earthy scent of the wet pavement.

Just as I was about to return inside, a movement caught my eye at the edge of the parking lot. A figure lingered in the shadows, partially obscured by the trees lining the street. My heart raced as I squinted, trying to get a clearer view.

"Hello?" I called out, my voice trembling slightly. "Is anyone there?"

The figure straightened, stepping into the fading light. My breath caught in my throat as I recognized the familiar face. It was someone I never expected to see again, someone who had vanished from my life like a wisp of smoke.

"Surprised to see me?" They smirked, their voice laced with mockery and a hint of menace.

"Why are you here?" I asked, struggling to keep my composure as panic began to bubble beneath the surface. "You shouldn't be—"

"Shouldn't be? Oh, I think you and I have a lot to discuss."

The words hung in the air, thick with tension, the shadows around us growing darker as the sun slipped below the horizon. I felt the weight of their gaze, the unspoken threat lingering like a storm cloud about to break. I could either step forward into this new reality or retreat, but the fear of what they might reveal held me frozen in place.

Chapter 17: Petals of Deceit

The rain drummed against the window like an impatient guest, eager to break through the glass and spill into the room. I stood in the small conference area of my office, where the ambient hum of fluorescent lights barely masked the rhythmic pulse of anxiety thrumming in my chest. Jude was sifting through a mess of files sprawled across the table, his brow furrowed in concentration. The air was thick with the mingled scents of damp paper and fresh coffee, a comforting contrast to the tempest raging outside. I leaned against the wall, arms crossed, watching him work as he flipped through pages, searching for the threads that would unravel the mystery ensnaring us.

"Here's the kicker," Jude said, breaking the silence. He held up a sheet that, under the stark fluorescent light, looked like a paper filled with vague figures and hastily scrawled notes. "The figures in this budget report don't match up with what we discussed last quarter. It's like someone's been manipulating the numbers right under our noses."

His voice had that familiar gravelly edge, the one that sent a shiver down my spine—part concern, part determination. I pushed myself off the wall, intrigued. "Manipulating them how? Are we talking embezzlement or just sloppy bookkeeping?"

Jude's lips curled into a wry smile that was almost a smirk. "Let's not kid ourselves; this town is built on deception. It could be anything from embezzlement to a concerted effort to sabotage our expansion plans. We need to dig deeper."

The urgency in his voice ignited a fire inside me, a strange blend of excitement and dread. I could feel the weight of Riverview pressing down on my shoulders, its long-standing histories of betrayal and whispered secrets creeping into the edges of my consciousness. I straightened up, shaking off the remnants of self-doubt. "Then we dig deeper. No stone left unturned, right?"

"Right," he replied, leaning closer, the warmth of his body a stark contrast to the cold reality of our situation. "And we need to be careful. Whoever is behind this isn't just trying to ruin us financially; they want to take us down completely."

His words lingered in the air, heavy with implications. I could almost see the shadows stretching beyond the walls of our little office, creeping closer, shrouding our plans in an ever-thickening veil of danger. My heart raced as I thought about the risks, but they paled in comparison to the thrill of working alongside him. Together, we were more than just two business partners; we were a force to be reckoned with, a volatile mix of ambition and tenacity.

"I'll call the accountant," I said, tapping my fingers against the table, a nervous habit I had developed. "Maybe she can shed some light on these discrepancies."

Jude nodded, his expression intense as he studied me. "Good idea. But don't go alone. Take someone with you."

I raised an eyebrow, curiosity piquing my interest. "You worried about me?"

"Not worried. Just... cautious," he replied, his voice lower, as if he was letting me in on a secret. "We don't know how far this goes. I want you safe."

His concern wrapped around me like a warm blanket, igniting a flicker of warmth that chased away the chill of fear. Yet, along with that warmth came a torrent of emotions I had fought to suppress. Jude had become more than just a colleague or friend; he was a tether to a reality I couldn't ignore. As I met his gaze, I felt the heat between us crackle, a silent acknowledgment of the tension that had been building over countless late-night discussions.

"Fine, I'll take Hailey," I said, trying to keep my tone light, even though my heart was thundering in my chest. "She can handle herself."

"Good choice," he said, a hint of a smile playing at the corners of his lips. "Just keep your eyes open."

After making the call, I felt the adrenaline spike as I prepared to meet Hailey. She had been my confidante and rock throughout this entire ordeal. There was something about her unwavering support that anchored me, especially now when the world around us felt so unsteady. But as I stepped out into the rain-soaked streets of Riverview, the reality of our situation sunk in deeper than the puddles gathering at my feet.

The streets, once bustling with life, felt ominously quiet. The streetlamps flickered, casting long shadows that danced in the rain. My heart raced, each footstep echoing in the emptiness as I approached Hailey's café, a cozy haven that had become a refuge amid the chaos. The warm light spilling out into the night felt like a beacon, drawing me closer to safety.

As I pushed open the café door, the bell chimed softly, the comforting aroma of coffee and freshly baked pastries washing over me. Hailey stood behind the counter, her vibrant smile lighting up the dim space. "There you are! I was starting to think you'd gotten lost in the storm." She gestured toward a table in the corner, inviting me to sit.

"Hardly," I replied, sinking into the plush chair. "But I might need a double shot of espresso for what's coming next."

Her expression shifted from playful to serious as she leaned in. "What's going on? You look like you've seen a ghost."

I recounted the developments with Jude, each revelation pulling her further into the web of deception that had wrapped around us. Her brows knitted together, concern etched on her features. "This sounds dangerous. Are you sure you want to dive deeper into this?"

"I have to," I insisted, my resolve firming with each word. "If we don't, who knows what will happen? We can't let whoever is behind this destroy everything we've built."

"Okay, but promise me you'll be careful," she urged, her voice laced with genuine worry. "And if it gets too intense, you have to back off."

"Deal," I said, but even as I spoke the words, a sense of foreboding settled over me. The stakes were higher than ever, and I could feel the invisible eyes watching us from the shadows, waiting for the perfect moment to strike. As we chatted over steaming cups, I couldn't shake the feeling that the storm outside was nothing compared to the one brewing within our lives.

The café buzzed with a low hum of conversation, punctuated by the occasional clatter of dishes and the soothing hiss of the espresso machine. I let the comforting chaos wrap around me, a stark contrast to the tension that clung to my skin like the humidity outside. Hailey leaned across the table, her expression a mixture of concern and excitement. "So, what's the plan? Are we going to infiltrate their lair or just bake cookies and hope for the best?"

I chuckled, grateful for her light-heartedness amid the dark clouds hovering over our heads. "If only it were that simple. But we need a more strategic approach. The last thing we want is to go in guns blazing and make things worse."

"Or worse, get caught in a very bad rom-com plot," she added, her eyes sparkling with mischief. "You know, the one where the unsuspecting heroine finds herself tangled in a web of corporate espionage while also juggling her love life?"

"Right? Because nothing says 'high-stakes drama' like a corporate espionage subplot," I replied, rolling my eyes playfully. "What I need is a plan, and maybe a superhero cape."

As I took a sip of my coffee, its rich bitterness grounding me, a sudden chill crept through the café. The door swung open with a gust of wind, rattling the wind chimes above it. I glanced up, and my heart lurched as I spotted a figure standing just inside the threshold, drenched from the rain. Jude's silhouette was striking against the café's warm glow, his hair slicked back and clothes plastered to his frame.

"Speak of the devil," Hailey murmured, a knowing smile tugging at her lips.

"Right on time," I replied, my stomach flipping as I met Jude's gaze. There was something intense in his eyes, a fire that matched the storm raging outside. I gestured for him to join us, and he slipped into the seat across from me, shaking droplets of water from his hair.

"Did I interrupt something?" he asked, his voice low and teasing, though his eyes flickered with a seriousness that belied his words.

"Just plotting world domination over coffee," I quipped, unable to resist the banter. "You know, the usual."

Jude's expression softened, but a hint of tension lingered. "I brought some files that might help. I didn't want to waste any time."

"Great, let's dive in," I said, eager to switch gears from the light-heartedness to the task at hand. I slid my laptop closer, and Hailey leaned back, content to be an observer. The dynamic between us shifted as Jude spread the files before us, the laughter replaced by a palpable intensity.

He flipped through the pages, his brow furrowed in concentration. "I reached out to a few contacts. There's definitely something bigger happening here. It's not just petty sabotage; this goes up the chain."

My stomach twisted at his words, a knot tightening as I considered the implications. "What do you mean by 'bigger'? Like corporate espionage bigger?"

"Exactly. It seems some key players in Riverview have been making moves to destabilize the competition, and it looks like we've become their target." He pointed to a list of names, some of which sent a jolt through me. Riverview had always been a tight-knit community, but the thought of betrayal from those I thought I knew was unsettling.

"Those names... they're all affiliated with—" I started, but Hailey interrupted, her voice laced with disbelief.

"No way. They wouldn't dare. It's too risky."

"Clearly, they're underestimating the risks," Jude replied, his voice low but steady. "This isn't just about business anymore. It's personal."

As he spoke, the reality of our situation settled around us, heavy and suffocating. I couldn't shake the feeling that we were playing a dangerous game, one that could cost us everything we had worked for. My heart raced as I realized how intertwined our lives had become, not just in business but in this complex dance of trust and betrayal.

"Then we need to counteract whatever they're planning," I said, my voice firm. "We have to stay one step ahead."

"Agreed," Jude replied, and I could see a flicker of admiration in his gaze, a spark that sent warmth rushing through me. "But we need to be smart about it. We can't act recklessly. We'll need allies, people we can trust."

Hailey nodded, her eyes sharp. "What about the others? The ones who have been loyal to you? They could help."

"Absolutely," I said, considering the small circle of friends and allies I could count on. "But we have to be cautious. We can't alert the wrong people."

The weight of the situation settled heavily on my shoulders, a storm of its own gathering momentum. I could sense Jude's presence beside me, strong and unwavering, grounding me as we faced the unknown.

"Let's do this," I said, my voice steady with resolve. "We can't let fear dictate our actions."

With newfound determination, we spent the next hour outlining our strategy, crafting a plan to confront the shadows that lurked just beyond our reach. Each idea we tossed around fueled my sense of purpose, and I could feel the camaraderie deepening between Jude and me. Our dynamic shifted, shifting from colleagues to something more, a partnership forged in the fires of adversity.

As the café began to empty, the warm light dimmed, and the rain continued to pour outside, I caught Jude watching me with an intensity that made my heart race. "You know, it's impressive how you handle pressure," he said, a slight smile breaking through the tension. "Most people would be cowering in fear right now."

"Maybe I've just had too much coffee," I joked, attempting to lighten the mood. "Or maybe I'm just stubborn."

"Stubborn is good," he replied, leaning closer. "It means you won't back down easily."

His words hung in the air, thick with unspoken possibilities. My breath hitched as I caught the glint of something deeper in his eyes. But just as quickly as the moment sparked, it faded as the bell above the door jingled again, and another customer stepped inside, shattering the fragile tension we had built.

As we resumed our discussion, I couldn't shake the sense that our lives were about to take a turn. Riverview was shifting beneath our feet, and as we faced the challenges ahead, I realized that every step we took would bring us closer together—or tear us apart. The stakes had never felt higher, and with each passing moment, I could feel the petals of deceit surrounding us begin to unfurl, revealing the thorns hidden within.

The air was thick with a mix of excitement and anxiety as we continued to devise our plan. Jude's presence loomed large over the small table, his focus unwavering as he sifted through the files spread before us. A light rain drizzled against the café window, creating a soothing backdrop to our hurried whispers. I could feel the gravity of the situation wrapping around us, yet there was an unexpected thrill in strategizing with Jude. Each stolen glance and shared smile felt charged with a sense of urgency that ignited something deep within me.

"Okay," I said, tapping my fingers on the table to regain his attention. "We need to consider our next moves carefully. If we're going to turn the tide, we can't just react; we have to anticipate their moves."

"Agreed," Jude replied, his voice steady, laced with determination. "We should gather as much intel as possible. I've got a friend at the local newspaper who might be able to dig up some dirt on our rivals."

"Perfect. And what about our allies? If we're going to confront this, we need backup," I suggested, my heart racing at the thought of rallying the troops.

He nodded, a flicker of admiration crossing his features. "We could reach out to the other business owners in town. If they're also feeling the pressure, they might be willing to join forces."

Hailey chimed in, leaning forward with interest. "I know a few people who've had run-ins with that same shady crew. They'd love a chance to fight back. But we'll need to present a united front if we want to make an impact."

"Then it's settled," I said, adrenaline coursing through my veins. "We'll gather information, reach out to our allies, and prepare for a full-scale response."

The door swung open again, and in walked a familiar face, one that sent a jolt of unease rippling through me. Carla, the rival business owner known for her cutthroat tactics, sauntered in as if she owned the place. The moment our eyes locked, I felt a chill creep down my spine. She exuded an air of confidence that masked something much darker.

"Fancy seeing you all here," she said, her voice dripping with feigned sweetness. "What a cozy little meeting you've got going on."

"Just enjoying some coffee, Carla. What brings you to this side of town?" I replied, keeping my tone light while my heart raced.

"Oh, you know, just checking in on the competition," she said, a smirk playing on her lips. "I hear things have been a bit turbulent in the Riverview business scene lately. Can't imagine that affects you all too much, though."

Jude leaned back in his chair, his eyes narrowing. "Always a pleasure, Carla. You must be eager to see how we weather the storm."

"Oh, I do love a good storm," she replied, her gaze flicking between us, sharp as glass. "You never know who might get swept away."

As she walked away, the tension in the room crackled like static electricity. I glanced at Jude and Hailey, our expressions mirroring the apprehension that hung heavy in the air.

"She knows something," Hailey whispered, her voice low. "We can't let her out of our sight."

"I don't trust her as far as I can throw her," I said, my mind racing. "If she's in on whatever's happening, we need to stay ahead of her."

"Let's keep a close eye on her and see what she does next," Jude suggested, his tone decisive. "We have to stay vigilant."

Our discussions shifted into high gear as we plotted our next steps, but the unease lingered, coiling tighter around me. I was acutely aware of how quickly the landscape had shifted, how the shadows that once seemed harmless now loomed with sinister intent.

As we left the café, the rain had turned into a torrential downpour, the streets glistening under the dim streetlights. The familiar path to my car felt treacherous, each step echoing with the foreboding sense that something was coming. The sense of being watched prickled at the back of my neck, a sensation I could no longer ignore.

"I'll drive you home," Jude offered, his tone authoritative yet caring. "It's too dangerous for you to be out here alone."

"Jude, I can manage," I protested, but there was a warmth in his insistence that soothed the apprehension gnawing at my gut.

"Just let me," he insisted, the determination in his voice leaving little room for argument.

Reluctantly, I nodded, and we made our way to his car, the rain drenching us as we hurried along the sidewalk. The inside of the car was a welcome refuge, warm and dry. As we pulled out into the slick streets, I glanced over at Jude, who was focused on the road ahead, tension radiating from him in waves.

"Thanks for this," I said, trying to ease the silence that had fallen between us. "I appreciate it."

"Always," he replied, a soft smile breaking through the seriousness of the moment. "Just looking out for you."

The drive was filled with an electrifying undercurrent, every glance exchanged holding unspoken words, each moment stretching out like a taut wire. I couldn't help but feel that the stakes were rising, and with them, the connection between us deepened.

When we finally reached my apartment, the rain had begun to relent, a soft patter echoing in the night. I stepped out into the damp air, pulling my coat tighter around me.

"Be careful," Jude called after me, his voice carrying an edge of urgency that sent a shiver down my spine.

"Always," I shot back, feeling the weight of his gaze as I walked toward the entrance.

Just as I reached for the door handle, a strange noise echoed from the shadows of the nearby alley. My heart raced as I turned to look, a fleeting instinct urging me to retreat. The darkness seemed to pulse, and for a moment, I was paralyzed, the chill of uncertainty wrapping around me.

Then, without warning, a figure stepped out, cloaked in shadows. My breath hitched in my throat as recognition hit me like a slap. It was someone I never expected to see here, not now, not ever. The figure moved closer, their intentions shrouded in secrecy, a smirk playing at the edges of their lips.

"Surprise," they said, their voice smooth and unsettling. "I think we need to talk."

My pulse quickened, and the air around me thickened with impending danger, leaving me teetering on the edge of uncertainty.

Chapter 18: Thorns in the Garden

The night air hung heavy with the scent of rain-soaked earth and the distant promise of thunderstorms, a rich aroma that should have brought comfort but only heightened the sense of dread clawing at my stomach. My flower shop, a riot of color and life just days before, now stood shrouded in shadows, its once-vibrant blooms twisted and torn. The sign over the door, which had been painted a cheerful sunflower yellow, now hung at an angle, the glass shattered and scattered like the pieces of my heart.

"Daisy, are you sure you want to do this?" Jude's voice was low, a blend of concern and urgency, pulling me back from the precipice of my thoughts. He stood beside me, the moonlight casting silver highlights through his dark hair, making him look almost ethereal—like something conjured from the depths of my imagination during quieter, happier days. The warmth of his presence reminded me that, despite the chaos around us, I wasn't alone. But the thought of facing whatever darkness awaited felt daunting.

I nodded, though doubt flickered like the dying light from the streetlamp. "I can't just let it go. This is my livelihood. Someone's targeting me—and you." The thought of Jude suffering because of my troubles twisted my insides tighter. Anger surged through me, a vibrant green vine of resentment choking my rationality. "This isn't just vandalism; it's a personal attack. We need to find out who's behind this."

With a resigned sigh, Jude stepped forward, surveying the wreckage. "What do you think they want?" he asked, crouching to examine a wilted daisy that had somehow survived the chaos. "To scare you? Or maybe it's just some kids acting out."

"Or someone who wants to ruin everything I've worked for," I snapped, the words sharper than I intended. The vulnerability beneath my bravado felt raw, like a fresh wound exposed to the harsh air. "And you've got a lot on the line too. Your bakery is practically the heart of this town."

"Don't forget that. It's worth fighting for." His eyes met mine, a silent promise woven into the depths of his gaze. The flicker of something more lingered between us, a tension that had been building like the storm threatening to break overhead. I wondered if he felt it too, this undercurrent of energy, a dance of unspoken words and what-ifs, waiting for the right moment to spark into something real.

Before I could say more, a figure emerged from the shadows across the street. Tall and cloaked in darkness, the silhouette was outlined by the pale light of the moon. A chill raced down my spine. "Do you see that?" I whispered, my voice barely above a tremor. "Who the hell is that?"

"Stay here." Jude's tone was firm, the protector emerging within him, and before I could protest, he moved towards the figure with a determined stride. The air crackled with tension, each heartbeat a reminder of how close we were to something dangerous. I clenched my fists, torn between following him and staying safe.

As Jude approached, the figure stepped forward, revealing a face I hadn't expected to see again. It was Miranda, my once-best friend, now turned bitter rival, her eyes narrowed like a cat stalking its prey. The hair that used to frame her face now fell in disheveled waves, the aura of chaos swirling around her, much like the wreckage of my shop.

"Fancy seeing you here," she said, a smirk playing on her lips, a weapon sharper than any blade. "I heard your little shop had a run-in with some rowdy kids."

"Is that what you're calling it?" I shot back, refusing to be intimidated. My heart raced, not from fear but from a rush of old emotions—betrayal, anger, and the remnants of the friendship we once shared. "This was no accident. Someone's trying to send a message."

She shrugged, feigning nonchalance. "Maybe you just don't belong in this town anymore, Daisy. You've always been too... colorful." Her gaze flickered to Jude, assessing, calculating, and I could almost see the gears turning in her head.

"What do you want, Miranda?" Jude interjected, his protective stance radiating a warmth that steadied me. "This isn't a game. People are getting hurt."

"Oh, darling," she cooed, her voice dripping with false sweetness, "I never play games. I simply enjoy watching others trip over their own feet."

A flash of something wild flickered behind her eyes, something dark and desperate. I felt a chill creep into my bones as I considered the lengths to which she might go to reclaim whatever she thought she'd lost.

"You think this is just about you? It's about all of us," I challenged, stepping closer to Jude, drawing strength from his presence. "You can't ruin our lives just because you're unhappy with yours."

"Unhappy?" She laughed, a sound that twisted my stomach in knots. "I'm thriving, darling. And you—" she pointed a manicured finger at me—"you're on the brink of disaster. It's poetic, really."

"Enough!" Jude's voice boomed, cutting through the tension like a knife. "We're not afraid of you, Miranda. We will find out who's behind this, and we'll make sure they pay for what they've done."

Miranda's smile faltered, and for a fleeting moment, I saw fear flicker in her eyes. But it was gone as quickly as it appeared, replaced by a mask of indifference. "Just remember, Daisy. You can't fight thorns without getting pricked."

With that, she turned on her heel and melted back into the shadows, leaving us standing amidst the wreckage, the weight of her words hanging heavily in the air.

As the wind picked up, rustling the trees, I glanced at Jude, whose jaw was set tight, eyes blazing with determination. "We can't let this go," I declared, adrenaline flooding my veins. "Not just for my shop, not just for your bakery. This is about taking a stand—together."

"Together," he echoed, and in that moment, a promise forged in fire and shared struggle sparked between us. The darkness loomed ahead, but as long as we faced it side by side, I felt an ember of hope igniting within me, illuminating a path through the chaos.

The morning after the confrontation with Miranda felt surreal, as if I had been plunged into a black-and-white film after a vibrant, technicolor dream. I awoke to the sound of raindrops drumming against my window, each drop echoing the turmoil in my heart. I pulled myself from the depths of a restless sleep, my mind replaying the events from the previous night. The remnants of our destroyed shop loomed large in my thoughts, and the sharp tang of anger mixed with the bitter taste of betrayal clung to my tongue.

With every fiber of my being, I wanted to fight back, to reclaim what was mine. I could already picture the soft pinks and yellows of my flowers, resplendent under the gentle touch of sunlight, blooming defiantly against the darkness. But right now, my sanctuary was a shadow of its former self, the shattered glass and ruined petals serving as painful reminders of the battle we were waging.

Jude's presence was a balm against the chaos swirling in my mind. He stood in my kitchen, brewing coffee, the rich aroma wafting through the air and wrapping around me like a warm embrace. The steam rising from the cup he held looked almost magical, dancing playfully in the air. I couldn't help but smile at the sight of him, that familiar warmth igniting a flicker of hope within me.

"Good morning, or should I say, what remains of it?" he teased, his eyes glimmering with that mix of mischief and sincerity that made my heart race.

I took the cup from him, my fingers brushing against his, sending a spark up my arm. "I didn't think I'd sleep at all after last night," I replied, cradling the warm mug against my chest. "But apparently, my exhaustion is stronger than my anger."

"Adrenaline can be quite the sedative," he quipped, leaning against the counter, the playful smirk never leaving his lips. "You should bottle that rage, though. I'd pay good money for a product that made me sleep as soundly."

"Just wait until I find the perfect blend of botanical goodness to infuse that anger into," I replied, my tone light but underscored with seriousness. "A little lavender to calm you down after a rage-filled day sounds like a bestseller."

We shared a laugh, the tension of the night before fading slightly, but the urgency to act loomed heavy over us like storm clouds ready to burst. "What's the plan?" I asked, setting my coffee down. "We can't just sit around sipping coffee while Miranda and her merry band of misfits wreak havoc on our lives."

"True," Jude said, his expression sobering. "But we also don't want to charge in blindly. We need a strategy. The last thing we want is to give her the upper hand."

I nodded, considering his words. "You're right. So where do we start? We can check the security footage from the shop. Maybe there's something—someone—who stood out."

"Great idea." Jude's enthusiasm returned, his eyes brightening. "Let's go. I'm ready to play detective."

We gathered our things, and I felt a surge of purpose replace the remnants of despair that had threatened to engulf me. As we walked to my shop, the rain began to ease, and rays of sunlight broke through the clouds, casting a warm glow on the damp pavement. Nature seemed to mirror the transformation happening within me—light piercing through the darkness.

Upon arriving at the shop, we pushed through the door, greeted by the overwhelming scent of earth and blossoms. The wreckage was still stark, but the sight of Jude alongside me renewed my resolve. "We can fix this," I murmured, the determination wrapping around me like a shield.

We began sifting through the remnants of our business, looking for any signs that could point us toward our attacker. My heart sank with each broken stem I picked up, the memories of past arrangements flooding back. Flowers were my passion, my escape, and seeing them marred felt like a personal affront.

Jude knelt beside me, picking up a mangled rose. "You know, if anyone can bounce back from this, it's you," he said, his voice steady and sincere. "You have a gift for turning chaos into beauty."

"Thanks, Jude," I said, my heart swelling at his words. "I guess it's what I've always done. But right now, I need to focus on the chaos before I can get to the beauty."

After clearing a small space, I set up my laptop to check the security footage. The screen flickered to life, and I felt a swell of anticipation as I navigated to the previous night's recordings. Each second felt like an eternity, and I leaned closer, my eyes glued to the screen.

The grainy footage finally showed a figure creeping through the darkened streets, their movements furtive. My heart raced as I squinted at the screen, trying to make out any distinguishing features. Then, suddenly, they paused outside my shop, their silhouette eerily familiar. I shot a glance at Jude, who was equally engrossed, his brow furrowed in concentration.

"Wait, pause it," I commanded, my voice a mix of excitement and dread. As Jude clicked the button, the figure froze, the shadows hiding their face but revealing a distinctive tattoo peeking out from under their sleeve. My stomach dropped. "No way. It can't be...."

"Who is it?" Jude asked, his voice tense.

"Trent. He used to work at the bakery, remember?"

"Yeah, the guy with the attitude. What's he doing here?"

I couldn't shake the chill creeping down my spine. "I have no idea, but if he's involved..." My thoughts trailed off, the implications too unsettling to voice.

"Then we have to confront him," Jude said firmly, determination etching his features. "We can't let this slide. If he's behind the vandalism, it's only going to get worse."

"What if he's just a pawn in this?" I replied, a pang of hesitation coursing through me. "What if someone's manipulating him?"

"We won't know until we ask him." Jude's voice was steady, reassuring. "And if he is being manipulated, we'll figure it out together."

I inhaled deeply, steeling myself for the confrontation ahead. "Okay, let's find him. But we need to be careful. This could get messy."

With newfound purpose igniting within us, we set off into the streets, ready to unravel the tangled web that had ensnared our lives. The storm may have darkened our doorstep, but I felt a flicker of hope amidst the chaos. If we could confront our demons—both external and internal—perhaps we could reclaim our lives, one thorn at a time.

As we stepped into the damp embrace of the evening air, the streets of our small town felt eerily quiet, as if the world were holding its breath. The usual sounds—the laughter of children playing, the distant hum of traffic—were replaced by an unsettling silence. Jude walked beside me, his presence a steady anchor in the tide of uncertainty that threatened to pull me under. The remnants of last night's confrontation still lingered, wrapping around us like a heavy fog, each breath I took thick with anticipation.

"So, what's the plan for our visit to Trent?" Jude asked, glancing sideways at me, his brow slightly furrowed. "Are we going in guns blazing, or do you prefer a more diplomatic approach?"

"Given the circumstances, I'd say diplomacy has left the building," I replied, trying to keep my tone light despite the heaviness weighing on my heart. "But I'm not looking for a brawl, either. If we can find out what's going on without setting off any alarms, that would be ideal."

"I'm all for avoiding jail time," he said with a chuckle, but the tension in his eyes betrayed his bravado. "Let's just make sure we don't end up in over our heads."

As we walked, I replayed the scene from the security footage in my mind, the image of Trent lurking outside my shop etched into my memory. He had always been a loose cannon, someone who thrived on chaos, and the thought that he might be involved in this mess made my stomach churn. If he was the one stirring up trouble, what had pushed him to it?

The path led us through the heart of town, where flickering streetlamps cast long shadows, stretching across the pavement like the doubts swirling in my mind. The bakery, Jude's sanctuary, glimmered in the distance, a beacon of warmth amid the encroaching darkness.

"Do you think he's acting alone?" Jude mused as we approached the entrance to his bakery. "Or could there be someone else pulling the strings?"

"It's hard to say. If he's been cornered into something, it might be a lot bigger than we think. Maybe Miranda is behind this, trying to make his life miserable as well as mine. She does have a way of getting into people's heads."

"Great. So, we're tangled in a web of petty vengeance and unresolved grudges," Jude replied with a smirk, attempting to lighten the mood. "I didn't sign up for a soap opera."

"Neither did I," I laughed, but the seriousness of our situation hovered just beneath the surface of our banter. "Let's just keep our eyes open and be ready for anything."

The warm glow of Jude's bakery enveloped us as we stepped inside, the scent of freshly baked goods wafting toward us like an old friend. My heart ached with nostalgia, recalling countless afternoons spent sampling pastries and trading secrets.

"Hey, Jude! Daisy!" shouted Ella, Jude's feisty younger sister, from behind the counter. "You two look like you just walked off a crime scene."

"Maybe we did," Jude shot back with a grin, his playful tone diffusing some of the tension in the room. "We're about to do some amateur sleuthing."

Ella raised an eyebrow, intrigued. "Count me in. I could use a little adventure—this place is way too boring lately."

I shot a glance at Jude, who shrugged, a smile creeping across his lips. "All right, but it could get messy. Are you sure you're up for it?"

"Bring it on!" Ella said, pumping her fist in the air, and I couldn't help but admire her enthusiasm. If only I had her unyielding spirit.

We gathered at a table in the back, the air thick with anticipation as we shared our plan. I relayed the details of the security footage and Trent's possible involvement, watching as Ella's expression shifted from excitement to concern. "What if he's part of something bigger? What if he's in too deep?"

"That's what we need to figure out," Jude replied, his voice steady. "We can't confront him blindly. Let's try to gather some intel first, see if we can find out what he's been up to lately."

Ella nodded, her eyes sparkling with mischief. "I can keep an ear out at school. You know how gossip travels faster than a speeding bullet. If Trent's up to something, someone's bound to know."

"Perfect," I said, grateful for her willingness to help. "And I'll reach out to a few contacts at the flower market. Maybe someone's seen him hanging around."

As the conversation flowed, I felt a sense of unity bloom between us, a fragile but potent bond forged in the heat of our shared struggles. Yet, underneath it all, a nagging doubt whispered in my ear—what if our efforts were futile? What if Trent was only the tip of the iceberg?

With our plan set, I took a deep breath, steeling myself for the confrontation that lay ahead. "Let's do this," I said, the determination surging within me. "No more running away from our problems."

The next morning arrived cloaked in a thick layer of gray clouds, a storm brewing on the horizon. I couldn't shake the feeling that we were hurtling toward something inevitable, a reckoning that would demand a price. The air crackled with anticipation as I opened the shop, the familiar jingle of the bell above the door echoing in the stillness.

I began tidying up, rearranging the surviving blooms as the morning passed in a blur of anxious energy. Each petal I touched reminded me of the battle we were fighting, not just against Miranda and Trent, but against the shadows that threatened to engulf us.

Around midday, I decided to take a break and check in with Jude. The bakery was bustling with customers, the warm aroma of baked bread filling the air. I found him behind the counter, flour dusting his shirt as he expertly worked dough, his hands moving with practiced ease.

"Hey, how's it going?" I asked, leaning against the counter.

"Busy, but good. Ella's been spying like a pro, gathering intel like she's some sort of undercover agent," he chuckled, and the warmth in his eyes made my heart flutter.

"Good to hear. Any updates on Trent?"

"Not yet, but I have a feeling something's brewing. We might not have to wait long to find out."

Just then, the bell above the door chimed again, and my heart sank as I turned to see a figure standing in the entrance, silhouetted by the sunlight streaming in. The moment I laid eyes on him, recognition struck me like a bolt of lightning.

"Trent," I breathed, the name slipping from my lips as the air around us grew heavy with tension. He stepped forward, a look of defiance etched on his face, and I felt my pulse quicken.

"What do you want?" Jude's voice was low, protective, as he stepped slightly in front of me, ready to shield me from whatever Trent had planned.

"Just wanted to chat," Trent replied, the corners of his mouth curling into a smile that felt more like a threat than an invitation. "I hear you've been asking questions. Figured it was time for some answers."

Before I could respond, a sudden crash echoed from the back of the bakery, followed by Ella's voice, shrill with panic. "Help! Someone's here!"

The world tilted on its axis as adrenaline surged through me. I exchanged a look with Jude, and in that split second, we understood: we were standing on the edge of chaos, teetering between confronting our past and defending our future. As we rushed toward the source of the commotion, the shadows lengthened behind us, a promise of danger lurking just out of sight, waiting to engulf us whole.

Chapter 19: In Bloom

The scent of lavender and rosemary drifted through the air, wrapping around us like a gentle embrace. The garden behind my shop was a riot of colors, where daisies and marigolds fought for attention amidst the climbing ivy that tangled with the wrought-iron fence. It was my sanctuary, a vibrant oasis where I had poured my heart and soul, planting each seed with hope, nurturing each sprout with care. And now, it seemed, this space had become a refuge for something far more complicated than the flora flourishing around us.

Jude sat across from me on the weathered wooden bench, a crooked smile lighting up his face as he playfully recounted the mishaps of our recent adventure. "You know, if I didn't know any better, I'd say you're the worst getaway driver this side of the Mississippi," he teased, his eyes sparkling with mischief. I couldn't help but chuckle, the sound bubbling up from deep within me, breaking the remnants of tension that had hung between us like storm clouds ready to unleash their fury.

"Excuse me," I replied, raising an eyebrow, "I was merely testing the limits of our escape route. A trial run, if you will. You can't blame me for wanting to keep things... exciting." I leaned back, feigning nonchalance, but my heart raced at the way he looked at me—his gaze steady, unyielding, as if he were trying to uncover secrets buried beneath the layers I had so carefully constructed.

The sun hung low in the sky, casting long shadows that danced playfully on the grass. It felt as though time had paused, allowing us to exist in this fleeting moment. The warm glow illuminated the features of Jude's face, highlighting the faint dusting of freckles across his nose and the way his dark hair tousled in the breeze. I had always admired the intensity in his gaze, the way it shifted from playful to contemplative in a heartbeat, but today, it felt charged with an energy I hadn't anticipated.

"What do you think we'll find next?" he mused, a hint of challenge in his tone. The question was innocent enough, but beneath it lay the unspoken acknowledgment of our shared predicament—the troubles we had stumbled into, the dangers lurking just beyond our garden's borders. I could see it flicker in his expression, the tension that still coiled within him, ready to strike at a moment's notice.

"I don't know," I admitted, my voice dropping to a whisper as I absently twisted a strand of ivy around my finger. "But I'm beginning to think we might be in over our heads. This isn't just some little mystery we can solve over a cup of tea."

He shifted closer, his arm brushing against mine, sending a jolt of awareness racing through me. "Maybe that's what makes it interesting," he said, his voice low and conspiratorial. "What's life without a little danger?"

My pulse quickened, and for a moment, I forgot the weight of our circumstances, the perilous situations we had faced. Instead, I found myself lost in the moment, in the way our shoulders aligned and the warmth radiating between us, a delicate tension that felt electric. I had never considered myself the type to succumb to such desires, yet here I was, craving more than just companionship; I wanted connection, a bridge between our tumultuous experiences and the uncharted territory of our emotions.

"Dangerous, indeed," I replied, my voice barely above a murmur. "But are you sure you're ready for what lies ahead? There's no turning back from here." I looked into his eyes, searching for any hint of hesitation, but all I found was a fierce determination that left me breathless.

"I've faced worse," he said with a confident grin, though I sensed a hint of vulnerability beneath his bravado. "And besides, I have you by my side. What could possibly go wrong?"

His playful tone made me smile, yet I couldn't shake the sense of foreboding that crept in at the edges of my thoughts. This was more than a partnership; this was an intertwining of our lives, our fates. I wanted to believe in the promise of our alliance, to think that together we could overcome any obstacle that dared to stand in our way. But shadows of doubt loomed large, casting a veil over the brightness of our connection.

As if sensing my unease, Jude turned serious, his expression softening. "Whatever it is, we'll face it together. I promise." There was sincerity in his voice that wrapped around my heart like a warm blanket, and I felt myself leaning into his words, allowing myself to believe, if only for a moment.

"I appreciate that," I said, my voice steadying. "But let's not forget the chaos we've just escaped. It's only a matter of time before it catches up with us."

Jude reached for my hand, intertwining our fingers in a gesture that felt both grounding and exhilarating. His touch sent a cascade of warmth coursing through me, a reminder that I wasn't alone in this—there was strength in our bond, a shared resolve that could weather any storm. The air around us thickened, charged with unspoken words and the possibility of what lay ahead.

"Then let's make the most of it," he said, a challenge in his tone that ignited something deep within me. "Let's bloom in the chaos."

His words hung in the air, a promise, a vow that wrapped around us like the vines in my garden. I felt the pulse of our connection—the thrill of adventure, the weight of uncertainty, and the intoxicating allure of what was to come. In that moment, I knew we were on the precipice of something profound, something that could change everything. I took a deep breath, ready to embrace whatever twisted paths awaited us, feeling the seeds of hope and desire taking root in the fertile ground of our shared experiences.

The fragrance of fresh earth mingled with the sweet notes of blooming flowers, crafting an olfactory symphony that made my heart swell. We were cocooned in a world vibrant with life, a sanctuary where the outside chaos felt distant, almost unreal. I shifted slightly on the bench, trying to find a comfortable position while simultaneously fighting the urge to lean closer to Jude. The sunlight painted him in warm hues, enhancing the contours of his face, and for a moment, I lost myself in the simple beauty of his presence.

"Do you ever wonder what it would be like to run away?" he asked suddenly, his voice soft yet teasing, as if he were inviting me into a secret world only the two of us could inhabit. "Like, just pack up and leave all of this behind?" He gestured vaguely to the shop and the garden, a hint of longing in his eyes.

I chuckled, shaking my head. "And go where? I mean, sure, I'd love to escape the daily grind, but I can't just abandon my plants. They rely on me for nourishment." I pretended to shudder dramatically. "What kind of monster would leave their beloved geraniums to wither in neglect?"

"Right, you wouldn't want to be known as the 'Geranium Killer' of Maplewood." He leaned back, hands clasped behind his head, his expression one of mock seriousness. "Imagine the scandal! A charming shop owner with a green thumb turned ruthless plant assassin."

I laughed, a genuine sound that bounced off the flowers and danced in the air. "I'd be the talk of the town! People would whisper about me at the grocery store, shaking their heads, clutching their organic vegetables as if I were some sort of monster."

His laughter melded with mine, and I could see the tension from our previous encounters dissolve like morning mist under the sun's warmth. In that moment, I realized that this connection was deeper than I had allowed myself to acknowledge. The light banter felt like a safe harbor, shielding us from the storms that loomed beyond our idyllic garden.

"Alright, maybe I won't become a fugitive just yet," he said, his tone shifting from playful to contemplative. "But what if we did find a place where we could be free? Somewhere we could discover new things without worrying about the mess we left behind?"

The question hung in the air like the last note of a beautiful song, and I felt the familiar tug of adventure at my heart. "What if we found an abandoned farmhouse?" I mused, my imagination igniting. "We could restore it, plant a garden together. Imagine waking up to fresh herbs and flowers. No gossip, no chaos—just the two of us and the wind rustling through the trees."

His eyes sparkled with mischief. "And maybe a few goats? I hear they make excellent companions, especially for garden guardians."

"Goats?" I laughed, the idea absurd yet strangely appealing. "I don't think my customers would appreciate their presence. Can you imagine trying to sell lavender with a goat nibbling on it?"

"Market trend: Organic Goat Grazing. Just think of the hipster clientele we'd attract! 'Buy our artisanal lavender, lovingly tended by a team of goats.' It would be a hit!" He was infectious, his enthusiasm bubbling over, and I found myself swept up in his daydream, a part of something larger than myself.

The laughter faded, leaving a comfortable silence punctuated only by the distant sounds of the town—children playing, the soft whirr of bicycles, and the occasional bark of a dog. It was idyllic, but beneath the surface, a current of unspoken thoughts lingered, and I could feel it threading its way between us.

"What's really going on, Jude?" I asked gently, my voice barely above a whisper. I needed to break through the jovial facade we had crafted, to peel back the layers and confront the truth lurking in the shadows.

He hesitated, the light in his eyes dimming as the laughter slipped away. "It's just... there are things happening that I can't control. I keep telling myself that it's fine, that we'll figure it out, but every time I close my eyes, I see what's out there, lurking."

A shiver ran down my spine, the remnants of our earlier chaos creeping back in. "The people we've encountered?" I ventured, searching his gaze for reassurance.

"Yeah. They're not going to forget what we did, and they won't just let it go." His words felt like a weight pressing down on us, and I could see the flicker of worry etching deeper lines into his brow.

"Then we need to be smart about this," I said, my voice firm as I leaned closer, gripping his hand tighter, willing him to see that we were in this together. "We need to plan. No more running blind into danger."

He nodded slowly, a reluctant acceptance clouding his features. "You're right. But planning means we have to think ahead, and I'm not sure I want to know how far ahead we might have to go."

His honesty resonated within me, igniting the same fear I had been pushing aside. "We can't let fear dictate our choices, Jude. We've come this far—there has to be a way to navigate through the chaos without losing ourselves in the process."

"Easy for you to say," he replied, a smirk creeping back onto his lips, though it lacked the usual spark. "You're the one with the green thumb. I'm just the guy who makes impulsive decisions."

"True," I said, a playful glint in my eyes as I tilted my head. "But sometimes, those impulsive decisions lead to the most unexpected adventures. Isn't that how we found ourselves here?"

He chuckled, a softer sound this time, and I felt the distance between us begin to close again. "Okay, fair point. But let's not end up on the front page of some tabloid for our next 'adventure.'"

"Deal," I said, my heart racing not only from the thrill of our conversation but from the very real connection forming between us. "We'll be smart. We'll plan. And maybe, just maybe, we can turn our chaotic encounters into stories worth telling."

As the sun dipped lower in the sky, casting a golden hue over the garden, I felt a sense of purpose igniting within me. In this moment of vulnerability, we stood at the precipice of something profound—an alliance forged not just in the heat of chaos but also in the steady warmth of understanding. Together, we could navigate whatever lay ahead, and with each passing moment, our bond blossomed into something beautifully resilient.

The sun dipped lower, casting an amber glow that bathed the garden in warmth, as if the very atmosphere conspired to keep us cocooned in this moment. My heart fluttered, caught in a delicate dance between the thrill of companionship and the looming shadows of the world beyond our sanctuary. Jude's laughter still lingered in the air, mingling with the scent of rosemary and the crisp bite of autumn that hinted at the change of seasons.

"You know," he began, his voice taking on a conspiratorial tone, "if we ever do run away to that farmhouse, I'd totally let you take the lead on the gardening. I can't even keep a cactus alive without overwatering it."

I feigned shock, placing a hand on my chest. "You, Mr. Adventurer, can't handle a cactus? This is a serious matter, Jude. Cacti are practically the definition of low maintenance."

"Low maintenance, yes, but that doesn't mean I won't create a drought in the process," he shot back, grinning widely. There was something comforting in our banter, a rhythm we had stumbled into as easily as two people breathing.

I tilted my head, gazing at him. "Okay, but let's talk about what it would really be like to live off the grid. What if I get attacked by a swarm of bees while trying to cultivate a bee-friendly garden? Do you have a plan for that?"

He chuckled, and I marveled at how effortlessly he kept my anxiety at bay. "I mean, I'd probably just throw you a can of honey and hope for the best. It's good for everything, right?"

"Right, because nothing says 'I care' quite like a can of honey." I laughed, but beneath the playful façade, an ember of worry smoldered. The unpredictability of our lives felt all too real, creeping in like the chill of evening air.

As the last of the sunlight faded, leaving a tapestry of stars to twinkle overhead, a chill crept into the garden, mingling with the warmth that had enveloped us. The shift was subtle but palpable, a reminder that our sanctuary was bordered by a world that thrummed with danger and uncertainty.

"What if we took some time to plan?" I suggested, a newfound seriousness threading through my tone. "You know, actually sit down and figure out what our next steps should be. There's a lot at stake, and we can't ignore that."

He nodded, the smile fading slightly from his lips. "You're right. We can't just play it by ear forever." His gaze drifted to the edge of the garden, where shadows danced like specters, and for a moment, I could see the weight of worry settle on his shoulders.

"Let's make a list," I said, leaning forward with renewed determination. "What do we know? Who's involved? What's our next move?"

Jude raised an eyebrow, amusement flickering back into his eyes. "You're really getting into this, aren't you? I can picture you with a clipboard, ready to take names and kick some serious ass."

"Clipboard?" I snorted. "Please, I'd go for a dry-erase board. Much more efficient. And yes, if we have to kick some ass, I want to make sure we do it right."

"Efficient and sassy. I think I'm falling for you, you know." The words slipped out so smoothly that I didn't have time to brace myself for the impact.

"Careful, Jude," I replied, my voice teasing but edged with genuine surprise. "I'm not sure I come with a warranty."

He laughed, but there was something softer in his gaze now, a depth that hinted at uncharted territory. "Maybe I'm willing to risk it," he said quietly, the air around us thickening with something electric.

Before I could respond, the sudden sound of shattering glass shattered the moment. It echoed from the direction of my shop, sharp and jarring, cutting through our cocoon like a knife. The tranquil night transformed instantly, a dark cloud cloaking the stars as adrenaline surged through my veins.

"What was that?" Jude's voice was tense, his playful demeanor vanishing as he shot to his feet.

"I don't know, but it didn't sound good." I followed suit, the warmth of our shared moment quickly evaporating. The shop stood like a fortress against the night, but even its sturdy walls felt vulnerable in the face of the unknown.

We moved towards the sound, my heart racing, each thud echoing in my chest. The garden's shadows shifted ominously as we approached the back entrance, and the familiar scents of earth and flora morphed into something more foreboding.

Jude reached for the door, but I held him back. "Wait. Let's not rush in blindly."

He hesitated, and for a heartbeat, I could see the conflicting thoughts racing through his mind—bravery clashing with caution. "You're right. But we can't just stand here."

"Let me check first," I suggested, summoning a resolve I didn't quite feel. I couldn't let fear paralyze us, not when something dark lurked just beyond the threshold.

Jude's eyes flickered with concern, but he nodded. "Okay, but I'm right behind you."

I took a deep breath, pushing the door open slowly, the creak of the hinges slicing through the silence. Inside, the dim light from the streetlamps outside barely illuminated the chaos. The shattered glass glimmered like shards of ice across the floor, casting an eerie glow that made my skin prickle.

"Hello?" I called out, my voice shaky, uncertain.

Silence answered, thick and suffocating, wrapping around us like a blanket of dread. Then, from the shadows, a low voice broke the stillness. "You really shouldn't have come back here."

The words hung in the air like a threat, chilling me to the bone. I squinted into the darkness, but I couldn't make out the figure looming just beyond the edge of the light. Jude's hand found mine, grounding me, a steady pulse of warmth in the cold reality of our situation.

"Who are you?" I demanded, my voice stronger than I felt.

The figure stepped forward, revealing a face twisted in a sardonic smile. "You've been meddling where you don't belong, my dear. And now, it's time to pay the price."

Jude's grip tightened on my hand as the tension between us crackled, a spark igniting a fire that would burn through the night, one we were powerless to extinguish. The weight of the moment pressed down on us, leaving us teetering on the precipice of danger, with no way to turn back.

Chapter 20: Secrets of the Heart

I could hardly believe my eyes as I stepped into Jude's shop, the familiar scent of fresh blooms and earthy soil a sharp contrast to the unease curling in my stomach. The sun poured in through the glass front, illuminating the delicate petals of hydrangeas and daisies, their colors vibrant and cheerful. But today, the warmth felt misleading, a veil over the cold truth that was about to unravel.

Jude had become a constant in my life—a presence so comforting that I often forgot to question it. His laughter had grown more familiar than the tick of the clock on the wall, and the way he tucked his hair behind his ear made my heart flutter. Yet, here in this sanctuary of flowers, the sweetness of my feelings was crushed by the weight of betrayal that clung to the air like a storm cloud.

I approached the counter, where the register sat innocently beside a bouquet of sunflowers, as if the world were still untouched by my doubts. But there, partially hidden beneath a stack of invoices, lay a tattered envelope marked with the logo of our rival florist, Blossom & Bloom. My heart raced, and I felt a rush of adrenaline as I snatched it up, my pulse pounding in my ears. The evidence was clear—a partnership that Jude had kept hidden from me. He had known more about their shady dealings than he had led me to believe, and the realization twisted like a knife in my gut.

"Jude!" My voice echoed through the shop, sharp and accusatory. He emerged from the back, a pair of scissors still in hand, his expression shifting from surprise to concern as he caught sight of the envelope crumpled in my fist.

"What's wrong?" he asked, his brow furrowing, the warm light catching the concern etched on his features.

"Is this what you call honesty?" I held the envelope up, shaking it as if the sheer force of my anger could make him see the gravity of what he'd done. "I thought we were building something real. I thought I could trust you."

His face paled, and for a moment, he seemed at a loss for words. "What are you talking about?"

"Don't play coy with me," I shot back, my voice rising with the frustration simmering beneath my skin. "You've been lying. You knew all along about Blossom & Bloom's tactics. Did you think I wouldn't find out?"

"Wait—" he began, but I cut him off, the fury and hurt bubbling over.

"I thought we were partners, Jude. I thought you were on my side. But this? This feels like a betrayal."

His gaze dropped to the envelope, and I could see the conflict etched in the lines of his face. "You don't understand—"

"No, I don't understand!" I interrupted, feeling my heart race in sync with my anger. "I thought I knew you. I thought we shared something more than just flowers and shop talk. You made me feel like I mattered, like I was more than just the competition."

As the silence stretched between us, the weight of my words hung heavy in the air. My heart thudded against my ribs, both yearning for his understanding and aching from the thought of losing him. I had given him a piece of myself, and now it felt like he was shattering it into a million tiny shards.

"Please, just let me explain," Jude pleaded, his voice softening as he stepped closer. The vulnerability in his eyes flickered like candlelight in a storm, and I fought against the pull of his gaze, desperate to hold on to my anger. "You have to know that I didn't mean for you to find out this way. I was trying to protect you—"

"Protect me?" I echoed, incredulous. "By keeping secrets from me?"

"By keeping you safe from the fallout. I didn't want you to get hurt if things went south," he said, his hands gesturing wildly as he tried to communicate the chaos swirling in his mind.

But his words only stoked the flames of my rage. "So, you thought lying was the answer? I would have preferred the truth, even if it hurt."

"I didn't want to jeopardize what we had," he said, desperation creeping into his voice. "You mean so much to me. I was afraid if you knew everything, you'd walk away."

"Guess what? You've already given me a reason to do just that," I shot back, my voice barely masking the pain.

The air between us crackled with unresolved tension, both of us standing on the precipice of something monumental. The familiar warmth of the shop felt foreign now, the petals and greens taking on a shadowy hue. I wanted to scream, to run, to hide away from the confusion swirling in my heart. But the truth was that beneath my fury, I felt a deeper anguish—the fear of losing the connection we had forged.

"I never wanted to hurt you," he whispered, his voice barely above a murmur. "You have to believe me."

"Believe you?" I scoffed, my heart pounding in protest against the pain. "You've just shattered that trust with your secrets. How can I believe anything you say now?"

As I stepped back, creating distance between us, Jude's expression morphed from anguish to pleading. "I'll do anything to fix this. Just give me a chance to explain."

I felt my resolve wavering, the ache in my chest threatening to burst through the walls I had built around it. It was a dangerous game we were playing—one where the stakes were our hearts, and the risks were too great to ignore. The remnants of our tenderness lay scattered around us like broken petals on the shop floor, and as

I grappled with the choices before me, the choice between love and self-preservation loomed large.

Jude stood before me, a mixture of regret and desperation flooding his features, yet all I could focus on was the growing chasm between us. The familiar scents of the shop—the heady aroma of lavender mingling with the sweetness of peonies—suddenly felt suffocating, as if the very air had turned heavy with betrayal. I tried to read the depth of his intentions through the hazel depths of his eyes, but all I saw was a man caught in the whirlwind of his own mistakes.

"I need time," I managed to say, my voice trembling with the effort to remain steady. I turned my back to him, wanting to escape the vulnerability that left me exposed. The bell above the door jingled, a whimsical sound that seemed incongruous with the turmoil brewing in my heart. As I stepped outside, the fresh air slapped me awake, a stark reminder that the world continued to turn while my life felt frozen in chaos.

The sun hung low in the sky, casting long shadows that danced along the pavement, mirroring the conflict within me. I could hear the laughter of children playing in the park across the street, their joy a stark contrast to the knot tightening in my chest. With every step away from the shop, I felt the weight of my emotions ebb and flow like the tide, leaving me adrift in a sea of confusion.

"What's going on?" My best friend, Marcy, materialized beside me, her brow furrowed with concern. She had a knack for sensing when something was off, like a bloodhound tracking a scent. Her curly hair bounced with each determined stride as she matched my pace. "You look like you've seen a ghost."

"More like I've uncovered a skeleton in the closet," I replied, frustration lacing my tone. Marcy's inquisitive eyes bored into me, urging me to elaborate. "It's Jude. He—he's been hiding things. Important things."

Marcy's expression shifted from concern to intrigue, her attention fully captured. "What kind of things? You know he's not the best at sharing, but I didn't think he was that bad."

"He's been in cahoots with Blossom & Bloom," I spat out, the name rolling off my tongue like venom. "I found evidence. He knew more about their shady business than he ever let on."

Marcy paused mid-stride, a mixture of shock and sympathy flaring across her features. "Oh no, that's...that's a problem. Are you sure? I mean, Jude wouldn't do that, right?"

"Wouldn't he?" I snapped, a hint of bitterness creeping into my words. "He had the chance to come clean, to be honest with me, and instead, he chose to keep it hidden. It feels like I was just a pawn in his game."

Marcy reached out, squeezing my arm gently. "What are you going to do? This isn't just about flowers; this is about trust. Do you think you can move past this?"

I shook my head, the weight of her question hanging heavily in the air. "I don't know. I thought we had something real. Something worth fighting for. But now... it feels like every sweet moment we shared was just a façade."

"Have you talked to him since?" she prodded, her voice softening.

"Not since the blow-up," I admitted, the guilt gnawing at my insides. "I just... needed space. To think."

"Space is good," she nodded. "But don't let it become a chasm you can't cross back over. If he means something to you, it might be worth giving him a chance to explain."

Her words wrapped around me, a gentle reminder of the complexity of relationships. Marcy had always been the voice of reason, the calm amidst the storm. But how could I listen to that voice when every instinct told me to run? As we walked toward a nearby café, the sun began to dip below the horizon, painting the sky with strokes of orange and purple. It felt poetic and cruel, a reminder of the beauty that existed even when my heart felt shattered.

Inside the café, the chatter of patrons filled the air, a comforting buzz that momentarily distracted me from my inner turmoil. I settled into a corner booth, the vinyl seats slightly sticky but familiar, like an old friend. Marcy ordered us coffee while I stared out the window, watching the shadows lengthen.

"What's the plan?" she asked when she returned, her coffee steaming between us. "Are you going to talk to him? Clear the air?"

I sighed, swirling the coffee in my cup. "I don't even know what to say. Part of me wants to confront him, demand answers. But another part of me wants to hide away until this all blows over. I'm tired of feeling this way, Marcy."

"Then don't let it linger," she advised, her eyes locking onto mine with a fierce determination. "You owe it to yourself—and to him—to at least have the conversation. If it's not worth saving, then you can walk away knowing you tried."

Her unwavering support wrapped around me like a warm blanket, but I felt the cold tendrils of fear creeping in, whispering doubts into my ear. What if I was wrong? What if Jude had his reasons, even if they were flawed? But in the end, I realized that staying silent would only prolong my suffering.

The following morning, I found myself pacing outside Jude's shop, the vibrant flowers inside calling to me like sirens. The bell above the door rang out as I stepped inside, the familiar ambiance a mix of warmth and tension. Jude was at the counter, his back to me as he arranged a bouquet of daisies, but I could sense the energy shift the moment I entered.

"Hey," I said, my voice surprisingly steady. He turned, his expression shifting from surprise to an unreadable emotion that made my heart race.

"Hey," he replied, his voice low and hesitant, as if he was testing the waters.

"Can we talk?" I asked, trying to keep my tone neutral.

"Of course," he said, wiping his hands on his apron before stepping closer. "I've been waiting for you to come back."

"Waiting or hoping?" I shot back, unable to suppress the edge in my tone.

"Maybe a little of both," he admitted, his eyes searching mine for a flicker of understanding.

As we stood there, the air thick with anticipation, I realized that this was a moment fraught with possibility. With each heartbeat, I could feel the weight of our shared history and the future we both desired, tangled together like the vines climbing the walls of the shop. I took a deep breath, steeling myself for the conversation that would determine the course of our lives.

The silence between us hung like a thick fog, heavy with unsaid words and palpable tension. Jude stood there, his expression a mixture of hope and apprehension, and I was struck by the familiar warmth of his presence battling against the icy betrayal I felt. The shop felt smaller, the blooms around us seeming to lean in, eavesdropping on a conversation that threatened to unravel everything we had built together.

"Look, I know you're angry," he began, his voice steady but tinged with urgency. "But I never meant to keep anything from you. I just—"

"You just what?" I interrupted, frustration bubbling over. "Thought I wouldn't care? Thought I wouldn't notice? It feels like you've been playing a part, and I was the audience clapping for a performance that was all smoke and mirrors."

His shoulders slumped slightly, the fight leaving him for a moment. "You have to believe me. I was trying to protect you.

Blossom & Bloom isn't just another competitor; they're ruthless. I didn't want you to get caught in their crosshairs."

"By keeping me in the dark? By pretending everything was fine?" I shot back, my voice rising. The hurt was morphing into anger, and with it came a surprising clarity. I didn't want to feel this way, but the truth was slapping me in the face like a frigid wind. "You think I'm too delicate to handle the truth?"

"Not at all!" He stepped closer, desperation written all over his features. "But I know how much this business means to you. I didn't want you to worry about things beyond your control. I wanted you to focus on the flowers, on us."

"Us?" The word left my mouth like a dare. "What us? The 'us' that you've kept hidden behind your carefully crafted lies?"

His gaze dropped, and I could see the weight of my words settling in. "I thought if I could keep you safe from this, we could focus on what really mattered. I didn't want to ruin what we had."

"By ruining everything?" I felt the air grow thick again, but this time with an uncertain energy. "And what exactly do we have, Jude? Was it ever real?"

"It was real to me," he said, his voice softening, eyes lifting to mine again, revealing a flicker of vulnerability that made my heart ache. "Every laugh, every moment, it was all real. But I was scared—scared of what could happen if you knew the truth."

"Scared of what?" I pressed, my heart racing. "That I would walk away? That I would hate you?"

"Maybe I'm scared of you seeing me as the villain," he admitted, rubbing the back of his neck, a telltale sign of his discomfort. "I never wanted to be the bad guy in your story."

"Then stop being one," I said, the fire in me dimming slightly as I searched his eyes. "Just be honest. Tell me what's going on."

He took a deep breath, and for a moment, the world around us faded. The flowers, the sunlight filtering through the windows, and even the clock ticking softly in the background seemed to vanish, leaving only the two of us suspended in this moment of truth. "There's a lot more at stake than just our rivalry, and I can't tell you everything right now. But if you'd just trust me—"

"Trust you?" I echoed incredulously, the bitterness rising in my throat. "That's a tall order after everything that's happened. What have you been hiding, Jude?"

"Okay, let me explain," he said, urgency coloring his tone. "Blossom & Bloom is planning something big, something that could hurt not just us, but everyone in this community. I was trying to figure out how to stop them without dragging you into it."

"By dragging me out of the loop instead?" I retorted, crossing my arms. "What makes you think I wouldn't want to help? This is my shop too, Jude. My dreams."

He stepped forward, desperation etched into his features. "I know that! I'm not trying to undermine you. I just thought—"

"Thought what? That I'd play along like a puppet on a string?" My voice quivered, frustration spilling over as I paced the small space between us.

"Please," he implored, his eyes earnest. "Just give me a chance to explain everything. Let me prove I'm not the enemy here."

I hesitated, the weight of his plea crashing over me. A part of me wanted to hear him out, to unravel the mystery that lay between us, while another part screamed at me to walk away before I could get hurt further. The conflict twisted in my gut, a gnawing reminder of how fragile trust could be.

"Fine," I finally said, the words tasting bittersweet on my tongue. "But you need to be completely honest with me. No more secrets. If this is going to work, it has to be all or nothing."

He nodded, relief washing over his features. "Thank you. I promise I'll share everything."

But just as we reached a tenuous understanding, the bell above the door jingled again, interrupting our moment. My heart sank as I turned to see a figure stepping inside, silhouetted against the bright sunlight. The newcomer looked familiar, but as the light shifted, I recognized him immediately. It was Evan, the owner of Blossom & Bloom, his smile wide and predatory.

"Jude!" he called out, the glee in his voice masking something darker. "Fancy seeing you here. And with a friend, no less." His gaze flicked to me, a knowing smirk creeping onto his lips.

"Evan," Jude said, tension pouring back into the room like a dark cloud. "What do you want?"

"Oh, just checking in on the competition." Evan's tone dripped with sarcasm, but his eyes glinted with malice. "You know how it is. Can't let you two have all the fun."

I could feel the air grow thick again, the silence stretching taut as we exchanged uncertain glances. The atmosphere crackled with danger, and I sensed the precariousness of the moment. Evan stepped further inside, the shadows lengthening around him, and I wondered if my fragile hope was about to be crushed underfoot.

"Just thought I'd drop by to remind you that the game is far from over," Evan continued, his words slithering through the air like a snake ready to strike. "You'd be surprised at what I've learned. Secrets have a way of unraveling, you know."

Jude's jaw tightened, and I could see the anger flashing behind his eyes. "Get out, Evan. This isn't your place."

"Oh, but it is now," Evan retorted, his grin widening. "You see, I've got plans, and you're all tangled up in them. Just thought I'd give you both a little heads-up before the storm hits."

"What storm?" I asked, feeling my stomach drop at the ominous tone in his voice.

Evan shrugged, his nonchalance chilling. "Let's just say that things are about to get very interesting in this little flower war of ours. You may want to hold on tight."

With that, he turned on his heel and sauntered out of the shop, the bell jingling mockingly in his wake. I stood there, my heart racing, the tension coiling tighter in my chest as Jude and I exchanged wide-eyed glances. The realization hit me like a freight train: the stakes had just escalated dramatically, and the secrets we thought we could handle were now spiraling out of control.

"Jude," I breathed, the words barely escaping my lips. "What did he mean?"

Before he could answer, my phone buzzed violently in my pocket. I fumbled to retrieve it, my heart pounding as I glanced at the screen. A new message blinked at me, and as I read the words, an icy dread washed over me, pulling me under like a rip tide.

"I know what you've been hiding. It's time for you to pay the price."

Chapter 21: A Fragile Alliance

The air crackled with an electric tension as Jude and I settled into the worn leather chairs of my office, the dim light casting a warm glow over our faces. Outside, the faint hum of the city blended with the rhythm of a late afternoon, but in here, it felt as though time had slowed, wrapping us in a cocoon of uncertainty. I couldn't shake the unease settling in my stomach, a reminder of the fragile alliance we were attempting to rebuild.

"Are we really doing this?" Jude's voice was low, tinged with disbelief as he leaned forward, fingers steepled together. His dark hair fell just so, framing his face, a mix of determination and vulnerability. The man was nothing if not infuriatingly handsome, even in moments of chaos, and I found myself wondering how we had let it come to this—two people, so caught in their own worlds, now thrust together by circumstance, each of us holding pieces of a puzzle that desperately needed solving.

"I don't see any other option," I replied, forcing my voice to remain steady. I gestured toward the documents spread across my desk, a chaotic mixture of spreadsheets and legal papers that chronicled our recent struggles. "If we don't confront this head-on, we risk losing everything. My company... my family's legacy... all of it is on the line."

He nodded, eyes flickering over the papers, absorbing the weight of what lay ahead. "Right. But we need to be smart about it. This rival isn't just some petty competitor. They're ruthless." He paused, letting the words linger in the air. "They'll come for us, and we have to be prepared."

A shiver ran down my spine at the thought, a reminder of the sleepless nights I had spent tossing and turning, haunted by the threats looming over our businesses. I had always prided myself on my independence, a fierce protector of what I had built, yet here I was, in need of a partner. It felt both exhilarating and terrifying.

"We'll gather our resources," I said, feeling the resolve harden within me. "We need to act swiftly and decisively. I have contacts who can help us dig deeper, find out exactly what they're planning." The words tumbled out with a newfound confidence, igniting a spark of hope.

Jude's expression softened slightly. "I'm glad you're willing to take this leap. I know it hasn't been easy for you to trust me again." He shifted in his seat, his gaze unwavering. "But I want you to know, I'm all in. I won't let you down this time."

I held his gaze, the gravity of his promise settling over us. There was a bond forming, one that was both fragile and resilient, stitched together by our shared determination to protect our dreams. "Let's make a plan," I said, my voice firmer now. "We'll meet with my contact tomorrow morning. After that, we can outline our next steps."

As we started to sketch out the details, the tension in the room began to dissipate, replaced by a flicker of excitement. We threw around ideas, strategies intertwining with moments of laughter that felt almost foreign but welcome. With each shared look, I felt the walls I had built around my heart begin to crack. Maybe this partnership could be more than just a means to an end; perhaps there was something worth exploring beneath the surface of our complicated history.

"Do you remember the first time we worked together?" Jude asked, a smile playing at the corners of his lips. "I thought we'd drive each other insane with all the back-and-forth."

I chuckled, the memory flooding back. "I remember you being infuriatingly stubborn, convinced your way was the only way."

He feigned offense, leaning back in his chair with an exaggerated gasp. "Stubborn? Me? Never!"

"Right," I retorted, crossing my arms playfully. "You practically wore it like a badge of honor."

The air between us shifted, laughter easing the tension, as if the shadows lurking outside had receded, leaving us momentarily safe in our little bubble. But I was acutely aware that this fragile alliance was precarious. Trust was an elusive thing, and while we had come a long way, I could feel my heart twinge with uncertainty. What if this all blew up in our faces? What if, once again, I was left standing alone, watching everything I cared about crumble?

"Okay, let's refocus," I said, steering us back to the task at hand. "We need to be strategic. We can't underestimate them, and we can't afford to be reckless."

Jude nodded, his expression turning serious once more. "We'll need to gather intel, find out their weaknesses. Every competitor has them, even the big players." He tapped his fingers on the desk, a sure sign that he was deep in thought. "We can use their arrogance against them."

I leaned forward, intrigued. "What do you have in mind?"

A smirk crept across his face, a spark of mischief igniting in his eyes. "I know someone who's been working inside their operation. If we can persuade them to share information..." His voice trailed off, the possibilities hanging in the air.

"Persuasion, huh?" I raised an eyebrow, a teasing smile breaking through my worry. "You mean charm them into spilling their secrets?"

"Or maybe we could just threaten them," he quipped, shrugging nonchalantly. "You know, nothing says 'trust me' like a little intimidation."

I laughed, a lightness blooming in my chest, momentarily forgetting the weight of our challenges. "I like your style, but let's keep it above board, shall we?"

As we dove back into the details of our plan, I felt the foundations of something new taking shape between us. Perhaps it was naive to think we could navigate this storm without losing ourselves, but the thrill of the chase, the prospect of fighting side by side with Jude, ignited a fire within me. It was more than business; it was about reclaiming control over our lives, our destinies.

The shadows outside flickered as night settled over the city, but inside, the spark between us glowed steadily, fueled by determination and an unspoken promise of something more. Together, we would face the darkness. Together, we would fight.

The following day dawned with an unusually bright sun filtering through the window, illuminating the chaos that had become my workspace. Papers lay strewn everywhere, each one a reminder of the stakes involved in our precarious alliance. I poured myself a strong cup of coffee, the rich aroma filling the air, hoping to drown out the underlying tension that clung to me like a heavy fog. Today was pivotal; we were set to meet with one of my contacts, a seasoned investigator named Claudia, who had a reputation for uncovering secrets buried deep beneath the surface.

As I gathered my notes, I couldn't shake the flutter of anxiety that had settled in my stomach. It felt like the calm before a storm, the kind of moment when you could almost hear the thunder rumbling in the distance, promising chaos. Jude arrived promptly at ten, looking sharp in a tailored suit that hugged him just right. He exuded confidence, but I could see the flicker of uncertainty in his eyes as he glanced around the room, absorbing the disarray.

"Nice place you've got here," he remarked, a teasing lilt in his voice. "Reminds me of my college dorm—minus the pizza boxes and questionable laundry."

I rolled my eyes, trying to suppress a smile. "Thanks. I like to think of it as organized chaos. It fuels my creativity." I shot him a knowing look. “Though I suspect you might prefer your meticulously arranged office.”

“Touché,” he replied, raising his coffee mug in a mock toast. “Here’s to chaos then, and may it lead us to victory.”

We shared a laugh that felt warm against the chill of our circumstances, but the moment quickly passed, replaced by the gravity of our task. With the time ticking away, I led the way to my car, the pavement beneath us warming under the growing sun.

The drive to Claudia’s office was filled with a comfortable silence, punctuated only by the occasional playful jab. It felt good to share this space with Jude again, even if the shadows of our past loomed nearby. The city whirled past us, vibrant and alive, a stark contrast to the brewing storm that loomed over our business dealings.

Claudia’s office was nestled between a bakery and a florist, the sweet scent of pastries mingling with the fragrance of blooming lilies. The moment we entered, I was greeted by the sight of Claudia hunched over her desk, thick glasses perched on her nose, pouring over a mountain of files. She looked up, her expression shifting from concentration to delight.

“Ah, the dynamic duo,” she said, her voice warm with familiarity. “I’ve been looking forward to this.”

“Hope we’re not interrupting anything too vital,” Jude replied, his tone light but his eyes scanning the room for clues of her ongoing work.

“Just the usual sleuthing,” Claudia shrugged, waving her hand dismissively. “Now, let’s get down to business. I hear you two are facing a rather slippery opponent.”

I exchanged a glance with Jude, the unspoken understanding between us echoing the tension in the air. “We need to know everything you can dig up about Harrington & Co.,” I said, diving into the specifics. “They’ve been pulling some shady moves, and we suspect they’ve got plans to undermine us.”

Claudia nodded, her fingers already flying across her keyboard as she took down notes. "I'll run a full background check, pull any public records, and see what whispers are floating around in the industry. But you both need to be careful. Harrington & Co. isn't known for playing fair."

"Fair is the last thing on their minds," Jude interjected, a hint of frustration creeping into his voice. "We've got evidence of their underhanded tactics, but we need to be smart about how we use it."

"Good. I'll get to work on that," Claudia replied, her focus sharpening. "But you two need to stay one step ahead. And if it were me, I'd consider gathering intel on their personnel—everyone has something to hide."

A sly smile crept across my face as an idea took root in my mind. "What if we hosted a networking event? We could lure some of their key players under the guise of collaboration. It would be a perfect opportunity to gauge their intentions while keeping our own close to the vest."

Jude's eyes widened in realization. "That's brilliant! We could mask our real motives with a friendly facade. It would give us an edge and keep them guessing."

Claudia chuckled, shaking her head. "You two are something else. Just remember, if you're going to play the game, you better be ready for the consequences."

"Consequences have never stopped us before," I said, a fierce determination rising within me. "We've come too far to back down now."

With Claudia's promise to gather intel and our newfound plan simmering with potential, we left her office feeling energized, the weight of our burdens momentarily lifted. As we walked back to the car, I could feel a change in the air, a stirring of hope that we might actually have a fighting chance.

"By the way," Jude said, his tone shifting to something more serious. "I wanted to apologize for how I acted before. I know I pushed you away when things got tough, and that wasn't fair. I should have trusted you more."

I turned to him, surprised by the sincerity in his voice. "You were trying to protect yourself. I get it. Trust is a fragile thing, and we both have our scars."

His gaze held mine, deep and searching. "But we can't let those scars dictate our future. Not if we're going to make this work."

The vulnerability in his words struck a chord within me. I had been so focused on the past that I had neglected to consider the strength we could find in each other moving forward. "Agreed. We have a chance to redefine what this alliance means. To be stronger together."

As we reached the car, the air shimmered with the promise of what lay ahead. The sun hung high in the sky, casting a bright light on the path we were forging together. I felt a renewed sense of purpose settle in my chest, intertwining with the threads of hope and uncertainty. We were on the precipice of something that could change everything, and for the first time in a long while, I felt ready to embrace the chaos of it all.

The journey was far from over, but with Jude at my side, I could sense that perhaps this fragile alliance was just the beginning.

The following day felt like a carefully arranged stage, with every detail poised for our upcoming networking event. The venue, a chic rooftop bar with sweeping views of the city, sparkled under the twilight sky, as if the stars themselves had conspired to lend us their glow. String lights danced overhead, casting a soft, romantic hue that belied the tension rippling beneath the surface. I busied myself with last-minute preparations, ensuring everything was in place while keeping one eye on the clock, the seconds ticking away like a countdown to battle.

Jude arrived just as the sun dipped below the horizon, the air thickening with anticipation. He looked effortlessly dapper in a tailored blazer, his dark hair tousled just enough to appear casual yet purposeful. There was something about him tonight—an energy crackling in the air between us that hinted at the shifting dynamics of our relationship. As we stood in the midst of mingling guests, I could feel the electric charge, the potential for what lay ahead.

"Nice setup," he said, nodding toward the crowd, his voice low enough that only I could hear. "You really know how to throw a party."

I couldn't help but smile, feeling a rush of pride. "It's all part of the strategy. Keep them entertained, and they won't notice the real agenda lurking in the shadows."

He chuckled, a warm sound that cut through my nerves. "Ah yes, the ol' misdirection. I hope you're prepared for the gamesmanship that will ensue. This is Harrington & Co. we're dealing with."

"Gamesmanship? I thought we were here to build connections," I retorted playfully, adjusting my dress and stealing a glance at the crowd. "Maybe I should hand out participation trophies."

Jude raised an eyebrow, amusement dancing in his eyes. "Only if you want to insult their fragile egos. Better to let them think they're all winners tonight."

The laughter that bubbled between us was a welcome distraction, but I could feel the pressure mounting. I had invited a mix of industry professionals, competitors, and potential allies—all while keeping an eye out for the key players from Harrington & Co. The idea was to create a space where they would feel safe to speak, unaware of the watchful eyes and hidden motives surrounding them.

As the night wore on, the atmosphere grew livelier, the clinking of glasses blending with the soft murmur of conversation. I moved through the crowd, exchanging pleasantries and smiling graciously, all the while scanning for familiar faces. My heart raced as I caught sight of one of Harrington's senior executives, a tall, imposing figure with a reputation for being shrewd and calculating. His presence sent a chill racing up my spine, but I pushed the feeling aside.

"Here we go," Jude said quietly, his gaze sharp. "Time to put our plan into action."

"Remember, keep it casual," I reminded him, my voice low but firm. "We're here to observe, not provoke."

With that, we approached the executive, whose name I had heard whispered like a cautionary tale—Markus Hale. He had a way of making deals disappear as quickly as they appeared, and I could sense the challenge he posed.

"Markus! So good to see you!" I greeted, injecting a layer of enthusiasm into my tone that felt slightly forced. "I hope you're enjoying the evening."

He turned, a sly smile spreading across his face, his eyes narrowing as he appraised us. "Ah, if it isn't the formidable duo. How delightful. I must say, it takes guts to throw a party right in the lion's den."

"Is that what this is? A lion's den?" Jude replied, matching his intensity with a well-practiced charm. "I thought it was more of a social gathering."

"Let's not play coy, Jude," Markus said, his tone dripping with disdain. "We all know the stakes."

I could feel the tension crackling in the air as the conversation twisted like a serpent. It was a verbal sparring match, and the stakes were growing higher with every word. "It's all in good fun, isn't it?" I added, forcing a lightness I didn't quite feel. "A chance for everyone to connect and collaborate."

"Collaboration," Markus echoed, leaning closer, his breath tinged with the scent of expensive cologne. "Interesting choice of words. Tell me, how do you plan to collaborate when it's clear that you've already been undercut?"

Jude's jaw tightened, but before he could respond, I jumped in, desperate to redirect the conversation. "I believe there's enough room in this industry for all of us, don't you? Friendly competition can drive innovation."

"Ha!" Markus barked a laugh, shaking his head. "Innovation, indeed. Or perhaps it's simply a mask for desperation."

The air grew thick with unspoken challenges, but just as I was about to counter, a voice sliced through the tension.

"Markus! There you are!" A striking woman in a sleek black dress glided into the fray, her presence commanding and confident. She flashed a brilliant smile that did nothing to warm the air. "I've been looking for you everywhere. We have some urgent matters to discuss."

"Of course, Hannah," Markus said, his attention shifting away from us. "Excuse me, but duty calls." He shot us a parting glance, one that promised this was far from over.

As he turned, I felt a mix of relief and frustration. "Great. Just when I thought we were making progress," I muttered, taking a deep breath to steady my racing heart.

"Not all battles are won in one conversation," Jude replied, offering me a reassuring nod. "We've planted the seeds. Let's see how they grow."

I appreciated his optimism, though doubt flickered at the edges of my mind. As the evening progressed, we continued to mingle, gathering snippets of information, all while keeping a watchful eye on the Harrington contingent. But with each passing moment, a sense of foreboding settled in the pit of my stomach, a nagging feeling that we were not the only ones with a plan.

Suddenly, the lights dimmed, casting an enchanting glow over the rooftop. A hush fell over the crowd as the owner of the venue stepped up to the microphone, ready to make an announcement. I caught Jude's eye, his expression mirroring my own apprehension.

"Ladies and gentlemen," the owner began, "thank you for joining us tonight. As we celebrate connections, I'd like to introduce a special guest who has something significant to share regarding our industry's future."

Before I could process the implication of those words, a figure stepped into the spotlight—none other than the CEO of Harrington & Co. himself. My heart plummeted as I locked eyes with the man who had been a shadow looming over our every move.

"Tonight, I have an important announcement," he said, his voice smooth and confident, every word dripping with authority. "Harrington & Co. is about to embark on a groundbreaking venture that will change the game."

The crowd erupted into applause, but I could barely hear it over the pounding of my heart. Jude's fingers brushed against mine, a reminder that we were in this together, even as I felt the walls closing in around me.

"Game-changing, indeed," I murmured, my voice barely above a whisper. "And we've got to find a way to counter it before it's too late."

As the applause faded and the CEO launched into details of his ambitious plans, I couldn't shake the sense that we were standing on the brink of a precipice, with the ground crumbling beneath us. And then, as if the universe had conspired against us, the lights flickered ominously.

With a crack that echoed through the space, a sudden explosion of color lit up the night—fireworks bursting against the sky in a dazzling display, a distraction that drew everyone's attention away from the unfolding chaos. But amidst the lights, I noticed a figure slipping away from the gathering, eyes focused, intent.

"Jude," I whispered, urgency clawing at my insides. "We need to follow that person. They might lead us to something critical."

He nodded, his jaw set in determination. "Let's move."

We wove through the crowd, the noise of the festivities drowning out the unease that clung to us. Just as we reached the edge of the rooftop, the figure vanished down a narrow staircase, and without a second thought, we followed.

The world above was suddenly distant, muffled by the urgency of our pursuit. The descent was steep, and as I hurried behind Jude, my pulse raced, the thrill of the chase mingling with the weight of our uncertain future.

As we reached the bottom, the dim light revealed a darkened hallway that stretched before us, a labyrinthine path filled with potential secrets waiting to be uncovered. And just as I was about to take the first step forward, a loud crash reverberated from behind us, followed by the unmistakable sound of shattering glass.

I turned, dread flooding my senses, as the realization hit me—this wasn't just a simple chase; it was the beginning of something far more dangerous. A chill settled over me, a premonition that whatever lay ahead could either be our salvation or our undoing.

With my heart pounding, I grabbed Jude's arm. "We have to go, now!"

But before we could make our next move, a shadowy figure emerged from the darkness, blocking our only escape. The air grew thick with tension, and I realized, in that heart-stopping moment, that the game had only just begun.

Chapter 22: The Final Confrontation

The scent of fresh blooms wafted through the air, mingling with the sharpness of impending confrontation. Each step toward the rival florist's shop felt like marching into a tempest. I could feel the warmth of the sun on my skin, a deceptive comfort against the chill of anxiety that knotted my stomach. The shop stood before us, a kaleidoscope of colors—a riot of petals framed by perfectly manicured hedges, its windows glimmering like a challenge. My heart raced as I glanced at Jude beside me, his expression a mix of determination and uncertainty.

"What if they've got some last-minute tricks up their sleeves?" I asked, my voice barely rising above a whisper.

Jude shrugged, his eyes scanning the shop's entrance, his hands clenched into fists at his sides. "We'll adapt. That's what we do. And remember, this is about more than just flowers." His words hung in the air, laden with unsaid complexities. Beneath his bravado, I detected a flicker of doubt that sent my own insecurities spiraling.

"Right. More than flowers." I tried to mirror his confidence, though the taste of it felt foreign on my tongue. The truth was, this confrontation felt personal, cutting deeper than I had imagined. As we crossed the threshold, I couldn't shake the weight of past grievances, every bitter exchange replaying in my mind like a broken record.

The bell above the door chimed—a stark contrast to the chaos brewing inside me. Inside, the air was electric, charged with tension. Shelves bursting with extravagant arrangements towered over us, each bouquet seemingly mocking our presence. In the center of the shop, the rival florist, Claudia, directed her employees with an iron fist, her auburn hair pulled tight in a bun that spoke to her no-nonsense demeanor. She spotted us and her lips curled into a triumphant smirk.

"Well, look who decided to grace us with their presence. The underdogs have finally come to face the champions." Her tone dripped with condescension, each syllable a taunt.

Jude stepped forward, his posture rigid, yet there was a vulnerability in his gaze. "We're not here to play games, Claudia. We're here to settle this once and for all."

Her laughter rang through the shop like glass shattering, sharp and unforgiving. "Settle what, exactly? Your futile attempts to compete with a real florist?" She gestured dismissively to the stunning arrangements that surrounded her, a stark reminder of our inadequacies.

I felt a flicker of anger ignite within me. "We may not have your flair, but we have heart. Something you wouldn't understand." My voice was steadier than I felt, a shield against her relentless mockery.

Claudia stepped down from her pedestal, her heels clicking against the polished floor as she approached us, her gaze piercing. "Heart doesn't win competitions, sweetheart. Skill does. And you, darling, are woefully lacking."

Jude's jaw tightened beside me, a silent storm brewing. "We're not here to trade insults, Claudia. We came to discuss the upcoming floral competition. We know you've been using underhanded tactics."

Her eyes flashed with a mixture of surprise and annoyance. "Tactics? Hardly. Perhaps you should focus on your own business rather than snooping around mine."

With every word, the weight of our rivalry bore down on me. Betrayal laced with deceit hung like a thick fog between us, stifling and overwhelming. Yet, I couldn't let her see how much her words affected me. I'd come too far to crumble now.

"Let's not pretend this is just business," I countered, my tone sharper than I intended. "You've been sabotaging our shop for months. We deserve a fair chance."

At that moment, the tension thickened, wrapping around us like a serpent poised to strike. Claudia's demeanor shifted; the bravado faded, revealing something darker beneath. "You have no idea what you're asking for. You think this rivalry is just about flowers? It's about survival."

Jude's voice cut through the air, low and intense. "Then let's cut to the chase. Are you willing to play fair this time?"

Claudia's lips pursed, a fleeting vulnerability crossing her face before the mask of confidence returned. "Fair? In this business? You must be joking. But I'll tell you what—I'm willing to make a deal."

My heart raced. This was unexpected. What could she possibly want?

"What kind of deal?" I asked, wary of her motives.

"If you want a fair competition, let's agree to a blind tasting. You present your arrangements, and I'll present mine. The judges will decide without knowing who made what. If you win, I'll cease all my... tactics. If I win, you back off. Deal?" Her proposal dangled like a ripe fruit, inviting yet perilous.

Jude shot me a look, his uncertainty mirroring my own. This wasn't just a challenge; it felt like a trap. Yet, a part of me couldn't resist. This was our chance—our opportunity to prove ourselves in a way that went beyond our previous rivalries.

"Deal," I said, surprising even myself.

Claudia's smirk returned, a serpent with its fangs bared. "Excellent. I do hope you know what you're getting into."

As we turned to leave, a sudden rush of exhilaration mingled with dread surged through me. We were in deeper than I had anticipated, tangled in a web of rivalry that threatened to ensnare us both. The day had transformed into something more—a confrontation not only with Claudia but with the doubts that had lingered in the shadows, threatening to derail everything we had worked for.

Outside, the world felt alive, vibrant colors reflecting my turmoil. I turned to Jude, his expression a mixture of resolve and anxiety. "Are you sure about this?"

"I am," he replied, the fire in his eyes igniting a flicker of hope within me. "We've come too far to back down now."

As we stood there, amidst the scent of flowers and the weight of our decision, I felt a shift. No longer merely competitors in a flower shop, we were warriors preparing for a battle that would challenge not only our skills but the very foundation of our dreams.

As we stood in the vibrant light of the afternoon sun, anticipation crackled like static in the air. The plan, a meticulously woven tapestry of ideas and dreams, felt frayed at the edges. I glanced sideways at Jude, whose jaw was set in a determined line, but there was a flicker of uncertainty in his eyes that mirrored my own. We were not just going to put our floral skills to the test; we were stepping into a battleground of wills, with pride and the very essence of our livelihood on the line.

"Do you think she'll actually follow through with her side of the deal?" I asked, adjusting the floral arrangement in my hands, which suddenly felt like a cumbersome weight rather than a symbol of our creativity.

"Claudia's nothing if not shrewd," Jude replied, his gaze fixed on the bright storefront adorned with cascading wisteria and peonies, a façade of beauty hiding the cutthroat nature within. "She'll play by her rules until she doesn't. Just keep your wits about you."

I swallowed hard, nodding, but the knot in my stomach tightened. The idea of competing against Claudia's elaborate arrangements was daunting, and as much as I wanted to believe in our chance, doubt gnawed at me like a persistent rat. We had to impress the judges, and the thought of them choosing her extravagant displays over our heartfelt creations made my palms sweat.

"Let's just do our best," I said, trying to inject some optimism into the air. "No matter what happens, we've got this."

"Right," Jude agreed, his voice steadying. "And if we fail, at least we can still eat cake."

A laugh escaped me, breaking the tension for a moment. "You and your sweet tooth. What are we, five?"

"Five with a flair for floral design," he shot back, a playful smirk on his lips. I was grateful for his ability to lighten the mood, even as the gravity of our situation loomed large.

As we set up in our shop, arranging the flowers with precision, I felt a surge of determination. Each blossom we placed was more than just a part of an arrangement; it was a piece of our hearts and aspirations, a declaration of our commitment to this dream. Jude and I worked in a rhythm, the unspoken connection between us guiding our hands as we transformed the cool marble countertop into a vivid spectacle of colors and textures.

"Okay, so we need a showstopper," I said, placing a large sunflower at the center of our design. "Something that'll make the judges gasp."

Jude arched an eyebrow, clearly skeptical. "And what, exactly, do you envision? Fireworks? A dance routine?"

"Maybe just a little pizzazz," I countered with a grin, the friendly banter between us easing my anxiety. "How about a cascade of hanging orchids? Something ethereal?"

"Orchid cascade it is," he agreed, his smile warming the chill in the air. As we worked, the sunlight streamed through the shop window, illuminating the petals and casting playful shadows that danced on the walls. Each bloom began to take on a life of its own, a reflection of our passion and resilience.

Just as we were about to add the finishing touches, the door swung open with a jingle, and in strode a figure I hadn't anticipated.

Claudia, looking every bit the part of a rival queen, stood in our doorway, arms crossed and a smug smile playing on her lips.

"Thought I'd pop in and see what the underdogs are up to," she remarked, her tone dripping with feigned innocence.

"Just preparing to lose," I shot back, not missing a beat.

"Ah, always with the sharp tongue," she replied, her eyes glinting with amusement. "Let's hope your arrangements can speak louder than your insults."

"Come to gloat or get advice?" Jude asked, his voice steady as he faced her without flinching.

"Neither. Just wanted to remind you of what you're up against." Claudia waved her hand dismissively, and I couldn't help but notice the subtle flourish—like a maestro conducting a symphony. "You do know I'm putting together something spectacular, right?"

"Surprise us," I replied, trying to project confidence even as uncertainty wormed its way back into my mind.

"Trust me, I will," she shot back, her eyes narrowing ever so slightly. "I just hope you can handle the heat." With that, she turned on her heel and sauntered out, her laughter echoing down the street.

As the door swung shut, an uneasy silence settled between us. "She's playing mind games," Jude said, tension etched in his brow. "Don't let her get to you."

"Easier said than done." I inhaled deeply, the floral scents swirling around me doing little to calm my racing heart. "What if we're not good enough?"

"Hey," he said, placing a reassuring hand on my shoulder. "We're good enough. You're good enough. You've got talent and heart—something she'll never understand. Trust in that."

His words steadied my fluttering heart, and together we returned to the task at hand. As we finished our arrangements, the sun dipped lower in the sky, casting an amber hue that wrapped around us like a warm embrace.

The competition loomed before us like an inevitable storm, yet I felt fortified, buoyed by Jude's unwavering support. Each petal we placed seemed to fortify the bond we had built—through rivalry, laughter, and shared dreams.

Later, as evening descended and the competition drew nearer, we gathered our arrangements, our creations a testament to our hard work. My mind raced with possibilities, an array of colors and shapes dancing in my thoughts, each a fragment of our journey.

"Ready?" Jude asked, his eyes sparkling with a mix of nerves and excitement.

"Ready as I'll ever be," I replied, grabbing his hand for a moment, feeling the warmth of his presence.

As we stepped outside into the fading light, the world seemed to hold its breath. We were no longer just competitors; we were artists, crafting our legacy in the heart of our community. Each step toward the competition felt like a step into a new chapter, a place where we would redefine what it meant to be a florist in our town.

The atmosphere buzzed with anticipation as we approached the venue, a gallery bursting with potential and adorned with floral displays that took my breath away. The array of colors swirled around me, but amid it all, I felt anchored by our work—our vision.

As we entered, the chatter of the crowd enveloped us, a symphony of voices filled with excitement and hope. The judges' table loomed ahead, and I caught a glimpse of Claudia, her expression unreadable as she surveyed the competition.

In that moment, everything shifted. This wasn't just about the flowers or the rivalry; it was about us, about standing up and fighting for what we believed in. The weight of expectations pressed against my chest, yet I stood taller, ready to face whatever lay ahead. Together, we would turn the tide, crafting not just arrangements but a future filled with promise.

The atmosphere inside the competition venue buzzed like an electric wire, crackling with anticipation and the scent of freshly cut flowers that mingled with a hint of anxiety. I scanned the room, taking in the dazzling displays that adorned every corner, each arrangement a statement piece, shouting for attention in a cacophony of colors. Our creations sat nearby, proud yet humble amidst the grandeur of the others. I could feel the weight of our work resting heavily on my shoulders, the stakes higher than ever.

"Remember, we're here to shine," Jude whispered, leaning in closer, his breath warm against my cheek. "No matter what happens, we created something beautiful."

I nodded, though the flutter of uncertainty in my stomach had morphed into a full-blown storm. "Right. Beauty before everything," I said, trying to inject confidence into my voice, but it came out sounding more like a mantra than a battle cry.

As the judges took their seats, I could see Claudia's arrangement glinting in the light, her signature opulence on full display. Each flower was strategically placed, the effect a whirlwind of vibrancy and chaos that somehow managed to look effortlessly chic. The judges seemed captivated, their eyes wide with admiration. I felt a pang of envy, the creeping tendrils of doubt inching closer to my heart.

"Focus on ours," Jude reminded me, catching my eye as he adjusted a rogue sunflower in our display. "We've got heart. She's all fluff and flash."

"Fluff and flash, sure," I muttered, my eyes still drawn to Claudia. "But that fluff is winning hearts."

"Enough of that!" Jude interjected, his tone playful but firm. "Our arrangements are not just pretty; they have stories. Let's make them hear our story."

His words resonated with me, igniting a flicker of determination. Our blooms told tales of late-night brainstorming sessions, laughter, and creativity, a testament to our journey. I inhaled deeply, allowing the floral notes to wash over me, invigorating my spirit.

The competition commenced with the judges making their rounds, each step sending ripples of nervous energy through the crowd. As they approached our arrangement, I held my breath, hoping my enthusiasm would translate into something palpable.

"What do we have here?" one of the judges, a silver-haired woman with discerning eyes, said as she bent closer to our display. "These colors are quite bold."

"They represent our resilience," I blurted out, the words tumbling from my mouth like petals on a breeze. "Each bloom symbolizes our journey—struggles, growth, and ultimately, a celebration of life."

Jude shot me a look that combined pride and surprise. "Right on, partner," he whispered, and I felt a rush of warmth spread through me.

As the judges took notes, Claudia sidled up beside us, her expression a mixture of amusement and disdain. "How charming. A touching little narrative to accompany your lackluster flowers," she quipped, her voice silky smooth.

"Better to have a narrative than a pretty shell," I shot back, surprising even myself with the sharpness of my retort.

"Touché," she replied, a flicker of irritation crossing her face. "But remember, darling, the judges want to be dazzled, not just moved. You'll need more than heartfelt speeches to win this."

Her words dripped with condescension, but I refused to let them penetrate my resolve. Instead, I focused on the judges, hoping they could see the passion woven into our arrangement.

As the competition progressed, I caught snippets of conversations from other competitors. Whispers of sabotage drifted through the air, igniting a fresh wave of anxiety. What if Claudia's tricks weren't just a thing of the past? I shot a glance at Jude, who seemed to be grappling with the same concerns.

"Do you think she'll try something?" I asked, my voice barely above a whisper.

"Most definitely," Jude replied, his brow furrowing. "But we can't let her distract us. Stay focused."

Suddenly, the lights dimmed, and a hush fell over the crowd. The final round of judging was upon us, and I felt the collective breath of the audience held tight in anticipation.

As the spotlight shifted toward Claudia's arrangement, I felt a twinge of dread. She stood tall, exuding confidence, her eyes gleaming with a dangerous mix of pride and ambition. I exchanged a look with Jude, who squeezed my hand reassuringly, his warmth a steady anchor against the rising tide of tension.

The judges began to deliberate, their expressions inscrutable as they moved from one display to another. I felt my heart race, each second ticking away like a countdown. My mind raced with thoughts of our future, the dreams we had woven together, now hanging in the balance.

Suddenly, a loud crash shattered the silence, and all heads turned toward the source of the commotion. One of Claudia's towering floral displays had toppled over, sending petals and stems flying in every direction. Gasps echoed through the room as the vibrant colors tumbled, creating a chaotic scene that contrasted sharply with the elegance of the competition.

"Oh no," I murmured, my heart racing as I watched Claudia's confident facade begin to crumble.

She rushed forward, her heels clicking sharply against the floor, eyes wide with fury and disbelief. "What the hell happened?" she shouted, her voice cutting through the stunned silence.

I exchanged a glance with Jude, who looked equally shocked. "Did someone bump into it?" I asked, perplexed.

"Or was it sabotage?" Jude muttered, his brow furrowed.

As the judges approached, a buzz of excitement rippled through the crowd. Claudia's arrangement lay in disarray, petals scattered like confetti across the floor. Her frustration transformed into a fierce glare directed at the judges, her competitive spirit unraveling before our eyes.

"Is this a joke?" she demanded, her voice a mix of disbelief and anger. "I've put in hours of work, and this—" she gestured wildly to the chaos around her "—is how you repay me?"

"Calm down, Claudia," one of the judges said, attempting to restore order. "Accidents happen. We're here to evaluate all displays, including yours."

As I watched the scene unfold, an odd sense of satisfaction bubbled up within me. Claudia had built her empire on intimidation and deception, and now, it appeared, the universe had turned the tables.

Yet just as I thought we might gain the upper hand, a realization struck me. If this was indeed a sabotage—if someone had orchestrated this chaos—it would only shift the scrutiny back onto us. The crowd, once a sea of curious faces, now shifted their attention between the chaos of Claudia's display and our calm, collected arrangement.

"What if they think we did this?" I whispered, panic rising in my chest.

"Stay cool," Jude urged, but I could see the tension rippling beneath his calm exterior.

As Claudia continued to shout, her frustration palpable, I caught sight of a figure slipping out the back door—someone I hadn't noticed before. The moment hung in the air, pregnant with potential danger. My instincts kicked in; something was off, and I needed to know what was happening.

"Jude, I need to check something," I said, my pulse quickening.

"Are you sure?" he asked, concern etched on his face. "This could get messy."

"Trust me," I insisted, the decision crystallizing in my mind. "I'll be right back. Just hold tight."

I slipped through the crowd, heart pounding as I made my way to the exit. The figure had disappeared around the corner, but I could hear the faint sound of footsteps echoing down the hallway. I pushed the door open and stepped into the cool evening air, feeling a surge of adrenaline propel me forward.

As I rounded the corner, the shadows deepened, and the figure came into view—a familiar silhouette cloaked in darkness. My breath caught in my throat as realization dawned. It was someone I knew all too well, someone who had their own stake in this competition.

"Why are you here?" I called out, my voice steadier than I felt, the chill of the night wrapping around me like a shroud.

The figure turned slowly, revealing a face I hadn't expected to see—a face that would change everything in the blink of an eye.

"Let's just say I have some unfinished business," they said, a smirk creeping across their lips.

And in that moment, I knew I was standing at the precipice of a revelation that could shatter everything I thought I knew. The stakes had risen higher than I ever imagined, and the real game was just beginning.

Chapter 23: Through the Ashes

The moon hung low in the sky, casting a silver glow that transformed Riverview into a realm of shadows and whispers. As I stood at the edge of the once-familiar woods, the night air was thick with a tension I could almost taste, sharp and electric. A few days had passed since the confrontation, but the echoes of that moment still reverberated through me. I could feel the weight of the secrets we had unearthed pressing down, heavy and unyielding, like the iron chains that had bound us to our pasts. Yet here I was, on the cusp of a new reality, grappling with the fragments of what had been and the possibilities of what could be.

Jude's presence beside me was a grounding force, a reminder that I was not alone in this chaos. His hand brushed against mine, a fleeting connection that sent warmth racing through my veins. The tenderness of that touch contrasted sharply with the tumult of emotions swirling inside me—fear, hope, and an unsettling mix of desire and uncertainty. The air crackled as he turned to me, his gaze dark and intense, searching for something that felt just out of reach.

"I never thought we'd end up here, you know?" he murmured, his voice low, almost reverent. The weight of his words hung between us, an unspoken acknowledgment of the fragile truce we had forged amidst the wreckage of our rivalry.

"Neither did I," I replied, my heart pounding against my ribcage. The realization that we had somehow transformed our animosity into something akin to partnership was bewildering. What had once felt like a battlefield was now a shared mission, albeit one laden with stakes higher than I had ever anticipated.

Our conversations, once filled with barbs and clever retorts, had shifted to strategies and plans. Each night we gathered with the others who had rallied behind us, weaving our lives and stories together like threads in a tapestry, our shared experiences binding us in ways I never thought possible. The firelight flickered in the depths of the clearing, illuminating faces etched with determination and fear alike, casting dancing shadows that echoed the turmoil within each heart.

"We can't let them take this away from us," Jude said, his voice a fierce whisper, punctuated by the crackling of the flames. He gestured toward the group huddled around the fire. "They're counting on us to lead."

A knot of anxiety twisted in my stomach at the thought. Could we really rise to the challenge? Each person who looked to us bore their own scars, remnants of a battle that had not been fought in isolation but as part of a community that had been shattered and shaken. I glanced around, taking in the faces of our neighbors, the laughter of children mingling with the solemnity of our purpose. The resilience reflected in their eyes filled me with a sense of responsibility that was both daunting and invigorating.

"Then we need a plan," I said, a spark of determination igniting within me. "We can't just react anymore. We need to anticipate their moves." I caught Jude's gaze and felt a surge of confidence. "If we know what we're up against, we can stand our ground."

"Absolutely," he agreed, his lips curling into that half-smile that made my heart flutter. "It's time to turn the tables. Let's show them that Riverview isn't backing down."

The air hummed with energy as we outlined our strategy, laughter breaking through the tension as we tossed around ideas. Our discussions turned into plans for community watch groups and information-sharing networks, a collective effort to fortify our defenses. The night deepened, and as stars peeked through the blanket of darkness, our resolve solidified like concrete setting in a mold.

In the days that followed, I found myself submerged in a whirlwind of activity. Together with Jude and our newfound allies, we canvassed the town, holding meetings in basements and living rooms, stirring up a collective strength that had long lain dormant. Our rivalry was replaced by a shared commitment, and the initial thrill of unity was soon overshadowed by the realities of what we were up against.

The shadows of our past began to creep back into my thoughts, uninvited and relentless. I could still feel the echoes of betrayal from those I had trusted, and doubt clawed at the edges of my resolve. Was I truly fit to lead? I watched as Jude flourished in his role, his confidence radiating like sunlight, illuminating the darker corners of my mind. He was a natural, commanding respect and drawing people in with his unyielding spirit. Yet as I stood beside him, I couldn't shake the feeling that I was trailing in his wake, a shadow of the person I aspired to be.

One evening, as we reviewed our progress over coffee that had gone lukewarm, I found myself staring into my cup, avoiding Jude's penetrating gaze. "What if I'm not cut out for this?" The words slipped from my lips before I could stop them, tinged with vulnerability.

"Don't be ridiculous," Jude replied, his voice steady. He reached across the table, fingers brushing against mine, and I felt the weight of his conviction. "You've brought everyone together. They believe in you, just like I do."

"But it's not enough," I murmured, frustration bubbling beneath the surface. "What if I lead them into danger? What if I can't protect them?"

His expression shifted, intensity flooding his features. "You won't know unless you try. We can't live in fear of what might happen. We have to confront it." There was a fierceness in his words, a rallying cry that stirred something deep within me.

The conversations morphed into a rallying call, igniting something in me that had been dormant for too long. The moment of doubt transformed into clarity as I realized that it wasn't about being perfect; it was about the effort to rise above the ashes of our past, to forge a new future. Each step I took was not just for myself but for everyone standing alongside me, their hopes intertwined with mine.

As days melted into nights, I felt the tension shift, the atmosphere thick with a sense of impending confrontation. The adversary we faced was no longer a mere whisper in the dark but a looming threat, bold and insistent. I could almost hear the drums of war echoing through the trees, a distant reminder that our peaceful existence was about to be tested in ways we had never imagined.

Jude and I stood together, hearts pounding in synchrony, our hands intertwined like lifelines amidst the chaos. Our journey had shifted from rivalry to partnership, but now, as we faced the horizon together, I knew that this was only the beginning. In the depths of uncertainty, our bond had become a beacon, illuminating a path forward that shimmered with promise. Together, we would confront the storm brewing in the shadows, ready to embrace whatever fate awaited us, united through the ashes of our past.

The dawn broke with a hesitant blush of pink and gold, spilling light over the remnants of the night like a painter reluctant to reveal their canvas. I stood at my kitchen window, coffee in hand, absorbing the quiet energy of Riverview awakening from its slumber. The sunlight danced across the dew-kissed grass, and I let out a slow breath, trying to center myself amid the chaos that still throbbed beneath the surface of our town. Every day felt like a new beginning, yet an undercurrent of tension lingered, reminding me that darkness was never too far away.

Jude sauntered in, his hair tousled and eyes still heavy with sleep. The way he moved through the kitchen was almost graceful, as if he were choreographed by an unseen hand. "What's with the early morning brooding?" he teased, a sleepy grin tugging at his lips. "You know the world doesn't start until at least nine."

"Maybe I'm just trying to get ahead of the chaos," I shot back, playful but serious, grateful for the easy banter that had begun to stitch our lives together. "You can't expect me to just wait for the trouble to knock on our door."

He chuckled, pouring himself a cup of coffee with that effortless confidence I found both comforting and infuriating. "What are you, a chaos magnet? Because that would explain a lot." His teasing tone made me roll my eyes, but inside, I felt a flicker of joy. It was nice to have moments of normalcy amid the storm brewing around us.

We had been thrust into a whirlwind of planning and preparation since that fateful night. While we had forged alliances and gathered our community, I often wondered if our combined strength would be enough. There was a palpable sense of urgency in the air, a feeling that we were on the precipice of something momentous. Each day brought new reports of disturbances—strange noises in the woods, flickering lights in the sky, and more sightings of those shadowy figures lurking on the outskirts of town. Riverview had become a battleground, and we were merely players trying to find our footing.

"I was thinking," I began, setting my coffee down to focus on him. "Maybe we should hold a community meeting, bring everyone together, and share what we've discovered. Transparency is key, right?" The thought sent a surge of determination through me, tinged with excitement. We needed to cultivate trust, to rally the town around a common purpose.

"Great idea," Jude said, his enthusiasm infectious. "Let's do it tonight. We'll need to make sure everyone feels involved. It's not just about us anymore; it's about the whole community. And you're right—if we don't share what's been happening, we might lose their faith."

The prospect of organizing a meeting filled me with an electric sense of purpose. We began planning, each step igniting our excitement and concern. As we made phone calls and sent out messages, I could see the shift in Jude's demeanor. The shadows of doubt that had occasionally clouded his expression were fading, replaced by a glimmer of hope. It was as if he was rediscovering a part of himself that had been lost in the turmoil of our shared struggles.

By dusk, the community center buzzed with energy as people trickled in, some familiar faces, others new. I stood at the front of the room, heart racing as I surveyed the crowd, a blend of anxiety and exhilaration coursing through me. It was time to transform our collective fear into action. Jude joined me, positioning himself just a step behind, an unspoken support that bolstered my courage.

"Thank you all for coming," I began, my voice steady despite the butterflies in my stomach. "We're gathered here tonight not just to discuss what's been happening in our town but to unite as a community. Riverview has always been a place of strength, and we need to embrace that now more than ever." My eyes scanned the room, catching glimpses of nodding heads and expressions that mirrored my own determination.

As I continued, sharing the unsettling incidents and our suspicions, I felt the tension in the air shift. It was no longer just my fear but a collective unease that resonated with everyone present. I explained our plans to establish a community watch and the importance of communication among ourselves. Each voice that chimed in, from the elderly with their wisdom to the teenagers with their sharp observations, transformed the meeting from a mere discussion into a powerful alliance.

"Let's face it," one of the older gentlemen, Mr. Henderson, said, his gravelly voice cutting through the chatter. "We've always been a little strange here in Riverview. We've survived floods, storms, and the occasional raccoon raid. A little darkness won't take us down."

His comment drew laughter, a welcome reprieve from the gravity of our situation.

"Exactly!" Jude interjected, a spark in his eyes. "We're not just residents; we're a family. And families stick together through thick and thin." His words ignited a sense of camaraderie that felt almost tangible, wrapping around us like a warm blanket.

By the end of the meeting, I could sense a shift—a determination to confront the challenges ahead rather than cower in fear. People began to mingle, exchanging ideas and offering help. The energy in the room crackled, and I found myself laughing with neighbors I had only nodded to before. I caught Jude's eye across the room, and the pride shining in his gaze filled me with a sense of belonging I hadn't fully realized I craved.

As the crowd began to disperse, I felt a soft touch on my arm. It was Marla, a friend I hadn't spoken to much recently. "I just wanted to say, you really brought everyone together tonight. It's like you awakened something in us."

"Thank you, Marla," I replied, a genuine smile spreading across my face. "I just said what needed to be said. It's all of us together that will make the difference."

Just then, Jude stepped over, his brow furrowed in thought. "Hey, can I talk to you for a sec?" The intensity of his gaze made my heart skip, and I nodded, curious about what he had on his mind.

We slipped outside, the cool evening air wrapping around us like a soft embrace. The stars glittered above, an endless expanse that made the worries of the day feel insignificant. "What's up?" I asked, leaning against the wall, the wood cool beneath my back.

"I was thinking about what Mr. Henderson said," he began, pacing slightly as if the thoughts were dancing just out of reach. "We're not just residents. We've got history, scars, stories that bind us. But... what if some of those stories are more than we know?"

"What do you mean?" I tilted my head, intrigued.

"I'm just saying, what if some of us have been keeping secrets? What if the darkness we're facing isn't just external but something that runs deeper?" His expression was serious, a shadow crossing his features.

An uneasy feeling settled in my stomach. "You think there's more to this than we realize? That maybe it's connected to the past?"

Jude nodded, his eyes narrowing as if piecing together a puzzle. "Exactly. If we dig deeper, we might find out that the answers are closer than we think. Maybe even among us."

The words hung between us, a thread of tension weaving through the air. Just as I was about to respond, the sound of a crash echoed from the direction of the woods, shattering the calm. My heart raced, a sudden jolt of adrenaline surging through me. Whatever had been lurking in the shadows was no longer hidden. It was here, and the time for answers was now.

The crash resonated through the evening air like a gunshot, slicing through the quiet comfort of the night and jolting me upright. Jude's eyes widened, his expression a mixture of alarm and determination. I felt my heart race, a wild thump against my ribs that threatened to leap from my chest. We were standing on the precipice of something monumental, and the sudden sound was a clarion call to action.

"Did you hear that?" he asked, his voice low and urgent, almost a whisper, as if the darkness itself was eavesdropping. "It came from the woods."

"I did," I replied, straining my ears to catch any further sounds, but the world around us had fallen silent, as if it were holding its breath. My mind raced through possibilities: a fallen branch, an animal startled by our gathering, or something far more sinister lurking among the trees. "We should check it out."

"Are you crazy?" Jude shot back, incredulous. "We have no idea what it could be."

"Exactly! Which is why we can't just stand here," I countered, adrenaline coursing through my veins, making me feel alive and reckless. "If it's a threat, we need to know. If we're going to protect this town, we can't let fear dictate our actions."

With a reluctant nod, Jude took a step forward, and I followed close behind. The air grew colder as we moved away from the comforting glow of the community center, the shadows lengthening and twisting in ways that made the hair on the back of my neck stand on end. We approached the edge of the woods, where the underbrush rustled ominously.

"Do you have your phone?" I whispered, feeling foolish for not having thought of it sooner. "We might need a flashlight."

"Yeah, I've got it," he said, pulling it out and illuminating the path ahead. The beam flickered like a beacon in the darkness, and I felt a rush of gratitude that he had decided to come with me.

As we ventured deeper into the woods, the silence was oppressive, a weight that pressed down on my shoulders. Every snap of a twig beneath our feet felt exaggerated, each sound echoing into the void like a countdown to something inevitable. The trees loomed overhead, their gnarled branches casting skeletal shadows that danced across our path.

"Are you sure about this?" Jude asked, his voice barely a murmur, uncertainty threading through his words. "I mean, we could just head back and let the others handle it."

"Where's the fun in that?" I replied, trying to lighten the mood with a wry smile. "Besides, I have a feeling we need to be the ones to uncover whatever is hiding out here."

He let out a low laugh, one that was both nervous and amused. "Only you could find the thrill in creeping into the woods at night. I swear, one of these days, I'll learn to talk you out of your wild ideas."

As if the universe had decided to respond to our banter, another sound shattered the silence—a low growl that sent chills cascading down my spine. I froze, the light from Jude's phone trembling in my hand. "Did you hear that?"

"Yeah," he replied, the playfulness evaporating from his tone. The tension between us thickened like fog, both of us aware that we had crossed into territory where laughter was no longer appropriate.

"Maybe we should—" I started, but before I could finish, a flash of movement in the underbrush drew my attention. I swung the light in that direction, and the beam caught the glimmer of eyes staring back at us—intelligent, predatory, and all too aware of our presence.

"Run!" Jude shouted, grabbing my arm, and the instinct to obey propelled me forward. We bolted deeper into the woods, the uneven ground beneath us threatening to trip us at any moment. The pounding of our hearts echoed in my ears, drowning out the sound of snapping twigs and rustling leaves as whatever was pursuing us gave chase.

Branches clawed at my arms, leaving stinging welts as we weaved through the trees, our breaths quickening with each passing moment. I could feel Jude's grip tightening around my wrist, grounding me even as panic threatened to take hold. "We need to find shelter!" I shouted over the cacophony of the night.

"Over there!" Jude pointed toward an abandoned shed, its silhouette barely visible against the moonlight. Without thinking, we raced toward it, the door hanging precariously off its hinges. As we stumbled inside, I glanced back to see the gleaming eyes now mere shadows lurking at the edge of the clearing.

Inside, the scent of damp wood and mildew filled the air, mingling with a metallic tang that made my stomach turn. We pressed ourselves against the wall, hearts racing as we strained to hear any sign of what was outside.

"Do you think it followed us?" I whispered, my voice barely above a breath.

Jude shook his head, his expression serious. "I don't know, but we can't stay here. We have to get back and warn the others."

"Right. But how?" My mind raced as I realized we were trapped in this dilapidated structure. The walls felt like they were closing in, and the darkness pressed down on us, heavy and suffocating.

Just then, the sound of claws scraping against wood shattered the stillness, followed by a low, menacing growl that reverberated through the shed. My heart lurched, panic surging anew. "It's right outside," I breathed, my eyes wide with fear.

"What do we do?" Jude asked, his voice a tightrope between calm and hysteria.

"Think! We need something to defend ourselves with," I said, scanning the cluttered interior. My gaze landed on an old, rusted shovel propped against the wall. "That could work!"

I grabbed it, the weight of the handle surprisingly comforting in my grip. Just as I turned to face Jude, I noticed a flicker of movement near the door—shadows coalescing into something more tangible, something that sent a surge of dread through me.

"We can't let it in," I warned, positioning myself defensively in front of Jude. He nodded, eyes wide but resolute.

As the door creaked ominously, slowly swinging open on its hinges, the dark figure beyond it seemed to swell and take shape. The air thickened with tension, and every instinct screamed that whatever it was, it was unlike anything we had ever faced before.

The figure stepped into the light, revealing a creature cloaked in darkness, its form shifting and writhing as if it were made of shadows. A snarl tore from its lips, echoing through the shed, and I felt the ground beneath me tremble as it advanced.

"What the hell is that?" Jude gasped, fear etched across his features.

"I don't know, but it looks hungry," I replied, heart hammering in my chest.

As the creature lunged forward, I raised the shovel, ready to defend our lives against the very embodiment of our nightmares. But just as I swung, the world around me erupted into chaos, a cacophony of sound and motion that shattered everything I thought I knew. In that instant, I realized the fight for Riverview was far from over—it had only just begun.

Chapter 24: Blossoms of Tomorrow

I wandered through the narrow aisles of my shop, inhaling the sweet scent of fresh blooms mingling with the earthy undertones of the potting soil. Each flower had a story, a burst of color that defied the drabness of the world outside. Sunlight streamed through the glass panes, casting playful shadows on the wooden floor, and I couldn't help but smile as I rearranged the peonies—pink and creamy white—gathered in a frosted glass vase. They were just as unpredictable as my life had become, blossoming beautifully despite the storms they had endured.

Jude's laughter broke through my reverie, a warm and melodic sound that danced in the air like the soft wind rustling through the leaves. I glanced over to see him at his shop across the street, his back turned as he spoke to a couple who were clearly enchanted by his charm. Jude had always possessed that effortless magnetism; it was one of the things that had first drawn me to him. The way he carried himself, confident yet approachable, made it impossible to resist his infectious spirit.

After the tumultuous events that had shattered Riverview, we had forged an unexpected alliance, united not just by the shop restoration efforts, but also by a deepening connection that felt almost magical. I watched as he gestured animatedly, a playful grin on his face, and felt a warmth blossom in my chest. My heart had once felt heavy with the weight of rivalry, but now it soared at the thought of our partnership—and perhaps something even more.

"Hey, flower girl! You think we have enough daisies for the festival?" Jude called out, his voice breaking through my thoughts. The sun glinted off his tousled hair, and for a fleeting moment, I found myself lost in the depths of his hazel eyes, where mischief danced like sunlight on water.

I rolled my eyes, but the smile tugging at my lips betrayed my mock annoyance. "You know, if you actually asked for help instead of yelling across the street, I might be more inclined to give you an answer."

He feigned a pout, crossing his arms over his chest. "But where's the fun in that? Besides, you can't resist my charm."

"Charming? More like infuriating," I shot back, but the laughter in my voice was unmistakable. "And yes, we should stock up on daisies. They're a favorite for the festival."

As I returned to arranging the flowers, I couldn't shake the feeling that something was shifting between us. It was as if the walls we had built during our rivalry were crumbling, replaced by a delicate bridge that connected our hearts. With each shared joke and playful exchange, I felt the distance narrowing, the air thick with unspoken possibilities.

The festival was only days away, and the excitement in Riverview was palpable. Vendors were setting up their stalls, the aroma of baked goods wafting through the streets, mingling with the rich scent of freshly cut flowers. The townspeople buzzed with anticipation, laughter echoing in the air as children darted around, clutching balloons and candy.

"Do you remember the first festival we competed in?" Jude mused, leaning against the doorframe of my shop, arms crossed casually. The way the sunlight caught his features made him look almost ethereal, and I felt a familiar flutter in my stomach.

"Of course! You thought it would be a good idea to create a life-sized flower arrangement in the shape of a unicorn," I replied, unable to suppress a laugh. "How did that turn out again?"

His grin widened, revealing a hint of nostalgia. "The unicorn collapsed before the judging began. I nearly lost my mind, thinking it would ruin my chances."

"It did ruin your chances! But I was secretly thrilled because it meant I had a shot at winning," I teased, unable to hide my delight. "And yet, look where we are now. The rivalry turned into this...whatever this is."

"Something beautiful," he said, the weight of his words settling between us, filling the air with unspoken promises.

The sun dipped lower, casting a warm golden glow over the streets, and I felt the magic of the evening settle around us like a comforting blanket. It was a moment suspended in time, where the world outside faded into insignificance, leaving just the two of us standing on the precipice of something new.

"Do you think we could recreate that unicorn, but this time with a little less drama?" I suggested playfully, my heart racing as I met his gaze. "Only if you promise to help me. I refuse to do all the heavy lifting alone."

He chuckled, the sound rich and inviting. "I promise I won't let you down this time. We'll create something that will outshine anything we've ever done before."

Our fingers brushed together as he leaned closer, and a spark ignited, a flicker of something electric that passed between us. In that brief moment, the rest of the world blurred into insignificance, and all I could focus on was the connection simmering just below the surface, waiting for the right moment to bloom.

Just then, the cheerful chatter of our friends pulled me back to reality, reminding me that the festival was just around the corner and that we had work to do. But I felt a newfound determination surging within me, an awareness that what was growing between Jude and me was more than just a partnership—it was the promise of something that could flourish, defying the odds. As we dove back into preparations, the vibrant colors of the flowers echoed the uncharted territory of our relationship, and I couldn't help but feel that the blossoms of tomorrow were beginning to unfurl before us.

As the festival drew nearer, the streets of Riverview transformed into a vibrant tapestry of color and sound. Banners fluttered in the gentle breeze, and the air was thick with the sweet scent of cinnamon and vanilla wafting from the nearby bakery. The excitement was infectious, igniting an energy that seemed to pulse through every corner of our small town. I stood behind the counter of my flower shop, arranging a bouquet of sunflowers that turned their cheerful faces toward the window, eager for passersby to admire their sunny disposition.

"Do you think sunflowers will be enough to distract everyone from your terrible dance moves at the festival?" Jude's teasing voice broke through my concentration, his silhouette framed by the open door. He leaned casually against the threshold, a playful grin on his face that made my heart flutter.

"Oh, please. My dance moves are a sight to behold," I shot back, trying to keep my tone light, though my cheeks flushed with warmth. "It's not my fault that the last time I tried to dance, I nearly tripped over my own feet."

He stepped inside, his laughter echoing off the walls. "You mean nearly tripped over my feet. I distinctly remember saving you from a tumble. You owe me, flower girl."

"Saving me? More like preventing a catastrophic flower disaster. I can't have the townsfolk thinking I'm a clumsy florist." I turned away, attempting to focus on my work, but the corners of my mouth betrayed me, curling into a smile. The light banter felt as comfortable as the worn-in jeans I wore.

With every moment spent together, the playful rivalry from before had morphed into a camaraderie that felt both thrilling and terrifying. I found myself yearning for more than just playful jabs and lighthearted teasing. Our partnership was blossoming into something more profound, a bond that wrapped around my heart like the delicate vines I often used in my arrangements.

"Come on, let's make a bet," Jude said, plopping a basket of daisies onto the counter. "If you can resist the urge to trip over your own feet at the festival, I'll treat you to the biggest slice of cake at Rosie's Diner."

"Deal. But if I win, you have to perform a dance-off with me," I countered, my competitive spirit igniting. "And no cheating!"

He held up his hands in mock surrender. "Fine. You're on. But don't come crying to me when I embarrass you in front of everyone."

"Right, because you're such a natural performer." I raised an eyebrow, the teasing light in my eyes mirroring the spark of excitement between us. "What will you do? A little shimmy and shake? The crowd won't know what hit them."

"Watch and learn, my friend. I might just surprise you." He winked, and I could feel the playful tension simmering beneath the surface. It was a strange sensation, that mix of exhilaration and anxiety, as if we were both standing at the edge of something extraordinary.

As we arranged flowers together, our hands brushed against each other's more often than necessary. Each accidental touch sent a thrill through me, a reminder of the chemistry brewing between us. It was intoxicating, exhilarating, yet unnerving. I couldn't ignore the way my heart raced whenever he leaned close, his breath warm against my ear as he whispered some outrageous comment meant to make me laugh.

"Do you think we'll actually pull this off?" I asked, the question slipping out as I gazed at our handiwork—a stunning display of flowers that felt like a perfect reflection of our journey together.

"Of course we will," he replied, his tone reassuring. "Riverview is tougher than we think, and so are we. Besides, we've got each other, right?"

His words settled over me like a warm embrace, and I nodded, my heart swelling with a mix of hope and something deeper. We had fought hard for this moment, and now, as we prepared for the festival, it felt like we were on the cusp of something monumental.

But as the days passed, I sensed a change in the air—a tension that prickled at the back of my mind. Whispers floated through the streets, and glances from townsfolk lingered a moment too long. There was an undercurrent of unease, as if the very fabric of our community was fraying at the edges.

I caught Jude's gaze as he prepared a new display of lavender, his brow furrowed in thought. "Do you feel that?" I asked, the weight of my words hanging heavily between us.

He paused, glancing around as if trying to grasp the invisible threads that wove through our town. "Yeah. Something's off, isn't it? People seem... uneasy."

"What do you think it is?" I pondered aloud, unable to shake the growing sense of dread that clung to me. "I thought we were finally on the mend, but I can't shake this feeling."

Jude's expression shifted, the lightheartedness of moments before dimming. "I don't know, but we'll figure it out together. Just like we always do."

The promise in his voice resonated within me, igniting a spark of determination. We had fought through storms before, and I refused to let anything tear us apart now. But as I looked into his eyes, I wondered if the challenges ahead would test us in ways we hadn't anticipated.

The day of the festival arrived with a rush of colors and sounds, a whirlwind of excitement enveloping Riverview. The streets thrummed with energy as vendors set up their stalls, each one brimming with homemade treats, crafts, and, of course, an abundance of flowers. I felt the pulse of the town quicken, and it mirrored the quickening in my own heart.

"Ready to show them what we've got?" Jude asked, his grin wide and infectious. I could hardly contain my enthusiasm as we stepped into the throng of the festival, laughter echoing around us like a symphony.

"Only if you promise to show off those dance moves of yours," I replied, nudging him playfully.

"Deal," he said, taking my hand and leading me into the chaos. The world around us sparkled with life, each smile and laugh adding to the atmosphere of warmth. Yet, beneath the surface of joy, I could still sense that something lurked in the shadows, waiting for the perfect moment to disrupt our celebration.

As the sun began to set, casting a golden hue over the festivities, Jude and I found ourselves pulled into the heart of the crowd. Laughter rang out, and the first notes of music began to play, a lively tune that filled the air with a sense of freedom and joy. We moved to the rhythm, our feet tapping along, and for a brief moment, I allowed myself to forget the unease that had crept into my thoughts.

But just as the evening reached its peak, a sudden hush fell over the crowd. I turned to see a figure standing at the edge of the square, silhouetted against the fading light. The laughter faded, replaced by murmurs that rippled through the gathered crowd like a wave.

"Who is that?" I whispered, my excitement faltering. Jude's grip on my hand tightened, his expression shifting to one of concern.

"I don't know," he replied, his voice low, but I could hear the tension beneath it. "Stay close to me."

The figure stepped forward, the glow of the festival lights revealing a face that sent chills down my spine. It was someone I had thought long gone from our lives—a ghost from the past that threatened to unravel everything we had worked so hard to build.

The figure in the shadows stepped forward, and as the light bathed their face, recognition hit me like a punch to the gut. It was Hannah, my childhood friend turned adversary, who had left Riverview years ago under circumstances that still sent ripples of unease through my mind. Her return stirred a storm of emotions within me—confusion, anger, and a reluctant curiosity about what had drawn her back to the place we once called home.

"Surprise!" she exclaimed, a wide smile spreading across her face, though it didn't quite reach her eyes. The crowd, once lively and carefree, seemed to hold its breath, anticipation thickening the air around us.

"What are you doing here, Hannah?" I managed, the words tumbling out before I could stop them. My heart raced, fueled by a mixture of disbelief and an old, familiar resentment that I thought I had buried.

"I thought it was time to come back and face my demons," she said, a hint of challenge lacing her voice. She glanced at Jude, a knowing look passing between them that made my stomach churn. "And maybe stir up a little fun in the process."

Jude's posture shifted slightly, a protective instinct flaring to life. "This isn't a game, Hannah. People are trying to rebuild here."

"Rebuild?" Her laughter rang out like broken glass, sharp and dissonant. "Is that what you're calling this?" She gestured to the festival, where the laughter had turned into whispers, eyes darting between us. "Look around. Is this truly what you want, or is it all just a facade?"

I stepped forward, anger surging through me. "You have no idea what we've been through, what it means to us. You can't just waltz in here and act like you have a right to judge."

"Judging? Oh, sweetheart, I'm not judging," she retorted, a smirk playing on her lips. "I'm merely pointing out the truth. This town is a powder keg waiting for a spark, and I just happen to be the one who's willing to light it."

The crowd shifted uncomfortably, and I could feel the tension coiling like a spring, ready to snap. "What do you want, Hannah?" I demanded, trying to maintain my composure as her presence unnerved me in a way I hadn't anticipated.

She tilted her head, feigning innocence. "What do I want? Why, I just want to catch up with old friends. Isn't that what a festival is for?"

"Cut the act," Jude said, stepping protectively beside me. "If you're back to cause trouble, you should know we're not playing your games anymore."

"Trouble? My dear Jude, you're the last person I'd want to cross," she replied, her tone dripping with mock sweetness. "But perhaps it's time someone reminded you how fragile this little paradise really is."

Her words hung heavy in the air, and I felt a chill creep up my spine. What did she mean? My mind raced with possibilities, each darker than the last. Just as I opened my mouth to confront her further, the sharp clang of a bell echoed through the festival, signaling the start of the evening's events.

"Let's all take a deep breath," a voice boomed over the crowd, and I turned to see Mayor Thompson stepping forward, trying to diffuse the rising tension. "Tonight is about community, about celebrating how far we've come together. So let's focus on the positives, shall we?"

The crowd shifted, eyes darting between the mayor and Hannah, the air thick with unspoken questions. I wanted to retreat, to hide from this sudden chaos, but I stood my ground, fighting to maintain my composure.

"Just remember," Hannah said, her gaze locking onto mine, "every flower has its thorns." With a playful flick of her wrist, she turned and began to weave her way through the crowd, a serpent slipping back into the grass. The crowd parted for her, whispers following in her wake, and I felt my heart race as unease took root in my chest.

"What do you think she's up to?" I asked Jude, my voice low, barely above a whisper.

He shook his head, his jaw set in a hard line. "Whatever it is, it can't be good. We need to keep an eye on her."

The mayor continued to speak, his words a blur as I struggled to focus on anything but the lingering presence of Hannah. Every laugh, every cheer from the crowd felt tainted, as if she had cast a shadow over our moment of celebration. Just when I thought I could shake off the unease, I felt Jude's hand find mine, grounding me.

"We're in this together," he murmured, squeezing my hand reassuringly.

"Together," I echoed, though doubt seeped into my thoughts like ink on paper. The festival resumed, the music pulsing around us, but my heart felt heavy.

As the night wore on, laughter returned to the air, but I couldn't shake the feeling that Hannah's arrival had set something sinister in motion. Fireworks lit up the sky, bursting in a riot of colors that felt almost mocking. Beneath the brilliant explosions of light, I could still feel the weight of uncertainty pressing down on us.

"Hey," Jude said, leaning in closer, his breath warm against my ear. "Let's go find some of that cake I promised you. It'll take our minds off... everything."

I nodded, grateful for his distraction. As we wove through the crowd, I felt the tension in my shoulders ease slightly, if only for a moment. The laughter of children, the chatter of neighbors—it all blended into a comforting hum, and I allowed myself to smile.

But as we reached the booth selling Rosie's famous cakes, I caught sight of Hannah out of the corner of my eye. She stood at the edge of the festival, her eyes scanning the crowd, a knowing smile on her face. My heart sank as I realized she was watching us, her gaze fixed and intent.

"Jude," I whispered, my voice barely audible over the crowd. "I think she's up to something."

He turned to follow my gaze, his expression hardening. "We need to keep her away from the main event. If she's trying to cause trouble..."

Before he could finish, the ground beneath us trembled—a low rumble that felt out of place amid the festival's joyful noise. Gasps echoed through the crowd as people began to turn, looking for the source of the disturbance.

Jude and I exchanged a worried glance just as the sky erupted with a loud crack. My heart raced, the air thick with panic as people began to shout, scattering in every direction.

"Run!" Jude shouted, pulling me close as the tremors intensified. My pulse quickened as I struggled to keep pace, my mind racing with a thousand thoughts.

Hannah stood at the edge of the chaos, an eerie calm in her demeanor as she watched the frenzy unfold. Her eyes gleamed with satisfaction, and a sickening realization struck me: this was no accident.

"What did you do?" I shouted, the question barely making it past my lips as Jude and I pushed our way through the throng.

She merely shrugged, the corners of her mouth twitching in that infuriating way that made my skin crawl. "Just a little reminder that life in Riverview is not as simple as you'd like to believe."

A deafening explosion ripped through the air, sending a shockwave that knocked us off our feet. The lights flickered, and for a moment, all I could see were flashes of color against the dark sky—vivid and chaotic, like the emotions surging within me.

Jude reached for my hand, pulling me up as we stumbled backward. The festival, once a haven of joy, had devolved into chaos, and all I could think was that we were standing at the edge of a darker chapter—one that threatened to pull us under, and Hannah was at the center of it all.

As the panic spread, a chilling realization set in: the festival wasn't just a celebration anymore; it had become a battleground, and we were caught right in the middle.

www.ingramcontent.com/pod-product-compliance
Lightning Source LLC
LaVergne TN
LVHW041017150826
845672LV00001B/116

* 9 7 9 8 2 3 0 0 7 4 2 3 6 *